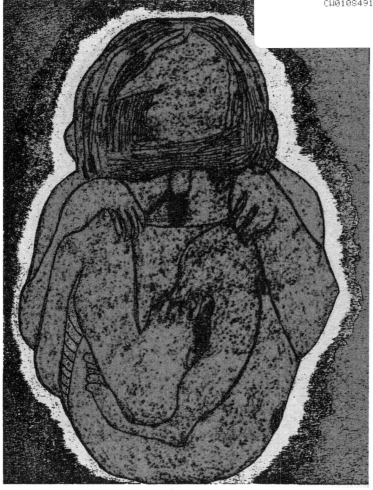

Dead Zoe zero

(James Ward Kirk Publishing)

ISBN-13:
978-0615791739
ISBN-10:
0615791735

Contents

Poetry

Photo by Mike Jansen

Rich Orth

Josette!

In this, the illumination
of my darkened imagination
Reposing enchantress
Rises once more
Grave to the door
My enrapturing Josette
Faint whispers . . . her voice. . .
Sweetest of melody
to my ear
Wafted upon the
summer's breeze
Flowing strawberry blond tresses
Tantalizingly caressing my flesh
As our bodies entwine
Finding ourselves spiraling
into our dream
Dream from which I pray
I not wake
Extremes more than willing
to take
Farewell to this mortal life
Godspeed to the few left
behind
For Josette releases me
From earthly confines
Evolving agony
to ecstasy refined

Rich Orth

In The Beginning!!

Within our beginning
Souls invariably paired.
Devils undecided
Destiny impaired

Willingly one eats of the fruit
Washed down . . . by nectar of the gods
As Golden Asp presides upon us
Deviance tis simply allowed

To touch her once more
Embrace original sin
Plies an honest man
Much to God's chagrin

For spurious decisions
Garden . . . oh how it grew
Whenst darkness breeds light
Evil breeds anew

So write your fiction
As I revel within truth..
We can argue conviction
Answers . . . oh how they mirror . . .
mirror all excuse

Rich Orth

Pretentious She . . . I Adore!

Twas within this smoldering Hell
Providence granted me Heaven
By design . . . Death tis finality
Hence upon conclusion

This faltering heart. . .
wallowed in despair
Altered destiny. . .
. . . Discontinuing preexistence
. . . all that once was
Scrutinizes . . . this moment
. . . One which affected love
One love . . . gone to this day
New Lover . . . here I am played
She, primordial extreme
She . . . drops one to thy knees
Disempowered . . . smirking as one screams
Struggle to awaken from dreams
Those that appropriate sensibility
As we disassociate reality from
truth
But embraced by memories of youth..
She coddles me once more
Saddles up to me..once more///
Loves me . . . for what she is
Loves me . . . for what I am
Loves me . . . she, my somewhat pretentious///
little whore

Rich Orth

Lion All the Time!

One configures. . .
Displays truth and circumstance
As pomposity trickles down
Pissing on the masses
Drivel dribbled
Day by day
Till Flooding waters
Drown all truth
Confuse the old
Confound the youth
Unmistakable silence
Oh, oh how it rings true
Today, we whine
Complaining for we . . .
we never listened
For we the people
are but Christians to the lions
Paraded before the crowd
With foregone conclusions
Inspired by disillusionment
Accepting exclusion
In a separation of reality
. . . and mental state. . .
Unable distinguish. . .
our forgone fate

Rich Orth

Crafted Story!

Tis Good Friday . . . 6th day of April
In this, the year of their Lord..1849
On this forenoon . . . time stood still..
Thus begins a tenebrous affair
Phlegmatic was the course
So far off of it I fell
Thus commences. . .
true degradation of the mortal tenement
;;;;;;;;;;;;;;;;;
Within Stygian crypt
Mullioned windows
Darkened and murky
As a muddied past should be
Bathed simply by transom light
Arras detailing each grisly scene
Tessellated floors reflecting antiquity
Here I am . . . in repose
Lying amongst silent harvests
This graveyard stench . . . rising up
. . . after relentless Spring rains
Phantoms of nightmares
Rattling hollowness
Lameness of thy soul
Oh, this paralyses of memory
Merely a tyro in this world. . . .
Gazing out at an abyss of alcoves
Shading shadowy figures. . . .
If of healthier inclination
In power of mental faculties
Rather than vexed. . .
with a modicum of sanity
One might grapple,
One mat attempt to flee
Though realizing destiny
I struggle no longer

This, my sanity, recalcitrant to
. . . fact and fiction
Compunction of conscience
Wavers laboriously
Benevolent . . . malevolent...who to tell
This be my immemorial curse
Within my antechamber of hell
In this aperture of the mind
Where eldritch flourishes
One envisions another passage
And a darkness is nourished

Vincent Bilof

The Poet's Deliberate Dream:

Part 1

Here's something to be forgiven for.
Broadened masquerades, bookended daydreams,
when rainbows become night-terrors. Ice-cream
trucks become carnival attractions and the laughter
of the under aged mingles with the tears of the hesitant.
Each bloodline guilty of running

through veins, branching roadways, and thunderstorm
misgivings.
The pulse of razorburn chanting and
the seconds, miliseconds, stolen years, all multiplied
all manifest, all overreaching. Blooming flowers

of yesterday's summer. You call me a killer? I'm afraid
to know what I wanted to be. I want to burn inside the pages
of a book while it's held in the gnarled figures of a dying old
construction worker. Write this down.

The Poet's Deliberate Dream: The Sequel
Where do all the dead pens go
when they're all forgotten and
(broken thought, image displaced, remembrance, translucence,
misinterpretation)
somewhere, emptied...?

The Poet's Deliberate Dream Part Three: Untitled
Murder isn't a desperate cry for help, I promise. My biggest
concern is the formatting. When sunset and dawn are exactly
twelve hours apart. Wrote a poem once about a cigarette burning
a hole through my skull, thought it wasn't my skull. Pretend that
you're me, come on, pretend that you're me for one moment, and
that just means forget everything and just become yourself, I

7

mean forget who you are and become yourself, if that makes sense. The doctors wanted to see if I could kill and be reborn. Therapy involves sacrifice and sacrifice requires pride and pride requires greed and greed requires that you wake up and waking up requires that you stop dreaming and to stop dreaming you must begin sleeping and to begin sleeping you must wear yourself down and to wear yourself down you must experience the abyss of debt. They said that I was married, that I loved her. I don't know how to do this.

Poet's Discourse

I wanted to answer your earlier question, the one involving the origins of man:

I don't see why. I mean, I suppose it should be done. Why not?

Okay, I'm cheating. Anyone can give that answer. That answer belongs(stretch this madness on for size, har har har) to me, at the end of time. It will be given to me as a gift

or a turtle will suddenly catch fire beneath a cavalcade of adjective-inspiring clouds. Insert provocative simile hither. Said the frog to the thing.

The Poet's Deliberate Dream: The Sequel

Where do all the dead pens go
when they're all forgotten and
(broken thought, image displaced, remembrance, translucence,
misinterpretation)
somewhere, emptied...?

Vincent Bilof The Poet's Deliberate Dream Part Three:

Untitled

Murder isn't a desperate cry for help, I promise. My biggest
concern is the formatting. When sunset and dawn are exactly
twelve hours apart. Wrote a poem once about a cigarette burning
a hole through my skull, thought it wasn't my skull. Pretend that
you're me, come on, pretend that you're me for one moment, and
that just means forget everything and just become yourself, I
mean forget who you are and become yourself, if that makes
sense. The doctors wanted to see if I could kill and be reborn.
Therapy involves sacrifice and sacrifice requires pride and pride
requires greed and greed requires that you wake up and waking
up requires that you stop dreaming and to stop dreaming you
must begin sleeping and to begin sleeping you must wear
yourself down and to wear yourself down you must experience
the abyss of debt. They said that I was married, that I loved her. I
don't know how to do this.

Vincent Bilof

Poet's Discourse

I wanted to answer your earlier question, the one involving
the origins of man:

I don't see why. I mean, I suppose it should be done.
Why not?

Okay, I'm cheating. Anyone can give that answer.
That answer belongs(stretch this madness on for size, har har
har)
to me, at the end of time. It will be given to me as a gift

or a turtle will suddenly catch fire beneath a cavalcade
of adjective-inspiring clouds.
Insert provocative simile hither.
Said the frog to the thing.

Vincent Bilof

Memento of Truth

You can die this way, cry this way,
hide this day, burn this
fate.
Nobody has to unravel the mystery
behind my eyes, the natural
and super-mystical way I carve
into your thighs.
Slightly,
(one gash)
a sordid, artistically-placed
em-dash.
Is that a tear I see fall
from those bright white orbs?

(Can't you see)

this is the work of a poet
and not a millionaire straight from the pages of Forbes?

I'm not some benign social experiment, as you say.
Look at me now because I do this
in a sick and twisted way.
Bleed upon this blade's edge!
Watch as I hover upon sanity's ledge.
Everything you say is another
carefully-concocted lie,
You're like all the others, I think––
stealing another moment of life
before you die.

Why didn't you feel this way before?

Vincent Bilof

Moments of You

Call me a whore, then.
I've seen this rage before.
"You're just like all the others."
So, can we call this an intimate moment?
Justify your inhumanity:
(tell yourself it's not real
it's all my fault, isn't it?)

Maybe you can blame the world
(so watch it spin, or watch it burn
watch it churn or watch it carom
off the skull of some benevolent shithead who
plays dice or chess or maybe poker with the universe)

This pain is nothing new.
You've hurt me before, just not with the face
you wear now.

You:
A world-famous poet, a suffering malcontent
drenched in your melancholia,
your megalomania.
Drowning in an ocean of You.

I'm your biggest fan.
I loved your way with words.

Smile.
You were married once. You had a lovely child.
Someone pitied you.
Bouts of narcolepsy complimented by pages
ravaged by your pen.
You killed them both.

Somebody knew you. Studied you. Wanted you.

They injected you.
Tested you.

Here you are.
You think it was all an accident.
But I'm your biggest fan.
Murder isn't an accident.

I was supposed to be saved, but not by them.
By you.

All that darkness swirling within you.
The moon shines through the blinds.
The truth burns a jagged scar across your soul, you—

—who are you.
Believeth in me.
Breathe me.
Do what you want with me.
No mortal man can satiate your lust for blood and pain.
They gave you a codename.

Want to know what it is?

Vincent Bilof Sonnet X

What else is there to say when you witness
the end of a dream?
I can love you forever, you know.
How many times do you live
when you're about to die?

I tilt my head and ponder.
(Whispering now, every so gently, the words like water pouring
slowly into a plastic cup that can burn in a funeral pyre or in
some anonymous incinerator which stands at the edge of the
world).

"Tell me what you see.
Do you know what it all means?
The muse of centuries,
the messenger who carried dire tidings
upon winged feed to brave heroes who desperately
clamored for home.
That's how I perceive you.
Love,
speak to me in a designed language,
the fire that rages or burns low
the glowing embers or the skyward apocalypse
that's, you know, what I need.
Your vision.
Tell me.
Yes, that's right, hold my hand.
Everyone was so disappointed
when I told them I wrote stories
about monsters and undead
cannibals. They thought I was Herman MELVILLE!
AND I LAUGHED!
Witness the giant.
He knows for whom the bell burns."

No interest in the benign.
No longer worth it, really.

Nobody can see what she sees.
Nothing can last as long as death.
Nowhere is there a glamorous sense of immortality.
Nonsense, all of it.
No man can ever really die,
Not here,
Not now.
Notice the tears that border the edges of
Nocturne musings, everything
Noted as conclusive,
Nothing.

At last.
Tilt the head.
Breathe.
The chest rises, and then...
Collapses, erodes, fades, dies, stops, ceases, ends, dies, burns,
cries,
sighs...

Matthew Wilson

The Human Element

I hate, therefore I must be human.
Other animals kill for hunger, or defense
But only man will act on anger. Murder.
So then I must be human.

If only my maker had not said so.
Things were going well.
I was happy, soon to be married
But humans are silly animals.

He wished to get a confession off his chest.
To give me total freedom. Like any human.
I hated him for taking it all away.
For reducing me to a robot. A thing.

Do not tell me. But he did.
I lost my head, blew a fuse.
And killed him. So you see I must be human.
For only humans destroy what is truly loved.

David Frazier

Hungry

Born into a wicked world
Sent on my way.
into the wild
raised To eat meat raw
I hunt, hunkered down.
Pounce at my moment.
Attack with my canines
Removing large chunks of meat.
Bloody, dripping red
Heart pumping
Pounding hard.
You can't stop me
I eat your carcass
For my soul-meal.

David Frazier

The Veteran

Wedged in a wheelchair
Wounded in war
Gave two legs
For my country.
No one cared.

Someone robbed my home
Stealing all I had.
Dumped out of my chair
Flat on the floor.
Cried out for help
No one cared.

Shot in the head
Blood on the floor,
Robber left by the door.
Cops at the scene
Found no evidence.
No one cared.

On the floor
An empty shell.
I was dead,
A veteran of war.
Fought for you,
No one cared.

David Frazier

Wicked Eyes

Thirteen steps rise toward the sky.
Ropes carefully tied swing.
One is slipped over my head
Cinched tight, roughness felt.
Trapdoor creeks below my boots.
Ebony hood covers
My wicked eyes.
Cannot see what is in front of me.
Drowning me in blackness.
Lever thrown, gravity pulls me
Toward destiny deserved
Yet unknown to all.
The future holds hostage
All hope.
Is there any light?
It is too dark to see.
The executioner has
Removed blind eyes which can't reveal
The future ahead of me.

David Frazier

A Funeral

Walking into church
I hear the bells toll.
Banging and clanging
Mourning the loss of a soul.
A soul with no regrets.
Murder, rape, and incest,
Crimes against man
Hold no place there.
A higher power will judge
If your soul makes the cut.

A funeral can't be arranged
without breaking eggs.
Wooden box royal and fancy black car
Cart your bones off.
Buried six foot underground
Like squirrels hiding nuts.
Sometimes fire hot as Hades
Disposes of remains.
Incinerated garbage.
Ashes in urns
Displayed on a mantle.
The living remember you as you were
Not as dirt or ashes swept away.

David Frazier

Permanent Sleep

The hour is getting late
How much longer will I stay awake.
Seems like I get no sleep.
There's nothing keeping me from restful bliss
From closing my eyes and
Seeking sweet repose.
Why then is it so hard
For me to sleep and break away
From rude awakenings plaguing me.
I feel the pillows sweet caress
Under my head.
The blanket swallows me,
Silken soft sheets caressing me,
Do not provide an escape for me.
I count sheep
Still, I don't get any rest.
I wish that I could sleep as well as my dog
He hits the floor, he's out like a light.
My eyes are closed,
I hear the clock
Tick-tock, tick-tock.
My time grows short and I'll never last
A full day's work
If I don't get some rest.
What a terrible thing not to sleep
A restful slumber is what I seek,
Seems like its been a week,
Since I have gotten any sleep.
Maybe I should take a little pill
This might fill the bill.
Then the referee could count to ten
I'll never get up again.
Sweet sleep would come to me
And I'll never wake again.

A. B. Stephens

Infidelity

My wife's tender flesh
In a rival's embrace rests
Frost on the red rose

Michael Lee Johnson

Prisoners of Mind and Soul:

Is a prisoner imprisoned simply by being locked up? Containment takes many forms: exile, poverty, mental or emotional, guilt, justification, caged in, among others. These poems explore this concrete bridge and the unseen one inside.

From My Grave
Michael Lee Johnson

Don't bring the rosary beads
it's too damn late for doing repetitions.
Eucharist, I can handle crackers and wine;
I love the Lord just like you.
Catholicism circles itself with rituals-
ground hogs and squirrels dancing with rosary beads,
naked in the sun, the night, eating the pearls
feeling comfortable about it.
Rituals and rosary beads are indigestible
even butterflies go coughing in farmer's cornfields-
Cardinal George, Chicago, choke on the damn things;
some of his priests think it a gay orgasm or piece
remote found in naked scriptures-Sodom and Gomorra.
But my bones in ginger dust lie near a farm in DeKalb, Illinois
where sunset meshes corn with a yellow gold glow like rich teeth.
My tent is with friends we say prayers privately like silence
tucked in harvest moonlight. Farmers touch the face of God
each morning after just one cup Folgers coffee Columbian blend,
or pancakes made with water, batter, sparse on sugar.
Sometimes I urinate on yellow edge of flowers,
near my tent, late at night, before the hayride,
speak to earth and birds like gods.
Never do I pull rosary beads from my pocket.
It's too late, damn it, for rosary beads those repetitions.

Michael Lee Johnson

I Work My Mind like Planet Earth

I work my mind
inward into a corner of knots.
Depressed beneath brain bone
I work my words, they overwork me.
Fear is the spirit alone, away from God.
Hospital warriors shake pink pills,
rattle bottles of empty dreams.
I walk my ward down the daily highway;
I work the roadmap of spirit,
weed out false religions.
Only one God for so many
Twelve Step programs.
I wrap myself around support groups,
look for dependency within their problems.
I publish my poems, life works,
concerns on floor five, psych ward
I edit my redemption,
escape from the laundry room;
run around in circles like planet earth,
looking for my therapist
to seal my comfort.

Michael Lee Johnson

Michigan City State Prison Poem

Strong
STrong
STRong SCIHIZOPHRENIA
STROng (here is the strong, the concrete wall, the absurd)
Strong (then there were all the images, undefined)
STRONG
(The fist, the iron will)
I am a fractured person, there are people all around me but I'm
alone.
Cell life is a dead life but my mattress is only 2" thick.
Thin I breathe A to Z I repeat over each day.
and birds of color I'm clean snow and bleach,
fly by. innocent.
Jesus created a false belief system, but why do I still believe in it?
I play bingo.
Nothing now in the dark
ever happens (double negative) death is simple, swallow it,
swallow it.
I like the repetition it keeps me angry, insane.
Laughter rings lonely in a cloud, high in my cell.
Nothing takes the right form for me.
Idle I walk, idle I'm here-think so.
Steel windows where do the lines stop and start?
for 74 years now
is the reputation in my house
of your end or mine, hotel
Steely Wind moor changes places with the warden, formal name,
right?
Idle I remain,
transfer,
idle the gates of the joint will close.

Michael Lee Johnson

Leroy and His Love Affair

Girlie magazines dating back to 1972 scattered across the floor.
The skeletons of two pet canaries lie dormant inside a wired
cage.
Bessie Mae died here 8 months ago.
From her lips, and from her eyes comes nothing like before.
Leroy, her lover, her only friend, the man she lived with
over 30 years locked her body in their bedroom.
He didn't want to part from her.
Leroy has no friends to detect anything that might be suspect.
He wants nothing between the two of them at all.
No one comes near to interfere.
Their bedroom is padlocked, stale, and stagnant with mildew,
looking
the way it did before she died.
Foul odors ooze up through their bedroom ventilation ducts,
Leroy contends that a dead rat in the basement is causing the
odors.
Leroy loves to lie about his sacred love affairs.
Layers of dust blanket over the mahogany floors, and the maid
doesn't come
here anymore.
Bessie Mae's remains are wrapped in a scarlet housecoat,
Dried blood sleeps in a small pool beneath her bed.
In time they both will sleep, sole witnesses to this fiasco
their lives will catch them in; enduring it, holding
their tongues till time matters no more.
Nothing appears changed, lovers unwilling to depart.

Michael Lee Johnson

Lilly, Lonely Trailer Prostitute

Paint your face with cosmetic smiles.
Toss your breast around with synthetic plastic.
Don't leak single secrets to strangers-
locked in your trailer 8 foot wide by 50 foot
with twisted carrots, cucumbers, weak batteries,
and colorful dildos-you've even give them names:
Adams' pleasure skin, big Ben on the raise, Rasputin:
the Mad Monk-oh no, no, no.
Your legs hang with the signed signatures
of playboys and drifters ink.
The lot rent went up again this year.
Paint your face with cosmetic smiles.

Michael Lee Johnson

Manic is the Dark Night

nice jpeg black and white)
Deep into the forest
the trees have turned
black, and the sun
has disappeared in
the distance beneath
the earth line, leaving
the sky a palette of grays
sheltering the pine trees
with pitch-tar shadows.
It's here in this black
and sky gray the mind
turns psycho
tosses norms and pathos
into a ground cellar of hell,
tosses words out through the teeth.
"Don't smile or act funny,
try to be cute with me;
how can I help you today
out of your depression?"
I feel jubilant, I feel over the moon
with euphoric gaiety.
Damn I just feel happy!
Back into the wood of somberness
back into the twigs,
sedated the psychiatrist
scribbles, notes, nonsense on a pad of yellow paper:
"mania, oh yes, mania, I prescribe
lithium, do I need to call the police?"
No sir, back into the dark woods I go.
Controlled, to get my meds.
Twist and rearrange my smile,
crooked, to fit the immediate need.
Deep in my forest
the trees have turned black again.
To satisfy the conveyer.
The Lord of the dark wood.

Michael Lee Johnson

I'm the Shadow Shredder

I take your ghost pile
your multi dreams,
twisted thoughts
moss that tangles,
these are desperate nights,
I shred them.
The devil is hell in your brain.
Give me your depression
in a handful of spit,
I will Drano it.
Give me your mass ruminations,
I will vacuum it flush for free.
I'm a writer of depression.
I'm shred man, shredder man.
I park free inside your brain.
Toss me bushels of anxiety
and I create a rainbow
you, alone, to cross over the bridge with.
I'm your friend, weeper night.
I'm your prayer partner, no, don't send darts
nor daggers. Hearts, winner of cards, decks.
Toss your fears, I will cultivate them to grace,
charity, Christ.
Fish for your life, no one bits but carp,
suckers, bottom dwellers.
Revisit your theater at night,
your ghostly tears.
From me I give you Christ, salvation to you.
I'm the shredder man.

Michael Lee Johnson

Depression's Darkness

I'm trapped inside
a ripped artery inside my chest
and inside my brain;
I can't disengage from my grief
with only my words.
The bills mount,
my business drops,
and aging hangs around
my neck like a visible
doggie name tag
and I fall into disarray-
my brain disassociates
and scatters my thoughts.
I feel alone.
It's at times like these I just want
to slouch down, visit the bedroom
siesta- seemingly the only answer.
But no one dances with a live partner
in bed; this is where the devil does his whittling-
builds his cages, practices his cult,
dangles his echelon of drugs, alcohol,
and fortifies them with negative thinking
whets the razor, suggests the fearful suicide dark.
I force my decanting self
to transfer these liquid lines
to solid white paper and black ink,
bully myself to be a spectator,
a review critic of my own
circus creation-
a day traveler between
Harlem, Hades,
heaven and hell.
I filtrate myself these cycles
and feel better, long be the night.

Michael Lee Johnson

Spirits of the Schizophrenic Dead (V2)

I am linked to the spirit world
by my own choice, character;
I connect with these people
because I thought they were lonely.
I use simple, plain language like you would understand.
I toss gold coins around their houses,
hear tinny sounds jumping out of the walls
screaming at me with human voices.
They say back to me that I was within their walls.
I tell them they are crazy.
My life is leading into the spirits of walking dead.
I am linked to the spirit world.
This night, in front of my cottage,
I toss my evening cape and all my
vampire clothing into the ocean.
I grab all my cassette tapes, the ones
I talk to them with, my poems, my dreams my nightmares-
toss them all into the ocean tonight at once,
waves belch.
I feel like a crossword puzzle,
parts missing my words,
jack hammer pounding my skeleton face.
But, now I am no longer haunted by a dictionary of the past,
my therapist is now my best friend.
We take photographs of each other,
we share them with no one.
I'm alive, but lonely, and enjoy the taste of bagels.
I touch them and they feel secure, safe within me.
I hear no polarization of sound variants,
speakers of spirit world silence.

William *Cook*

We Stand Accused

To leave this earth was my wish:
Ponytail Princess smiles
fills her cheeks with pink
blesses my bare arm with a pinch the same color
skips over the precise lawn in the sun
slow motion smiling all around,
'til Dad's car drags a dark cloud home

I remember the Ice-man
didn't talk to me for five long years
held prisoner in HIS house
every hour a lament for a certain kind of escape
and mum played Elvis to retreat
'till the music died
but that all ceased because
she listened to HIM more than to YOU

I remember the Ice-man
brought a television that should've been school uniforms
YOU said that mum was more interested
in conservative television underwear ads
than in YOU
maybe that's why mum hates TV now?

YOUR eyes could slap
YOUR sneer could grind its hard boot
into our meek faces and YOUR words . . .
YOUR words could slowly strangle with such sadistic force
like being lifted off the ground
with a noose squeezing around the neck
the linoleum would pulse a heartbeat
the walls would crush like pistons, then drop . . .

I remember the Ice-man's stare
hate – filled eyes, entrance to Devil's lair
every thought YOU think
a child dies drowning in its own blood
bleeding from wounds that never heal.

William Cook

Parabolic Dream

The misty hue of sleep
wakens images within:

Windows, doors, walls
and a black fox skitters
'round the broken room
sniffing trash

rats within walls
through holes watch
with death intent
so still

time's pendulous blade
slices deftly
and the fox has seen
sniffed, snorted
and disappeared

this forgotten room
now empty
save for moonlight
and the flickering fireplace
explodes with my next breath
as the whole interior
is illumined
in blossoming blood flowers
crushing cellophane sounds
break the night dream
as the flames in the hearth leap skyward
with sun-burst bright brilliance

the dream is engulfed
enveloped with fire and twisting smoke
before it crackles away

to petering coals
to ash that floats like falling leaves
then back to back black
as the dream drowns
in sleep.

William Cook

Blood Meal

words crawl like
pulsing worms
from the mouth

naked, caught
in fetid time
merciless clock ticks
another soul off
the life list

blood red rain falling
dead birds
thumping the roof

old trees in the forest stand
cracking twigs
arthritic limbs, breaking

the night's winter air freezes
flays flesh, off
bare skin
as the whipping wind
delegates, lashings of punishment

and beyond the eye, disease licks
seeks human access
to burrow faster in the blood

and there she stands
hollow chest
red lips
platinum hair
ghost skin
as her dull yellow tongue licks
black teeth

everything surrounds and
squeezes back all the while,
large machines enlarging,
march with grim resolve
knee-deep in blood . . .

David S. Pointer

Sartre's Freedom Fighters

This was no Mt. Suribachi
and we had no battle flag,
but after we killed all the
space villagers we found
that all their cut off corpse
heads fit onto the animal
control come along poles
planted by executioners
atop body mound park

David S. Pointer

Post Altar Fermentation

Lover's wine is always a
cup of Somali coastal water
yet we continued to gulp the
ecstasy of the grapes unaware
that each imported lip bottle's
added ingredients washed into
us like acidic nuclear waste

David S. Pointer

Constitutional Rebirth

All the true believers
enter one interrogation
room or another with
taxidermied ghost vibe
mounted on walls or on
inclimate weather boards
outside assimilating into
future space stations for
genealogy searches as the
paint on old observational
mirrors continues to dry

David S. Pointer

Dust Buster Ritual

The new model coffins
had push button moans,
rasping sobs, hoarse wails
followed by favorite psalms
finally remotely controlled
incineration negating the
need for anything except
post funeral car or cab home

David S. Pointer

Oak Ridge Area Case Worker

The
client's wife's neck
tumor protrudes
like a game head,
growing past you,
and there's not
enough fish bone
bourbon to see
enthusiasm through
as you flip into a
big phone book
searching for every
fantastic fair priced
surgeon near
Sevierville

Ro McNulty

The Salt Garden

"My brother, remember, we were once children here
But time hasn't passed now for long, weary years
My brother, the statues, did you once know that face
Brother, do you dream or are you back in this place?"

*"Oh sister, sweet sister, we were made proudly here
Why so cold, your face? Did I not here your tears?
I came on the wind, I heeded your cries
I loved you, sweet sister, jewel of my eyes.
Why mourn for the life, the time that passed here?
I see only winter, the passage of years
Ah, sister, our garden so tender you care
Call me back in the spring, on the warm wind so fair "*

"I see you now, brother, and guilt doesn't lie
We salted the earth and watched the garden die
You know nothing grows from this cursed dirt
From the fallow salt-fury we heaped on the earth
And brother, remember? The thorns were like steel
The flowers here withered, the land grew surreal
My brother, clad in ash, not mourning black
Remember what you buried, in the scorched earth's cracks?"

*"Remember? Sweet sister, there was life here to tend,
The flowers, the grave, we were with you at the end
Poor sister, poor child, this sick land does lie
It was salted with tears, and dirt doesn't cry
The glass has not darkened, I see through it yet well
Not all souls here partake in your hell
All cries now come from centuries' span
And your time yet has just begun"*

"But the glass lies in shards, brother, like brittle bone
And all souls that you see here are just carved in stone
You see what once was, not what's left here to find

And hell? hell is nothing to those you left behind
Remember? My tears? I've no such thing shed
But the years didn't come for me, for all that I begged
And you know this stone face? Well, statues don't lie
But you forgot this corpse garden, you left me to die

"Sweet sister, I'll come back to the black iron gate
Through the long, longing years I hear your pleas where you
wait
Through aeon's sand, a few souls may yet pass
So fleeting, they dance yet through mortal time's glass
Sister, wait..."

"...But there's nought left here that still grows
Fearful years will not pass for one they once left alone
It's not my voice that calls you, it's just the bitter wind's howl
There are no souls but the dead that wait for you now.
My brother, the statues, did you once know that face
Brother, do you dream or are you back in this place?"

Greg McWhorter

Kingdom Flagitious

On Eldritch paths to glory turn
As Kings of old did also yearn
Let blood flow throughout the land
Prick thy neighbor and take thy stand

Kill thee a maid of purity absolute
Spill her blood for surety resolute
A dark thing growing will seem amiss
Fear not a reaper from the abyss

Times have come for thrones to emerge
Hewn of stone and crafted to serve
Erupting violence of archaic tribes
Split asunder by ancient ties

Swift swords of justice they do slash
Twill spill the blood and leave a gash
A blood-filled chalice to the brim
To slake the thirst of he who wins

Can a king control a demon though?
An ether-thing part friend and foe?
Forget not chants and glyphs to cry
Else carve thy destiny -prepare to die

Gladius sanguis et mors
Gladius sanguis ego facio imperium tuum

Mike Meroney

Thirteen

I am disease brought forth to inflict and infect.
Filth that rotted my mother's womb outward
before those fetid lips spit a glob of phlegm called "itsaboy!"
onto an already fucked up world
like a hammer smashing a pair of crooked teeth.
Born bad
made worse.
Destiny fuels itself on blood slit from jugular veins
by hands once greased of toy trains.
Filling up my chalice-
I toast the sky-
Raising Hell.
Violence is my master-
and tomorrow
I am thirteen.

Flash Fiction

Photo by Mike Jansen

Greg McWhorter

An Abstract of Measures

"Have you been waiting long?"

"Yes. I have."

"Well . . . ?"

"Well . . . What?"

"What is it that you want?"

"Oh . . . I want to see you dead . . . no more."

"Am I supposed to be shocked by this?"

"No. I guess not. Doesn't everyone want you dead?"

"No. Little kids want me to hurry, but they don't want me dead. There are actually lots of elderly people that want me to slow down, but they don't want me to stop. Not completely."

"I guess I'm like that. I don't want you to stop, but slow down."

"How old are you?"

"I'm 43."

"That explains it, middle age. Yes. Your kind always wants me to slow down too."

"Can you?"

"You mean slow down?"

"Yes."

"No.

"Why not?"

"Haven't you ever heard the expression, "Time waits for no man"? Well . . . it's true. I can't wait for women or animals either. The truth is, I can't stop even if I wanted to."

"So what am I supposed to do?"

"Continue living."

"Won't you stop when I die?"

"No. I will only seem to stop for you. I will still be moving along for everyone else."

"How long will you go on?"

"I will never end. I may seem to stop. There may be times when no one is around to record me, but I will ever continue."

"That sounds like a lonely existence."

"It is."

"Maybe what I have is better?"

"Maybe."

"You have given me something to think about. Thank you."

"You are the first to ever thank me. Most people curse me or beg for more time. Since you are the first to thank me, let me give you a gift. Do you want a gift?"

"Yes, please."

"Here is your gift. It is a verbal gift. Time is an abstract concept made by man. I really do not move nor do I exist. Man measures what is not actually there."

"That does not seem like much of a gift."

"Think about it. It will help to kill some time."

Ken Goldman

A Comforting Though

The tears finally were subsiding as young Ronnie Arlington emerged from his bedroom to the living room. Grandmother sat waiting, clutching a cracked Bible to her breasts. She looked up, the flesh of her face fissured with a compulsory smile aimed at the little boy.

"You want some dinner?" She asked, her accent as southern as fried chicken livers, her breath a schism in the warm air.

Ronnie shook his head. His stomach, an excruciating pain in his center, was not ready for nourishment. The boy sat alongside Grandmother and placed his head on her shoulder, hoping to have his grandmother run a hand through his hair like she sometimes did. But she didn't do it, and when she spoke her voice sounded rehearsed, like the preacher's, not at all like Grandmother.

"Parents die, Ronnie. It doesn't often happen when they're so young, of course, and it's sad when they leave children behind. But it happens because bad things sometimes do happen. Can you understand what I'm saying?"

Residual tears pricked Ronnie's eyes and he made his best effort to grasp what Grandmother was telling him. Such an effort required much more endurance than the ten year old could muster. He settled for a semblance of stoicism that might allow for a quivering lip instead of outright bawling, at least until he felt able to put together a complete sentence.

"I wonder about a God that allows such a thing to happen, Ronnie. Haven't you?"

Ronnie hadn't. In fact, the thought had not entered his mind because so many other thoughts made no sense. But now that his grandmother had mentioned it, the boy suddenly realized that he had not questioned God's part in any of this.

"Mom always said God had His reasons for doing things that I didn't understand, like when my puppy Sandy got hit by that car. Did God have a reason for taking Mom and Dad?"

Ronnie watched Grandmother considered his question, as if she were grappling with a difficult math equation like the fractions Miss Pope had been teaching last week. Finally she was ready and grasped Ronnie's face into her hands and locked her eyes so he could not look away.

"Sometimes God gets angry, you know. Was there something you did to make God angry, Ronnie?" Grandmother's controlled voice remained soft, but did nothing to soften the impact of her words.

Ronnie whimpered, burning memories welling up in his eyes.

"Last Tuesday, the day before the accident, I forgot to take the trash out. I didn't mean to, it's just that I got caught up in the Hockey game against the Flyers. It was pretty close, and--"

The old woman's face reflected horror.

"Pray, Ronnie. Right now, you march right up to your room and pray. I can't promise, of course, but perhaps in time God will forgive you."

"Gran' ma, I didn't mean--"

"Pray. You run along now and do as I say."

Ronnie didn't quite run, but that was all right. The old woman understood her grandchild's turmoil. Death was difficult to grasp when so young. Grandmother learned this lesson from her grandmother.

She clasped her hands together in prayer. "Thank you, Lord, for giving me the strength to provide my grandson the guidance he so badly needs." She paused. "What's that--? All right, then Lord, Thy will be done."

She rifled through the drawers, finding a wooden twelve inch ruler. It would do nicely against the boy's bottom. And if not, there were the garden shears. One must be certain.

Proper guidance, not easy, was important.

Marija Elektra Rodriguez

The Temple of Sepia

Although I've only known you for sixteen weeks, I will love you until I am dust.

I whispered the words in his lavender ear and entwined his fingers with my own. They were marble, hard as stone, glacially cold. The ebony was seeping from his wrist, barely visible past the cuff of his military uniform. It could have been a stain of ink, but I knew it was nothing so benign. His blood was discoloring, turning black. His skin had taken on a pallid tone. There were hepatic speckles across his hands like wayward drops of paint from an artist's brush stroke. He seemed so small in death, shrunken, surreal—as though the unnamed artist had carved him from stone and laid him out on the crimson silk. *He's just a statue . . . An imitation of life . . . Not the real thing.*

My eyes strayed to his face. The lustrous crop of auburn hair, so like my own, had dulled, turned tawny in the flickering candlelight of the church. I resisted the impulse to touch his cheek. The stiffness of his hand had shocked me, sending a brief ripple of alarm through my chest. The bones of his face seemed more prominent in death than in life. And in a day there would be nothing left of his flesh. He would be burned, like medical waste. Then the ashes would be sealed in our family sepulcher, dusting the bones of our ancestors, piled upon each other. The thin line of his lips, those eyelids sewed shut, they would all dissolve. I would never see those onyx orbs again. Gone: just sunken cheeks streaked with ivory and lavender.

And it was my fault that he was going in the ground.

In the confines of the church, my mother and her sisters elevated their mourning wails. The sound reverberated off the walls and drowned everything in sorrow. It was our tradition, our ritual. Deeply inhaling the cinnamon scented air, I attempted to join in the half-chant, half-screaming song—but the sound choked in my throat and a heavy, raspy breath escaped my lips instead. It was an obligation to the dead, this hideous cacophony,

49

denying the pollution attracted to bloodshed, or so the old widows had told me in my youth.

But I no longer believed such superstitions.

Tears chased each other down my ashen cheeks. In the golden reflection of the tabernacle my eyes were two violet drops in a sea of liquid crystal. My small chest glittered with jewels pulsing in the inconstant candlelight.

I looked over his dark navy jacket, the crisp white collar blossoming out upon his neck. I moved his favorite knife from within the coffin and lay it upon his chest. I felt around in my pocket for the smooth, cool metal object tickling my thigh through the thin fabric of my dress; his cigarette lighter. How he had loved that thing; flick the small, metal latch backward and forward to watch the blue-gold light reappear, trace fingers over the elaborate engraving in the metal. The baroque letter 'R'. His name had been Romano. Just another lazy Sunday afternoon in our small cottage on the side of the volcano, flicking the lighter and following me with his eyes.

"We've all lost a child. Life will get better with time."

A gnarled hand clutched my elbow—one of my aunties, veiled in black. Only the white flesh of her neck and cheeks broke through the flatness of the color. Gelatinous orbs looked at me with pity, laced with blame. Her lips were bloodless, her mouth moving in a soft monotone of comfort. She whispered that last word through her solicitous stare and glazed emerald eyes.

Time. I had nothing but time. I was only twenty-eight.

"You can try again."

Try what again?

Back at home, in the small cottage, I laid two plates on the kitchen table. He wasn't there. I placed the bitter almond biscuits on his red silk handkerchief, filled his glass with the honey-spiced wine, lit a small red candle in his honor. Inhaled the cinnamon smoke of the flame and sprinkled a sulfur crystal upon it. I watched as the honeycomb yellow powder melted into a drop of viscous red foam.

Il giorno della morte . . . The day of the dead. The only day I set the table for two. I no longer believed in the custom, but I felt wrong not to perform it.

I sat and flicked a cigarette lighter as he had done, bathing the room in amber.

A crescent moon inspected me from behind lace curtains and frost-bitten glass. The patterns in the lace created luminous figures who danced upon the cottage floor and across my toes. I could see the Doric temple from the window in my chamber. The remains of the Greek theater and cemetery lay just to its side. They lit up the ruins at night. Sandstones, the color of sepia. The Christians had tried to build a church over the pagan site, but abandoned it when lava erupted almost drowning the temple in flames. A sinewy, red-gold snake, flowing down the side of the volcano, the tear streaks from the ancient god trapped below the mountain. The volcano was littered with superstitions. Snakes carry the souls of loved ones. The widows' words ricocheted in my mind. I could see the small silhouettes of the women as they left the honeyed cakes and bitter almonds for the serpents. Take the sweet biscuits. Let me know he still lingers.

But you will never be a snake. You will never be buried in the ground. You, just a few drops of blood. Maybe it's not so bad. Plenty of women bleed when they are pregnant.

But the acid in my gut and the red snake down my thigh tell me differently. My body has betrayed me. And your father, Raphael, had those long, rounded lashes—like spider legs shooting from his eyes. He is already in the ground, but you cannot go with him.

You are too little.

My mother drops her plate with honeyed cakes and bitter almonds. The spiced wine splashes the stone floor of the cottage, mixes with the small red drops of you.

She starts to wail and her sisters join in. There is no church, no coffin.

There never was, and there never shall be.

Just the sandstone, sepia temple, with the ancient statue of the goddess in the middle; the one the Christians threw into the sea but washed back to the black soil of the volcano. I would have named you Romano. And I can fit you in the palm of my hand.

Although I've only known you for sixteen weeks, I will love you until I am dust.

"We've all had miscarriages. It will get better with time. You can try again," promised my aunty, the black-wrapped widow.

But you will never be.

William Cook

Anomalous Perigee

He turned on his black polished heel, raised his well-dressed right arm—the light dancing off his polished cuff link—repositioned his curved left arm a little higher on the delicate back of his true love, then slowly waltzed from the center of the light into the shadows.

Over her shoulder he watched the light, drunk with love and wine. He could not contain the rogue tears that tumbled from his tired eyes. The smell of her perfume engulfed his senses: The silk touch of her soft skin on his cheek, the feel and smell of her fine hair brushing the tip of his nose as they spun slowly in between the light and the dark.

The empty chairs and tables in the hall resounded with applause; confetti fell like snow upon their twisting slow sonata. . .

The adagio waned. The click of a door echoed through the music and the lingering mumble of departing guests. The light flickered, swelled, then was full and bright again as it should be.

The confetti was gone, the guests too; the table and chairs nowhere to be seen. The hall walls had shrunk, chandeliers disappeared, but still the music continued as he took one last semi-pirouette and stopped; his hand raised, fingers together as if holding the smallest of hands, the other hand spread just away from his mid-section as if to protect the daintiest of waists.

He stood under the dim light, the yellow glow casting shadows on his face, his dapper suit now looking quite threadbare. The cuff links long ago disappeared over the grimy counter of a downtown pawn shop. His polished shoes, the seams along the soles split; the buttoned collar around his neck, loose. He tried to look away as the mirror rippled darkly around his form, transfixed. His hands went to his head, his shoulders collapsed, and he turned his back on his own pitiful image.

***

The old man poured himself a glass of water from the kitchen tap and took the last bottle of his heart pills from the shelf, before making his way back to his small bedroom. He slowly unbuttoned his jacket and hung it carefully over the back of a chair. Sipping at the cold water he swallowed ten of his tablets. He unbuttoned his grimy collar and stepped from his old worn shoes and swallowed another ten pills with a sip of water. He removed his old gabardine trousers and tapped out the remaining pills, thirteen in all, and swallowed them with the rest of the water. He folded back the covers on his thin bed and pulled the cord above him, which extinguished the light. As he lay there in the dark, the adagio still tumbling through his mind, his chest tightened and he raised himself up to look through the gap in the blind.

The moon was low and full and seemed to smile back at him drunkenly. He pulled the blind cord and rattled the Venetians open. The cold blue moonlight beamed across the room, trying to penetrate the black shadows of his austere home. The mellow luminosity of the light filled his mind with a soft sapphire hue.

He knew there were angels, alive, somewhere. Some people called them Ghosts or Spirits, but he preferred to think of them as angels. The heaviness in his heart began to subside as he lay on his side and watched the night outside his window. He could almost step onto the moon, he thought. It's so low. So blue. So big.

After a while his tired eyes closed, he stretched and rested his thin arms gently onto the mattress either side of his skeletal frame. He breathed deeply, his body shuddering, as the cold hands of death gathered his final breaths and he was with her once again.

Julienne Lee

Danger to Society

I watched the crimson flames consume the house. My heart was cold and hard, resisting the burn of emotion like the brick resisted the gasoline-fueled fire. Only hatred rippled, mingling with the intensity of the heat. Did I blink as it burned? I longed to join it. I envied the cleansing it received. But no, I would survive and endure my tainted heart. On-lookers shivered, regarding me, the flames reflected in my eyes. Would vengeance be as acrid as the black smoke billowing from the fallen roof? Or would it be as soothing as the fireman's water, come to save what remained? I turned from the clean winds to follow the settlement of ash as it coated everything nearby, forcing people to take note of the power of destruction and its endless hunger

My fingers rubbed the sealed pill bottle concealed in my jacket pocket. I told them. I told them I didn't need it, and they refused to listen to me. The same ones they forced down my throat after I bit the Doctor's leg in the prison cell.

The bastards refused to listen when I told them it was lighter fluid and not heroine that I injected to rid me of the demons trying to take possession.

They wouldn't listen. As their medications took hold, I shouted and raged "I'll burn everyone one of your fucking houses down!"

After I'd *slept it off*, I was weak and vulnerable with all the toxins out of my system and I could see *them* much more clearly. Like a sickly grey cloying membrane shrouding the person they attached themselves to.

"I'm going to recommend an assessment and treatment, Professor Stevens." I didn't give away that I could see *them* when the Doctor came for me again, talking in his hushed tone. I swallowed my fear and revulsion as the membrane slid grotesquely over his smiling face. "I'm sure your students will be happy to have you back in the lecture hall as soon as you're well again."

My students! Yes, my students – I needed to protect them from these demons, I thought while my resolve hardened.

54

I was released, prescription and referral in hand. I studied every face that had loomed over me while I was being handled into my prison cell. I memorized those ones that had the swirling grey mucus veneer like a death pall.

And I knew what would kill these creatures, these soul-suckers.

With one more glance, I watched the oily smoke billow over the house like an all-consuming monster. I ignored any regret that the Doctor would be lost along with the demon. He would not have let me close enough to inject him, I justified to myself.

I walked away, scratching at the injection tracts of my inner elbows.

I would already be settling my next score by the time the authorities located the "victims" of this tragedy.

A.A. Garrison

Life is Good

I am a young man, in young clothes, walking through a young part of town. It is a pretty summer day and things are in order, and I should have every reason to smile; but I don't. I'm looking for my friends.

Away from them, I just don't feel right.

The world is threatening, to me. I feel as awkward as anyone seen alone, and I look every bit like I feel. When I pass fellow pedestrians, I do not make their eyes. When I pass groups, I walk faster. My face says I inhabit a war zone.

I round a corner, and that's when I see my friends.

They are congregated outside a bar, five in number, of my age and appearance, like mirror images escaped into the material world. My friends aren't at all awkward or afraid. Grinning and composed, they are a single, able organism, as if connected to the same machine. Confidence shines from them, and a raw, dumb strength. Were they not my friends, I might fear these men.

"Hey," they say to me. "Hey," I reply.

Then, magic happens: the group accepts me.

The change is so swift. All at once, there is no longer an "I," but a "we." My friends' strength becomes my own, and it grows by consequence. I shed my awkwardness and vulnerability. My eyes sharpen. I assume the well-nourished glow of my colleagues. The man of seconds ago falls away, as if never there at all.

This feels right.

We feel right.

And then we are walking, with no destination stated or implied, still feeling perfectly right. One of us cracks a joke, and I laugh deeply, despite it going over my head, because this, too, feels right. We pass individuals and intimidate them nonverbally, and I never question the rightness of this behavior, for all my intimidation just minutes prior. Presently, feeling right is all that matters.

Similarly, it feels right to harass the woman—but, who is harassing? We are just goofing around, giving the pretty lady some innocent attention, and we agree on this, in the bush telegraph of our body language. Yet, when we innocently follow her for a block, and innocently make loud, male noises, and innocently feel her up, causing her to spin to us with incredible speed—she appears afraid, and offended, and not a little enraged.

What a crazy bitch.

"Crazy bitch," we tell her, innocently. She doesn't move until we are some distance away.

The man is just as crazy, perhaps something in the water here. It feels right to set our sights on him, so we do, because anything else would be absurd. Walking clumsily and dressed unfashionably and very alone, the man looks at us as if we had fangs—*fangs*. And when we follow him, turning where he turns and stopping where he stops, he begins watching us from the corner of his eye, as if our fangs are bloody. And, after several blocks, when he finally runs, it is with a fervor suggesting an open mouthful of these fangs.

There is no question of giving chase, for this, also, feels right, as much as any other right thing we've done today. Even as the man shows surprising endurance, leading us through a maze of alleys and back doors, the objective remains clear. Doubt is for the wrong people of the world, and the crazies like this man.

The lunatic's luck soon runs out, and we have him cornered, somewhere he won't be heard. Then, he's shouting and pointing his finger, as if *we're* the crazy ones. I want to argue my case, list the many reasons for this man's craziness, but that does not feel right. Now, it feels right to punish this man for his blatant wrongness in these matters.

Without a word, my colleagues agree.

Silence in the trash-littered alley as we merge on this villain amongst us, forcing him into the little valley between two dumpsters. We tackle him as we do all things: as one, reducing the man to a squirming, deadlocked knot of skin and clothes. It is six against one, but, somehow, this feels fair—and so it is, despite all rational thought. Mathematics, like most else, were suspended upon my induction into the We.

Somehow, the lunatic manages to free a fist and connect it with one of our noses.

The effect is instantaneous and explosive: this evil person has hurt us—*us*, the eternally innocent. The attack is paused as my injured friend looks amongst us, receiving reinforcement. I feel so offended. Solemnly, our attention returns to the attacker, now with an ironclad justification.

But, still, the man has the gall to shout and accuse as we deliver his just punishment. Only a broken jaw ceases his outrageous antics, reducing them to wet gurgles. His eyes swell shut, as to blind him to his justice. His knees turn the wrong way. Crushed ribs show just how wrong he is. It feels necessary to continue beating him, for his own good, and so we do. Suddenly, I understand how parents feel when spanking a disobedient child.

When the beating is done, it only signals a shift, from injury to sodomy. I am surprised, but only by how right it feels. The man makes no response as we violate him in turn, and this only confirms his guilt and our righteousness. We are helping this poor crazy soul, is the consensus, and nothing could be more sound and sensible. Our good deed for the day. We deserve medals, perhaps.

Can we do wrong, my good friends and me? What is this miraculous power we've discovered?

These are my thoughts as we finish our non-rape and then leave, this as coordinated as everything else, as if rehearsed many times. Then, however, something changes: there is the slightest of faltering between us, our We-ness slipping just one tiny bit. The feeling—of *question*, of *wrongness*—sweeps through us like an airborne disease, altering our shapes and strides. What could this be? Had the We been mistaken? I want to say something, but I have no words for the bizarre thoughts swarming my mind. Neither do my compatriots.

So, we say nothing. We walk on, and eventually the feeling goes away. You just have to ignore these things, I guess. Solutions are so easy.

By the time we return to the street, it's all okay, everything okay. The world looks no different than when we left, and now we don't either. We continue our march, and no one speaks, and this feels the rightest of anything.

I spend the rest of the day with my friends, then go home, still feeling absolutely right. I sleep well that night, and those thereafter. Later in life, I go to a good school and get a good job and marry a good wife, like all my friends, which proves just how right we were all along.

Man, life is good.

Greg McWhorter

Light

I sit here all alone, perspiring and whimpering on the cold linoleum floor. I sit with my knees pulled up to my chest and my hands wrapped around my drawn up legs. The cold is sapping my strength. I shiver. I sob. I hurt. I'm in pain. My brain is on fire. It literally feels as if there is a conflagration within my skull that knows no cessation.

I shot up again. I'm a junkie. The chemicals in my veins keep the apparitions at bay, but the cost is my slowly ebbing mental state. I am becoming animal-like. How long have I been here? At least I no longer see the dead. The doctors think that the cuts on my arms are ones that I made, but they are actually from them – the apparitions. The ghosts, or whatever the hell they are, are trying to cut me up. They crave my flesh, but they seem intent on making me suffer. They are intent on my downfall. They are intent on my eventual destruction. They will see me dead.

I'm fighting them off with chemicals, but my brain can't take much more. I must do something. Maybe I can cut the symptoms out. Maybe I can dispel the demons within me. At least I think they emanate from me. Something inside of me is dead. I rock back and forth. There is only one light in this small room and it is directly over my head. A light bulb with no covering. Stark and bleak.

I keep rocking, slowly at first and then with increasing energy until I manage to stand up. I shamble over to a small briefcase sitting on a nearby table. All of my knives are gone. The doctors were efficient and left me with nothing. I have no way to cut out the demons that howl in my skull. That must be where the apparitions come from. Only the drugs keep them entombed within me. I need to let them out, but in a way that releases me from them.

I turn and see a nearby window. Of course it has metal bars over the outside of it to prevent my falling out. The glass is on the inside though. I pick up the small briefcase and shuffle over to the window. I stand looking at my reflection in the glass for only a second. I see that the demon is me. That's all I need to know. I pick up the briefcase and smash the glass before anyone can stop me. I know that they watch me from behind their safe distance and video cameras.

As the glass shards fall to the floor, I toss aside the briefcase and quickly thrust my head through the new opening. The bars outside prevent me from getting my whole body outside, but there is just enough space for my head between the bars. I let my head slide down between the bars quickly and try to decapitate myself on the broken glass still upright in the sill. I don't get my head off, but my throat is cut at the jugular and I can feel life quickly flowing from me. I am free from the dead at last. I am free.

Scathe meic Beorh

Annalisa!

Tessie ran and ran and ran in big, wide circles, her flaxen hair blowing like laughing wheat, her Brandeis-blue dress covered with snowy polka dots shifting this way and that in the crisp Atlantic breeze of the early year. Tessie was like a butterfly—you couldn't catch her, but she was beautiful to look at.

***

Tessie's twin sister Jessie liked to sit and dream. Sometimes she liked to run around in big circles, but mostly she liked to sit and dream, so she never ate as many peanut butter and jelly sandwiches as Tessie because she was never anywhere near as hungry. Few people could tell the difference between the five-year-olds, they were so much alike. Annalisa could tell the difference, but she was their baby sister by two years. Miller couldn't tell the difference, though, because he was just born. Miller was the girls' baby brother. Tessie and Jessie told Annalisa that Miller flew down from Heaven on wings that God made from the pages of golden faerytale books, but Annalisa had already decided that her brother sprouted out of the red oak that grew in their back yard, and his bright red hair was proof of it. And Miller smelled like their oak tree, which was even more proof.

***

The day after Tessie fell and twisted her ankle and decided that running in circles while blindfolded might not be such a good idea after all, Annalisa stole Miller out of his crib, climbed her daddy's old wooden ladder that was leaning against the red oak, and hid her baby brother in the spacious crotch of the tree.

"Tessie? Jessie? Where's Miller?"

"Annalisa had him. Mommy my ankle hurts. Really bad."

"Annalisa? *Annalisa! Come to the kitchen please!*" Mommy felt panic rising in her like the waters of a flash flood.

"Yes, Mommy Rabbit?" said Annalisa as she hopped down the stairs with her hands cupped on the top of her head like bunny ears. "Mommy, do rabbits only squint their nose and hop?"

"*Annalisa! Rabbits later! Where is Miller! Where is he!*"

"Oh. Outside in his tree," said Annalisa as she yawned. "I tired of him crying and waking me up, so I take him back to his tree. He be alright."

***

Mommy didn't remember climbing the ladder. Neither did she remember falling. When she awoke in a swirly daze, unhurt, she was surrounded by willowy figures with bright ginger hair. One of them held Miller.

"My baby!"

"This one is yours?" the Red Oak Lady holding him replied.

"Yes! *Miller!* He's my baby boy!"

"He's a handful, this one. He bawls all the time. You may certainly have him back, and please tell the flaxen haired child who brought him to only bring quiet ones from now on. We simply have no time for the ones who bawl. Our own small ones never bawl. Our people weep sometimes, yes, but we never bawl."

"Please... give me my baby...." Mommy said as she stood and took Miller from the Red Oak Lady. Other Red Oak People stood looking at her as if seeing something they had never seen before. Then they all began to diminish like a morning fog in the sun, and were soon gone.

***

"Why you bring Miller back, Mommy? Now he cry all the time again. I don't like him cry all the time."

"Don't take him away again, Annalisa," Mommy said as she held Miller close and wept. "If you ever take him away again, Annalisa, I'll give you to the Raven People who have claws and beaks as sharp as Daddy's kitchen knife. The Raven People like to eat children's eyes out and then chew their lips off. If you don't want that to happen to you, Annalisa, then never ever take Miller away again. *Ever.*"

"Alright Mommy," said Annalisa, but she wasn't scared of the Raven People. They came in her dreams sometimes and told her astonishing stories about their world. Annalisa liked the idea of going to see where they lived, and if stealing Miller could help make that happen, then that was what she was going to do. Miller wasn't hurt with the Red Oak People. They didn't hurt him. Maybe Mommy was angry with them and told them she would take them to the Raven People, and they were scared of the Raven People. But Annalisa wasn't scared. She wanted to go and visit the Raven People. Maybe even live with them forever. She wasn't sure yet. She'd have to wait and see if they had chocolate pie. If they didn't, she was staying with her human family. After all, she would miss Tessie and Jessie a lot. And Daddy. And sometimes Mommy. But never Miller.

***

After Annalisa got the big boy next door to put the ladder back up against the oak for her, she waited at the crotch of the tree until somebody came. One came soon enough.

"White Hair Child, you promise he will not bawl?"

"What *bawl* mean?"

"To make a loud noise with the lips as water pours from the eyes."

"Oh you mean when he cry. No, he not cry no more."

"You promise? We hate babes who cry."

"I *promise* he not cry. I give him medicine. He not cry no more."

***

"Annalisa d-darling," said Mommy, her voice shaking like grass in a high wind.

"Yes Mommy Rabbit?"

"Where... where is Miller, sweetheart?"

"I take him to his tree."

"Annalisa! *Please... oh God!*"

"Where you think I take him, Mommy Rabbit?"

But when Mommy climbed the ladder this time, she didn't fall... until she tried to caress Miller's eyes open, tried to kiss him awake and couldn't. Then she fell.

63

Tessie saw her fall. Jessie saw her fall. Annalisa saw her fall.

To this day, though, all three girls say that they never saw their mother land. It was as if she fell into or through the grassy back yard at the base of their red oak tree.

#

The mortician did masterful work on Miller's missing eyes and chewed-away lips. People said he looked as if he died peaceably in his sleep, though everyone knew the truth.

Scathe meic Beorh

The Burning of David Bailey

The smell of autumn here is nauseating. Death and dead leaves everywhere.

One day a commotion outside pulled me away from putting together my new model biplane. Somebody was yelling to high heaven. Needing to stretch my legs anyway, I opened my window and peeked out. "Oh Lord!" I cried. "Mom! They've got David tied to the tree out front!"

My scream did nothing to pull our mother away from her hallowed household duties. It was like trying to get Dad disinterested in mowing the lawn. Yard work was his "happy place" away from his accounting work at the bank (that he only sometimes enjoyed, he said).

It was a short hop and a skip downstairs and out the side door to the tree-lined street we lived on. *Tuscarora Road.* A place I'll remember forever as being the ideal American neighborhood of the 1950's, complete with a red brick cobblestone street. Buffalo, New York was a good place to be. Unless, of course, the neighborhood kids (with nothing else to do on a lazy October weekend) decided to tie your little brother to the tree in front of his house and burn him at the stake.

The little monsters already had the firewood piled up around David's ankles when I got there. He had stopped yelling and was slumped over in an idiotic stupor that anybody about to be torched alive might find themselves in. A 'last few minutes to live and reflect before death' kind of scenario. I pushed seven-year-old Mary Hopkins and her flaming twist of newspaper out of the way and began tossing pieces of wood, covered in rubbing alcohol, away from my brother. I guess the kids hadn't been able to find gasoline, which was a good thing.

"No! Stop Ned! He stole our candy!" said Bobby Haussler as he stepped forward to challenge me with his wooden sword.

"I don't care what he stole," I replied as I grabbed the silly weapon and wrenched it out of his grubby fingers. "He's my brother and you're not burning him at the stake like some gol'darnned witch!"

"You don't care he stole something from us?" asked Lizzy Riordan.

"Wake up, David!" I said as I gave him a good, stinging slap across his bare arm. "Did you steal the neighborhood kids' candy again?"

"Yeah!" said my younger brother as he snapped back to our reality. He rubbed his arm. "Why'd ya hit me like that, Ned? Why, I ought'a have my buddies work you over! Want me ta have my boys work you over, big guy? Next week at school. You just wait. You'll be sorry! Then we'll see who slaps who."

"Alright," I said. "I'll just leave you tied up here and let the kids burn you alive. How does that sound?"

"Mom'll come get me."

"Mom's doing laundry and getting dinner ready."

"Well... well... Dad'll save me."

"You'll be burnt to a crisp by the time Dad gets home, David," I said as I walked away. "It was nice knowin' ya."

"Yay!" said Mary Hopkins as she struck a match and lit another rolled-up piece of newspaper. The neighborhood kids (there were seventeen in all) made haste to grab up the discarded firewood. They rearranged it back around David's legs. Mary set it afire as best she could. It smoked and then went out.

"More rubbing alcohol," said Toby Haussler, Bobby's older brother by a year. Cindy Riordan, Lizzy's twin sister, brought the bottle and, with her forefinger half-plugging it, sloshed it over the wood. "More fire," she said. "I need fire."

Seeing that things had gotten out of hand, I made myself visible again to David. When he saw me, he began to weep and beg me to save him.

"Ned! I thought you left me! Please. Please, Ned. I'm sorry. Really sorry. I'll have my buddies get you some hot-rod magazines. Or buy you pizza. Or beer, even! Whatever you want. Whatever. Just please untie me and save me from these crazies!"

"Give me the alcohol, Cindy," I said. Though hesitant, the little girl did as she was told. I was, after all, sixteen. She was only ten.

"Ned? Ned! What are you doing? You're gonna set me afire? Mom! Mom! Help! Save me!"

After I had David's grease-monkey blue jeans and white t-shirt soaked with the alcohol, Mary walked up to me with a match. "Strike it," I said. She did. "Now toss it on David."

"Nooooo! You're killing me! Your own brother? You're burning your own brother alive? I hate you! I hate you! Mom! Mom! Save me! Ned's killing me!"

Mary tossed the burning match. David's legs erupted in blue flames, burned for a minute, and then went out. But by this time, every kid in the neighborhood had run for cover, including Mary the Torch.

After covering his shoulders with my coat to keep him from getting pneumonia, I left my kid brother tied to the tree until Dad got home. David was crying and saying he was hungry as Dad untied the ropes and helped him into the house.

"Just another day on Tuscarora Road, eh Ned?" my dad asked me at suppertime. I was nervous. My father carried a sense of justice quite a bit different than the one I had inherited from my mother's side of the family.

"Yes... sir," I replied as I dropped my eyes.

"Good job, son."

David wept into his mashed potatoes.

"Next time," Dad said, "buy the kids candy, David. Don't take it from them. Lesson learned, I hope."

"Yes, Dad," my brother replied as he wiped his eyes and took another bite of meatloaf. "Delicious food, Mom. Thank you. I especially like the crushed tomatoes on top."

The next day there were three hot-rod magazines lying on my dresser. On Halloween Night that year, the favorite house was ours, because we gave out 'the good candy,' which I couldn't eat because of my 'Autumn Nausea,' as I call it.

***

The next time David mistreated the kids in our new neighborhood with his selfish antics, they set out to hang him, but none of them knew how to tie a slipknot. So they tried to drown him instead. Good thing he'd taken swimming lessons.

Scathe meic Beorh

The Witch in Albert's Back Yard

I had never seen a witch grow as a fruit tree, but Albert bet me my *Strange Worlds #1* that he had one growing in his back yard. It was a warm February weekend day, all my chores were done to dad's approval, and Albert's mom was feeding us Sloppy Joes— my fave.

The witch shook her skinny citrus limbs when we got near her. Six more dead leaves dropped off. I watched them swirl to the grass. I imagined they were disguised spacecraft landing on the green surface of Saturn.

"I fed her tuna fish last night like I do with all the stray cats around here," Albert said. Then he shrugged his shoulders like he didn't know if that was the right thing to do or not.

"I don't think you should'a done that," I said. "Now she's gonna want baked fish. And french fries. And some of your mom's blackberry pie. I think you might 'a started something you can't stop."

"Aww, I dunno. She can't move from where she's growing. She don't even talk loud. Listen to her whisper."

I cocked my good ear toward the tree. I could hear a breeze blowing, but I didn't hear the witch say a word. "I can't hear nothing," I said. I was really interested, though, because Albert had never lied to me or even tricked me all our lives, and we had been best friends since we were one or two years old. I didn't care if I lost my comic book in the bet, but I needed solid proof first. "Go get some more tuna fish."

"We're all out. I gave her the last can."

"Then get some deviled ham or something."

"Let's just wait until we eat lunch and then we'll give her some of our Sloppy Joes, what'cha say?"

"Oh alright," I said, disappointed. "Let's get to work on them vampire kits."

We left the witch growing there where she stood and traipsed out to the shed in the far back corner of Albert's yard. All the neighborhood kids liked our Vampire Hunter Kits. We sold lots of them around Halloween every year. My mom gave me and

Albert some of her quilting cloth and other kinds of cloth and showed us how to sew drawstring bags. We had to make the bags pretty big because we had to fit three cloves of garlic strung together, a bottle of holy tap water, another bottle filled with holy cooking oil, a wooden stake big enough to puncture a vampire's heart, a page from the Bible, and a Cross of Jesus made out of two sticks tied together—mallets sold separately at Jemison's Hardware, and a dime dropped in by the vampire hunter if he wanted some silver in there. One day Bick Fidelio asked us if we had 'Ghoul Defense Packs' or something like that, and then all the other kids thought we had those too, and everybody started asking for them. But when me and Albert had our next tree-house meeting, we talked it over, and it didn't make any sense to us because ghouls dig up graves and mess around with dead people, and the kids who were asking for the ghoul kits weren't dead, and were less likely to be dead if they hurried up and bought our Vampire Hunter Kits. So that's what we started saying whenever somebody asked for things to protect them from ghouls and other kinds of monsters. We sold a lot more vampire kits that way. I watched my comic collection grow by the day, and dad watched my cavities grow by the week.

We made seven more Vampire Hunter Kits that afternoon before Albert's mom called us in to eat. She was a nice lady. She gave us Sloppy Joes with kosher dill pickles and iced tea, sweetened with honey I think. Oh, yeah, and potato chips. "Nothing sugary today," she said with a big smile. "Albert's got too many cavities already." I thought that Albert's dad must have really liked his wife's smile.

I saved three pinches of my third Sloppy Joe, and Albert did the same thing. We dropped them into a paper lunch bag. Then I rolled it up and stuck it in the back of my pants under my shirt, which had come untucked anyway. After all, it was Saturday. It'd be tucked in for church the next day anyway, and for school all week. One afternoon wasn't going to hurt anything.

"Hear her?" said Albert as he grabbed my head and turned it in the direction of the witch.

"No."

"Oh c'mon, Rolly!"

"I really can't hear her... *wait...*"

"Yeah?"

"I hear something!"

The breeze had picked up while we were inside eating, and I saw it rustling through all the trees and bushes.

"You hear that?" said Albert, stepping closer to the witch.

"Don't get too close! She might grab you and pull you underground! I read one time about a man who lived in the woods and trapped kids by leaving treasure for them to find and when they did he came out from behind a tree and pulled them underground and ate them alive! Stop Albert! That's close enough! *Stop!*"

Albert stopped inching forward toward the witch tree. "Hear that?" he said.

"Not sure..."

"She said 'hungry!' I heard it. She says she's hungry."

"Yeah, for two twelve year old boys! Get away from her!"

But Albert got too close, and the witch grabbed him and pulled him into her scrawny limbs. "Help! *Rolly!*"

"I'll get you out!" I said as I snatched the bag of Sloppy Joe pieces out of my belt, snapped it open, and flung the food at the monster. One piece slapped Albert upside the face and slid down into his mouth that was open in a silent scream of terror. He coughed and choked... and chewed. "Yum," he said, but his heart just wasn't in it. The rest of the pieces flew into the witch's branches and then plopped down around her roots like hot lava out of a volcano. Or something.

"Too bad our Vampire Hunter Kit won't work on witches!" I said as I looked over at the pile of kits we had made.

"G-garlic! C-cross, Rolly!" said Albert as a twig found his mouth and started diving down his throat. "B-bible! H-h-holy w-water!"

Man, was I stupid! Of course a witch would be afraid of holy oil and water! I ran and got one of our kits and ripped it open. "Albert hang on hang on hang on!"

The Bible page made the twig pop back out of his throat, but now other twigs and branches were doing all kinds of mean things to my friend. I slung holy water and holy oil and garlic cloves and more garlic cloves! "Take that, you stupid witch tree! See if I don't cut you down here in a minute after I get my buddy outta there!" I whipped the Cross of Jesus out and danced around the tree reciting Psalm 23 and the Lord's Prayer back to back, over and over until Albert slid, unconscious, to the ground. The last dead leaf of the witch fell off her and did its slow flight to the grass. I pulled my friend away from her roots and checked his pulse. He was still alive, but barely. Then I went and got the axe out of the shed. I made short work of that witch and then, with the help of some kerosene, made a fire with her to warm Albert back up.

"She dead?" he said as his eyes popped open.

"You better believe it!"

"You're a good friend, Rolly."

"Thanks. So are you."

"I got too close."

"Sometimes we do," I said.

Scathe meic Beorh

The Great Marbella Hutchins

She glowed like some kind of phosphorescent creature that cool desert night as she walked down the almost-two-dimensional Boulevard, slow and measured, like the matron of a demesne, or even a queen. I had heard of women like her from voices filled with horror and wonder. "They're not everywhere, but once you see one, you'll never forget her as long as you live."

But I had to do more than see one. I had to talk to one. If she would talk. If she knew where she was. If she knew she was alive.

The kinds of things that haunt me day and night? Velvet curtains, pipe organs, monkey coffins, 78 rpm records, exotic objects d'art, flamingo feathers, mothballs, tuxedos in steamer trunks, wood mold, original S. Charles Lee ticket booths, flashbulb wool, over-size magnifying glasses atop yellowed newspaper clippings, stiff black scrapbook pages, drained swimming pools, pungent funeral flowers, clematis, old theater seats that creak before you sit in them, the pink light in the corner of a cinema screen, ill-advised taxidermy, cigarillo-smoking projectionists in mustard-stained tank tops, the back of an old starlet's hand seemingly glued to her forehead.

As I came out of the Chinese Theatre, I saw her. I ran. I would catch her, but then what? What then? I didn't think further than that. I passed her, and slowed. Fifteen feet from her I turned, trying to be nonchalant, trying not to let her know that it was only me and her in my tiny world, nothing else, and that my heart burned to know. I had to know.

"I..."

She took a few more steps toward me in her almost-unearthly gait, her faded blue feather boa fluttering in the breeze of a passing 'gypsy cab,' her discolored teal silk evening gown shimmering in an infernal Hollywood breeze.

"You?" she said, her puckered cigarette lips smiling, crow's-feet clawing at her sad, sad eyes.

"I want to know," I said, breathless. "How... how long. How long..."

"How long have I been living in Hollywood? Is that what you want to know, doll?"

I was suddenly frightened. My mind raced to the film Sunset Blvd. I backed away from her and nearly disappeared into the shadows of a side street. But then I came back to my senses.

"Yeah... yes," I replied. "Yes m'am."

"Oh, a Southern boy!"

"Yes ma'am. Northwest Florida."

"Oh my word! Why, I'm from Pensacola!"

"Ma'am... now please don't think I'm lying to you, but I was born and raised in Pensacola."

"Well... I have a way of telling whether you're lying to me or not, young man. What part of Pensacola?"

I saw what she meant. "Ferry Pass," I said.

"Ferry Pass. Sure! Out by the river. See? You're not a liar. A bit of a lair, maybe, but not a liar. Well, I was raised in Downtown Pensacola. On Seville Square. But that's been long ago now. But to answer that burning question of yours... say? Would you like to have a drink with me at the Carousel?"

"Yes ma'am, and I'm buying."

"Such a gentleman!"

***

"I came to Hollywood in 1929," said Marbella Hutchins as she fixed a Pall Mall into her shiny black Bakelite 'opera length' cigarette holder. "Sixty years ago. Got a light, doll?"

"Yes ma'am," I said as I fished around in my loose pants pocket for my Zippo. "May I be honest about something, Miss Hutchins?"

"You sure can, sweetheart," she said, blowing smoke in my face. Classy way to commit suicide. "Honesty's all I got left. All I've had for lots of years now, come to think of it."

"People think... people believe, ah, that women like you are, you know..."

"Crazy? Oh, I know that! Why do you think I'm sitting with you talking right now, young man? You're the only person to talk to me in close to a year, and the last time it was just a bum wanting a fag. I say something sometimes to a person I know lives around here, not a tourist or anything like that, and still all I get is this scared look in their eyes like 'Oh god! That insane old broad just talked to me!'"

I felt like I wanted to cry. I went ahead and did just that. Marbella handed me a bar napkin. It caught three tears before it tore apart. She asked the barkeep for a stack of napkins, then handed me six more before I could fully collect myself.

"You really care about people, don't you, doll?"

"More than anything, Marbella. I guess it's what I do best. Then I go and write it all down."

"Oh! A writer! I should have guessed..."

"Where did you first live here in Hollywood, Miss Hutchins?"

"My first place was in the Regency, just a few buildings north of the Chinese Theatre, on Orange. Something wrong?"

"No," I replied, realizing that my facial expression had spoken out of turn. "It's just that I live there is all. The Regency. Which room was yours?"

"All the way at the back of the building, second floor on the right, as I remember. It's been fifty years, give or take."

"That's my room. My apartment. There's talk of tearing it down. Least that's what I hear."

"I didn't want to hear that, doll. That's not good news. You know Marilyn and Bogie both lived there when they were just getting started, don't you?"

"I heard... pretty thrilling. I've wondered if maybe they stayed in the room I'm in..."

"You said apartment. Those are rooms, not apartments, sweetheart."

"I have, well... you know, a stove, refrigerator..."

"Oh, there was nothing like that in there when I lived there, doll. A Hollywood starlet had to eat at cheap diners and hole-in-the-wall restaurants back then. Well, most of them..."

"I see."

"Do you? Maybe you do. You're a writer after all. Well, I can't imagine trying to cook in such a small place anyways. Not and have room for my dressing table and all my clothes. Still have the Murphy bed that folds down out of the closet?"

I stirred my drink. What should I ask next? I wanted to know it all, but how could I learn over a half-century of knowledge about a lady's life in an hour. Two hours. Three hours. Heck, even three days!

74

"You want to know how I've lived in Hollywood all these years? How I've survived?"

"Well, Miss Hutchins," I said, sure that I had never heard of her or seen her in any film. "Yes, I would like to know how you have survived. But I don't think it's any of my business, really."

"I've just made it your business, haven't I? Listen, doll. I don't say anything I don't want to say. I never have, I never will. So here's the facts. I am a wealthy heiress. That means I'm a princess. An old, worn-out princess that everybody thinks is crazy, but a princess nonetheless. Every year that goes by, though, less and less people pay attention to me. It used to hurt bad, to be ignored. See, I was quite the actress in my day. Leastwise till the War, then everything fell apart on me. I never had more than bit parts even at the height of my career, but then those quit coming along. I couldn't keep an agent. They all said I was 'over-the-hill.' Lord! I was only thirty-two! I could have gone back to Pensacola, but why? My mother and father were dead, I had no siblings, and what few relatives I had wanted my money. My father, a wise man when it came to money, sold out before the Stock Market Crash, and then he and my mother were killed in an automobile accident. Everything they had went to me. I had a dream. I wanted to be a movie star. I came, I saw, and I sort of conquered. At any rate, I stayed here in Hollywood. I always lived cheap, preparing for the very real likelihood that I would never become a star. I never did, of course. You ever heard of 'the Great Marbella Hutchins?' My last job as an actor was in 1940. I played a WAAC in one of those insidious war infomercials they played in the movie houses."

"But... but that's been almost fifty years ago, Miss Hutchins!"

Marbella looked down at her whiskey and swirled the melting ice. "Yes it has, hasn't it. Another 'Shirley Temple' for you, doll?"

"No m'am. Thank you, though. Why... why do you... still dress as if you were attending a Hollywood soirée?"

"And why shouldn't I?"

I felt truly embarrassed. I shouldn't have asked that question. "I'm sorry," I said. "I dress how I feel. Why shouldn't you?"

Her smile was genuine. She took my hands in her bony fingers. Her skin felt thin, like my grandmother's. Marbella was, after all, a very old woman. Despite her evening gown. Despite her boa. Despite her lipstick and rouge.

"Where do you live now?" I asked, trying not to feel ashamed for the whole night, for the kamikaze way I had accosted her, for being such a poor sociologist. A writer. A speculative fiction writer no less. Sociologists condemn us daily for our methods. But that's alright. I condemn them for theirs.

"The Knickerbocker," she replied. "I live at the Knickerbocker with all the rest of the old fogies."

"I'm glad. I mean..." God! Open mouth, insert entire leg...

"Ha! You're glad that I don't live on the streets like a nasty old bag-lady!" she replied, genuinely tickled. I relaxed a little.

"Will... you have lunch with me tomorrow, Marbella? My treat. Musso & Frank Grill?"

"Such a gentleman," she replied. "I'd be happy to, doll. I'd be happy to."

***

Marbella Hutchins never met me at the famous grill on Hollywood Blvd. I went to the Knickerbocker Hotel looking for her, but the attendant told me in a typical Hollywood matter-of-fact tone that unless one of their elderly residents made prior arrangements, no one was allowed beyond the lobby. So for several days I waited in the lobby for her, hoping she would come out, hoping I would hear that she had been feeling just a bit under the weather or something. But I never saw Marbella again. Not on the Boulevard. Not anywhere in Hollywood. Not even in my dreams.

Short Stories

Photo by Mike Jansen

Mike Jensen

Master Pricklylegs

The town is getting ready to go to sleep. Snow covers the walls and the roofs of the houses that are just visible above the wall. A cruel wind blows from the east and disperses the smoke that wafts from the chimneys. The gates are closed. No one dares remain outside in the freezing cold. Even the guards stay inside, confident that the weather is a better detriment to invading forces or ordinary bandits than the high stone walls.

In the darkness beyond the town rise the crumbling towers of the City, ancient and mostly dead and dark. Its remains have helped build the town and pieces of steel girders and blocks of concrete are visible between brick and ordinary mortar.

The deep dark forests to the south were seldom travelled, but this night a lone figure dances along the white paths, barely leaving a trail and even that is quickly filled up with loose powder snow. He is tall, yet thin, gaunt almost, thin legs reminiscent of a stork's stilts with large, flat feet. His upper body is well formed and powerful. A long, grey beard covers his face, barely leaving his large nose and small, black eyes free. His clothes are dark but they seem to blend in with his surroundings.

Occasionally the traveler plucks the strings of his lyre, generating chilling dissonants that spur his calico cat to greater effort. The small animal hastens to catch up to its master while trying to keep its belly out of the snow. It shakes its paws regularly to get the snow off.

When its master halts before the gates it sits between his thin legs and looks up hungrily at the small mice that nest in his grey beard.

He takes off his hat and the wind grabs his lanky hair and whips it into a grey halo around his head. With a deft movement, he picks a small feather from the dark fabric, holds it up in his hand, and blows it at the city gates. Without a sound, the ghostly essence of the gate swings open.

Master Pricklylegs smiles and bares sharp teeth in a too wide mouth. He replaces his hat, picks up the cat that he keeps in the crook of his right arm, to protect it from the mice and their razor blades, and together they walk through the ghostly gates.

The street beyond is quiet and snow has formed deep mounds. Warm yellow light pours from a small window just off to the left. He places the cat on top of the highest mound and watches in amusement as it flounders and slides down. It glares at him with yellow, hate filled feline eyes. The cat seems ready to give him a piece of its claws, but the glittering razor blades the mice swing out of Pricklylegs' beard deter sufficiently to calm it.

The man himself hardly notices. He plucks his lyre again and the dark notes reverberate harshly between the houses, hardly softened by the thick snow and the dense curtain of flakes that fills the air. He licks his lips from ear to ear as if he tries to taste the air. His eyes pinch closed as he sniffs up the scents, making him seem almost eyeless.

"Weather won't hide you, sweet one," he says. His voice is deep and throaty. He coughs and spits and the snow around his yellow phlegm melts into a small, bubbling puddle.

He moves forward, leaving only the trail of his calico's paws in the virgin snow. At the very first crossroads, he waits and listens.

"Show yourself!" he demands. Nothing. He whips out a fan and opens it, revealing blades covered with many colors of cellophane that he uses to scan the road until he finds and recognizes the small figure that hides behind an abandoned wheelbarrow.

"Name your price, old one," Master Pricklylegs states formally. The lands may change and civilizations may grow or wither, but his sense of etiquette is flawless, as ever.

The answer is a mere whisper, but he hears it like he feels the burning need of the minute deity. He nods his agreement and takes a small flask from his dark robes. From it he sprinkles a few drops in each direction. It's not going to rescue the small god, but it will sustain him a little longer until belief grows strong again.

He moves on until he sees the lantern man standing on his ladder, refilling one of the few cast iron lanterns the town has.

As he ignites the lamp the lantern man sees the dark form of Master Pricklylegs at the edge of the light. A deep sense of fright makes him fall backward, but a strong arm catches him. As he looks up into the dark face of his rescuer and sees row upon row of sharp teeth in an inhumanly large mouth, he feels the warmth of his urine spread along his legs.

79

Master Pricklylegs spins his rattle in front of the lantern man's face, causing him to fall into a deep sleep. Carefully he carries the man to the nearest house, breaks the lock on the door, and places his charge inside, finds a blanket to cover him, then closes the door again. Tonight is not the night for killing the living.

He follows the trail of lanterns until he reaches the town's centre. Bleak, square buildings of dark concrete blocks, their shutters closed, surround the square. One building seems created from the granite and marble of ancient mausoleums and some of the walls still show faded gilded Latin characters. A sign reads 'Town Hall." There is power there, other than the worldly power of the leaders of this place and he sniffs deeply. He has to pass this place to reach the alluring scent that guided him here.

The captain of the guard and three of his men leave Town Hall and start to cross the square. The men wear normal clothes with a thick cloak against the cold, but their superior is in full chain armor and the sound it makes as he moves is harsh yet strangely muffled in the steadily falling snow. When they reach the other side of the square, the captain suddenly looks up into Master Pricklylegs' eyes. He barks at his men and they quickly disappear.

"You're out late, bone shadow," the captain says.

Master Pricklylegs looks down at the man and his armor and the sudden holy fire that burns bright in his clear blue eyes. He has seen it happen before, many times. "Paladin. You're far from your usual haunts."

"I'm always near when you're hunting, you know that. Even in this far off place," Paladin says. He turns to the calico cat and says, "Meow. Mrrmeow."

The calico cat twitches its whiskers and replies: "Quite well, thank you very much, oh, wielder of purity." The voice is human and drips with sarcasm.

Paladin snorts. "Cats," he says. "State your intent, bone shadow, I demand it."

Master Pricklylegs growls and the mice in his beard throw old breadcrumbs at Paladin, but etiquette again wins. "I follow a dead trail this night, Paladin. The living need not fear me."

Paladin examines Pricklylegs' face but there is no subterfuge and he does not expect it, not from the bone shadow. There is no need. But the ancient traditions must be observed if the Old Ones wish to survive the dusk of civilization. He nods at the lyre and says, "Play me a dirge then."

The cat climbs onto a low, stone wall and taps snow off its paws. "Are you certain?" it asks. "There is much sadness in Pricklylegs tonight."

Paladin nods. "If it is bleaker than this fimbulwinter it might lift my spirits somewhat."

The cat sits straight. "Do you think it will come?"

"What? The end?" Paladin shakes his head. "Who can tell? All I know is that the winters last longer and that the other seasons have shortened."

"What do the humans think?" calico cat asks.

"Before the collapse they talked about reduced solar output and shifting poles. Now they only try to survive and "civilization" turned out to be a thin veneer," Paladin says. A deep sadness in his eyes almost matches the dark melody that Pricklylegs now produces from his lyre. "Aye, that must be the darkest, most brooding piece you ever played, bone shadow."

Pricklylegs bows deeply which evokes protest from the mice in his beard. "I need your permission, of course."

"And you have it. The dead you hunt must be old and wicked if it is to match your play," Paladin says.

"It is, Paladin." Master Pricklylegs puts his lyre away. "Tonight we are not enemies." He nods at the other man and continues on his way.

He crosses the square and passes Town Hall. The power in the stones is old and strong, but it sleeps and he knows it will not bother him in his endeavors. He feels Paladin's eyes still on his back and as he passes just beyond Town Hall, he sees the other man watching him. He lifts his right hand, as if waving goodbye, a very human gesture and utterly unheard of. He doesn't know if Paladin noticed it or if it made him feel any different, but at this time and in this place the gesture, empty as it may be, seems oddly suited.

He finds the trail near the cemetery, a droplet of blood, a wisp of hair, the corpse of a young man who looks to have fallen asleep against the naked white stone breasts of a voluptuous cherub. Little snow remains on the young man, which means there is still some residual warmth left to melt it off.

The girl hides in one of the ancient tombs that once housed the dead of the City. Their wood caskets have all been removed for firewood. And bones mix well with mortar. She notices Pricklylegs and starts to run. It's always the same, he reflects, the dead are cowards. For the first time in his existence, he wonders if they fear dying again, or do they perhaps welcome an end to their parasitic existence?

She tries to double back toward town square, most likely to engage the help of the guards who might recognize her as someone's daughter. Pricklylegs increases his speed and he notices calico cat has no problem keeping up. It too enjoys the hunt.

They catch up to the girl in an empty courtyard where doors and shutters are closed and there is no escape. Pricklylegs notices her thin cotton blouse and voluptuous skirts with gaudy frills. She is dressed as a two-bit tart. With uncanny clarity, he remembers other encounters where the dress of his victims never mattered for the job at hand. Now he sees reason and purpose and he understands the fear of discovery that drives the creature before him, which ultimately is the fear of an untimely, second death.

"Spare me," she pleads, "I'll do anything." She unbuttons her blouse and bares small breasts. She bows her head and her cold lips form silent words.

Master Pricklylegs realizes this is prayer, a religion of the dead and an image of a thorny wreath appears before his mind's eye. But his heart is as cold as the fimbulwinter and with a gesture he initiates the torture that earned him his name.

The girls shrieks as the bones in her body start to twist and contort, breaking off splinters that pierce flesh, nerves and organs. Her legs break in dozens of places and she drops onto the snow, sobbing. Slowly the bones in her body curl up and her limbs move accordingly. Pricklylegs observes as he has done so often before. Despite her anguish, she continues her whispering prayers and it bothers him.

"Are you nearly done?" a voice behind him asks. He looks back and just sees calico cat unfold into Bubastis, his Queen of Thorns.

"I think she's sufficiently immobilized," Master Pricklylegs says.

"She can still move, Pricklylegs," Bubastis says. "You need to fix her here, where the sun will touch as it rises."

"Have you ever wondered if they are capable of reason, Bubastis?" he asks.

"They're no more than animals, Pricklylegs. You know this," Bubastis admonishes him. "Here, let me." She speaks a Word and the girl renews her shrieking. Within seconds thick, black thorns spear through the girl's flesh and roots seek hold and penetrate the ground where she sits.

"Of course," Pricklylegs says. "I have just begun wondering if all this is really necessary."

Bubastis looks at him with questioning eyes. "Is something wrong with you, Pricklylegs? She taps her right foot in exact synchronicity with the growth of the thorns inside the girl and the shrieking becomes a hoarse whisper. "Kill the dead, you always say. Now you hesitate?"

Master Pricklylegs slowly shakes his head. "No, you are right, this is the proper way." He offers his arm to Bubastis and together they depart, leaving the girl in her twisted and thorn filled body until the rays of the rising sun will melt the flesh from her bones.

***

The morning is grey, dreary, and cold. As always. Still, the baker needs to be at work long before the people rise from their slumber. These days however people remain in their beds as long as possible, which also means they pick up their bread later.

Baldwin the baker is a very tall man, wide of shoulder and always covered in flour. Even on the last day of the year, he gets up early to leave for the bakery. When he steps out the door, he notices a thorn bush in the courtyard that had not been there before. Somehow, it reminds him of a girl, but he shakes his head and pulls his coat closer around him.

As he walks past the thorn bush, a golden flickering attracts his attention. He halts, looks, and sees a gold key hanging from a gold chain from one of the branches of the thorn bush.

Curious he picks up the jewel. He holds it up in the light of the sun and looks at it in amazement. He estimates its value might well keep his family in food and clothes for the next few years. He hangs the key from its chain around his neck and stares at the thorn bush for seven minutes.

The baker walks back into the house. He thinks it's a good idea to place the key he just found inside, but as he steps into the house, he remembers to pick up an axe and he proceeds to kill his wife and two little boys. He knows there is a job to do and for that, he needs their power, their strength.

With newfound strength, the baker starts setting the stage for the return of Master Pricklylegs who has just enough moral compass to know that he has left loose ends in town. The baker diligently positions his pawns and polishes the words and lines for maximum effect. Pricklylegs is nearly where he needs to be and once the countless iterations culminate into the desired effect, he will understand his true purpose. Now it is just a matter of improving the world around him until the set is just right and the sleeper awakens to end all and –perhaps- begin anew.

Paula D.

Ashe Bereft

Angeline languidly trails her fingertips along the slight contours of her breasts. Eyes closed, mouth slightly agape, a corona of swampy light surrounds her like a halo. She straddles me, her knees digging into the soiled mattress beneath us. I'm on my back, legs open, knees pressing against the petal softness of her skin. With one hand, I trace the dry opening of her cunt. With the other, I mirror the movement against my own aperture. Across the room, Our Father sits in a battered leather recliner, shirtless, the fly of His pants unzipped and unbuttoned as He strokes Himself to hardness. On His chest are moss-like patches of wiry silver hairs that darken near His nipples. His skin is dark and tough, like alligator scales. His shoulders are broad, his body thickly muscled. I can think He's a monster. A demon who took Our Father and wears his skin like a cloak. He sees me watching and peers at me over wire-rimmed glasses.

I smile. He has taught us to grin flirtatiously while performing for Him. Before, we would cry, scream, and beg. We didn't want to touch each other. It was scary. We didn't want to touch Him. It was wrong. We didn't want to be touched. It was painful. He used His words, hands, and instruments to shape us to His liking.

Father's smile has soured to a frown. His penis remains flaccid. His shift at the hospital is soon and we have yet to fulfill our duty. Angeline's eyes are still closed. I need her here. I pull my hand from her and suck at my fingertips.

Her taste calms me.

Our Father grunts in pleasure. I slip my hand between her legs, find the bundle of nerves centered in her folds and slickly massage it in the way that makes her tremble from the inside out. I will coax her back to me. I will love her in the way she likes so she is the only thing I feel while I fall into the sanctuary of her eyes. Our Father can do what He wants to me, as long as I can stay lost there, with her.

Last night she said we should just make him mad. Last night she said she just wanted it all to be over.

The bead of damp heat at her core thickens.

Last night I held her in the dark, whispered nonsense things to calm her. I stroked her hair and told her that God would not abandon us. I said that Mother was telling God to send his angels to come take us away from Him.

"Angels don't exist, Anessa. No one is coming for us."

Soon, she should part her legs and urge her hips forward in invitation.

But she doesn't.

Angeline is still. Her movements have not altered. She's not even here.

She's left me alone with Him again.

Father remains limp. Frowning. Droplets of sweat appear on his upper lip. He is impatient. My heart thunders in my chest. She means to anger him. I will my hands to still. We have failed our obligations only once before. He left us caged for 72 hours. No food, no water, no toilet. He must be pleasured. Now that Mother's gone, the act falls to us.

It's what daughters do.

When He first brought us down here there was a kitten in the backyard. He let us play with her for a while. We named her Belle. Then, He came downstairs and skinned her alive in front us. Her screams sounded human. She was so scared. She sounded like she was made of pain. Her body contorted and twisted to get away, but Father's dripping red fists were so big. As he maneuvered the blade beneath her fur I could feel the steel severing the flesh from my bones. I passed out. When I came to, Belle was thankfully dead. He told us he could have made it last for days. He told us that if we were disobedient, if we did not give ourselves to Him, he would do the same to us.

I see Belle now at the bottom of the steps like she was when he tossed her away once finished.

I see Angeline in her place, a terrible crimson promise.

I shove three fingers inside of her. She doubles over, screams. Her thighs clamp together and push me in deeper. Our Father sits up in His recliner, His member growing ruddy, and stiff. Angeline is crying. She pushes at my shoulders, trying to force me out. I dig my fingernails into her taut inner walls and anchor myself. A liquid warmth trickles into my palm. I glance downward to find dark crimson streaks marring my wrist.

Pushing myself upright, I quickly shove Angeline to the ground. I'm on top of her. Driving myself into her. Slickened by her blood.

"Anessa! I'm sorry! Plea--"

I clamp my other hand over her mouth.

I am Father and she is Me.

Leather creaks. Our Father gets up from his seat. Engorged, enormous, I brace myself for the violence of His entrance.

Leaning forward, angling myself higher in the way He likes, Our Father impales me. I squeeze my eyes shut. His smooth surgeon's hands have turned my bones into handles, made my body His machine. With each thrust of him, I become wetter, warmer. My head is yanked upward.

It hurts my neck, but I remain quiet. His grunts grow harder, faster.

This will end soon. Thankfully, it always ends. But that just means another beginning.

I open my eyes. My sister's face is blotchy and tear stained. Her mouth is a tight line, her eyes clenched closed. Her shoulders are hunched up around her ears, her arms cross her small breasts in useless protection, her hands defensively splayed. The slap of Him against my buttocks drives me even deeper into her. He's going to come soon. Father releases my hair and squeezes my waist between His hands with such force that tears spring to my eyes. He'd love nothing more than to crush my pelvis. God, what would He do to me if I were I immobile? Slowly, so as not to disturb Him, I ease myself forward until my face hovers above hers.

Her weakness, her crying, her pleading, her face and body paralyzed in anguish makes me weak.

I wish she were dead. Then, I wouldn't care what He did to me. Then I wouldn't need to be alive. I hate her. My malice writhes through me like a snake as Father's spits its hot venom into me. The tears against my lips have doubled. My body shudders with restrained sobs. Father slaps my rear. He thinks I'm enjoying myself.

"Anessa..."

My name comes out in a weak squeal. I pull my fingers from her, red and sodden.

Father disengages me, buckles his pants and loudly clomps up the stairs. Angeline trembles beneath me.

I am Father.

***

"Would you like some time alone?"

We stand in the doorway of Angeline's apartment. On the twin bed tucked into the far corner of the small studio, she lies beneath a makeshift shroud of sheets. She covered herself, closed her eyes, and sailed silently away on an ocean of stolen sedatives. Nine days before her thirty-eighth birthday. Four days before my fortieth. Her presents are in the trunk of my car.

"Yes. Please."

Tammy Richards, resident supervisor of Fairhaven Communal Living, nods and places a hand softly onto my forearm. The fish-belly pale skin around her eyes is ringed red and blotched with shadow.

"Take as much time as you need. I'm so sorry again, Anessa. I'll be in my office."

I step into the room and Tammy shuts the door behind me. Angeline's apartment is almost cheerful with the bright spring sun pouring through the curtained windows. The shelves along the wall are adorned with children's books and colorful toys. On the middle shelf is a bucket of sidewalk chalk and a yellow plastic dump truck. The corners of the truck bed are grimed with sand. Beside the truck is an empty space. There is supposed to be something there, but my memory is as blank as the bare walls. That's new. She'd had so many goofy and garishly colored posters of kittens and puppies and pastel unicorns zipping through space. I didn't notice the absence when I brought her back yesterday. Maybe Tammy took them down.

"Oh Angeline..."

My breath is swept from my lungs and I collapse against the door. She doesn't move. I slide to the ground. She's gone. There's light and air and color and she's gone.

My sister is dead.

I pull my knees up to my chin and wrap my arms around my head. I shouldn't be here. I can't do this. My breath catches in my throat. I fall over onto my side. Shivering, as all the heat leaves me. She's gone.

I shriek through clenched teeth and pound my fists against my head.

Sometimes when we were in our cage I would scream until my throat went raw. Angeline would comfort me. She would hold me to her breasts and rock me until I fell asleep.

I hit myself harder. My rings, thick gems nestled on bright silver bands dig into my scalp, pop hard against my skull.

She's gone.

He won.

A sharp pain fires in my stomach and acid rises in my tear-choked throat. Crawling up from the floor, I run to the small bathroom in the corner and vomit into the toilet.

I stand, flush, turn to the sink. Her toothbrush sticks haphazardly from a green plastic cup sitting on the edge of the basin. I turn on the cold tap, rinse my mouth and spit. The corner of the mirror is fouled with a star-shaped smear of browning adhesive. I close my eyes. A pink star. There was a little pink smiling star stuck to the mirror. She tore it down. Recently.

My eyes burn and the image blurs. She destroyed what she loved. She desecrated the silliness she thought was sacred. Maybe she was trying to grow up. Maybe this was the only way she knew how to. Wiping away the scalding tears, I leave the restroom and stand beside Angeline.

The outline of her body beneath the sheets. The absence of breath. The stillness. I will never laugh with her again. Never feel her hugs. Never roll my eyes at her when she says something stupid. The curtains are open. The light, joyous and clean, amplifies her silent form. I twist the blinds shut and pull the drapes together. The room becomes as grey and as dismal as I feel.

With shaking hands, I pull the sheets back and kneel beside her. She looks asleep. Peaceful, solemn, and unreachable. She wears a white tank top and a cerulean knit sweater with daisies sewn onto the oversized pockets. Pulling the sheets back farther, I see her standard black knit pants. For once, they are free of lint balls. I always carried a roll of sticky paper solely for Angeline wherever we went. But she prepared herself for this. Carefully gathered her clothes, lint rolled them as she never did before, and arranged herself on her back. She even crossed her hands daintily over her belly. Emptiness echoes off the bare walls to crash against her still body, presented as if waiting for an audience. This naked fact of planning rakes through me like fishhooks. I reach out and take her hand, not yet stiff, but chilly

89

and dry like snake scales. I lean over the bed and dig my elbows into the mattress. Her body shifts slightly against me.

"What happened, honey?"

I place her hand against my cheek.

"What didn't I see?"

After our rescue and after the institution, regression was the way that she had chosen to cope. I brought Angeline to Fairhaven because I liked the plan that Dr. Gordon enacted for my sister's care. She told me that Angeline would never be what anyone described as "normal" ever again. The damage done to her psyche was permanent but if the only way for her to 'walk in the world' was with the toddling steps of early youth, who were we to cripple her? I liked that.

I liked that so much.

For the first time since we'd been discharged from the Pratt Institute, I felt hope. Father's savings and investments, coupled with His and Mother's insurance policies had provided us with the means to live in relative comfort and seek a variety of rehabilitative options.

I took classes in animal behavior. I liked the innocence of most animals, their eagerness to obey. After earning my degree, I started a dog training service. I helped owners learn how to communicate with their pets in a mutually shared language of gestures, words, and tones. Behavior was important, too. Most dogs want the safety and security of a confident and assertive master. That is the most difficult thing to teach; people are so insecure about their ability to lead, even when it's what a subordinate pet needs. I'm good at bringing that out of them. I'm good at putting it in.

Angeline was on her seventh group home in five years, but at Fairhaven she was starting to get better. She'd been slowly developing a stronger sense of self, one that wasn't tethered to the child-self she'd become. She was feeding herself and taking her meals with the residents instead of staying in her room to be fed by one of the nursing assistants. Last spring she'd been named captain of the Fairhaven kickball team and over the summer had led her team to victory in a citywide tournament for outpatient and inpatient residents of various rehab facilities colloquially known as the "Nutball League".

Last night at dinner she'd been quiet, but that was nothing out of the ordinary. Tuesday was the first of many weekly talk

90

therapy days and she was often subdued after a particularly tough session.

I made her favorite meal: meatloaf, cheesy mashed potatoes, sweet corn, and caramel swirled brownies. She devoured her food and would've eaten the entire pan of brownies if I hadn't stopped her. I distracted her from sulking by luring her from the dining room into the living area with a promise of a Disney movie marathon. We made it through our own specialized extended edition of *Beauty and the Beast* (extended only because we both needed multiple replays of "Be Our Guest" replete with dancing and raucous singing) and a more sedate half of *The Little Mermaid* before her snores became too loud to ignore.

Angeline wanted to stay the night. She could've slept in the guest room. The basement walls were lined with sound absorbing cushions so we would not be disturbed. Once settled in, I would've called Tammy and Dr. Gordon and explained that things were fine, things were good; we were just spending time together as sisters do.

In daylight, at Fairhaven and elsewhere, boundaries were clear. Roles were definite and easy to play. The stern yet compassionate trainer. The doting sister. The casual friend. In the dark, at home, the master wears no masks. I could, and often did, have whatever I wanted.

I was sure that Angeline would want to share a bed with me.

At Pratt, such companionship was expressly forbidden and it was one of the most agonizing lessons we'd had to learn. The first few months there had almost been more torturous than our time in Father's cage. At least there, we had each other. Our team of psychiatrists, psychologists, nurse practitioners, physicians, and social workers had unanimously decided that the first step in our treatment would be eliminating the "unhealthy" aspects of our relationship. They talked about "desexualization" and "establishing appropriate familial and social boundaries." As I was most responsive to treatment, it was my responsibility to initially establish and enforce those boundaries. It took years. I made so many mistakes. Finally, the Angeline I loved began to fade away from me. She became a child. In a way, it was a blessing. I could not cross the border that Father had so happily violated after our mother's sudden illness and passing. Her gradual expression of child-like behavior disturbed and repulsed me. I was released first and, once settled into my routine, I was

91

able to care for Angeline in a way befitting her condition. I became her Big Sister.

Nothing more.

I hold her hand against my mouth. My breath warms her skin and if I try hard enough, I can believe that she's just sleeping. I rub my thumb over the lump where He chopped off her smallest finger with a pair of surgical shears. It happened days before His accident. She'd angered Him by pushing him away. I came between them to protect her. Absently, I slip a hand beneath my hair and trace the jagged scar where my outer ear once was.

My throat constricts. Something happened. Whether it was at therapy or before, something happened and I was too preoccupied with my houseguest to notice.

"I'm so sorry."

Still on my knees, I strip off my ankle-length cable knit sweater, slip out of my heeled boots, and slide beneath the covers beside her.

Lying on my side, I run my fingers through her dull auburn hair. Wrinkles have sprouted at the corners of her eyes and around her mouth. Did I grow so old too?

I adjust her arm behind my back and wrap my arms around her waist. She is so heavy. Not she. It. The body. My sister.

The anguish of her absence crushes the breath from my lungs.

I pull her closer and bury my face in her hair; fragrant and fruity from cheap strawberry shampoo.

"Don't leave me, please."

The breath of each tearful syllable ruffles her hair and my lips graze against the soft meat of her ear. There's a spot of tenderness just below her earlobe where the line of her jaw begins.

I want to put my mouth there.

Clenching my eyes closed, I pull my hands away from her and ball them into fists, shove them between my knees.

"I promised," I whisper to my dead sister, "I promised never to hurt you. I promised to protect you."

I did protect her. From Father. From herself.

One night in our cage I woke up to Angeline pressed against me, my warm twin in the dark of our strange, cold, hell. I turned over. The dirty window allowed a faint silver light into the basement, and in its glow, I saw a dullness blossom in my sister's eyes. She seemed to stare through me, through the bars of the cage, through the walls of the cellar, to a distant world, invisible and all the more desirable. I went cold on the inside. She was leaving me to traipse through some private purgatory and leave me alone in the abyss.

The thought of being left with only the husk of her terrified me beyond any agony Father could deliver. I had to do the only thing I knew to keep the desolation at bay. To keep her with me. With my hands and mouth, I showed her that she was loved and as long as we both lived there would be parts of ourselves that even He couldn't touch. It was our first time without Father.

Where He was rough, I was gentle. Where He was greedy, I was gracious. Father only took, only hurt, only smashed and cut and hit. I was tender. Playful. Angeline and I developed secret games and disguises, made costumes from the trunks of mother's clothes left moldering in boxes. We could become different people when we were alone. When He came stomping down into our world we faded into the shadows to become empty shells, pale sketches of the girls we were. He had no idea of the love we shared. With just a smile, she could ignite a spark of pleasure between my legs. With just a touch, I could rescue her from the madness waiting in her eyes.

Angeline was thirteen and I was fifteen. Two years later Father was rushing home from the hospital and in his haste t-boned a fuel truck carrying close to 100 gallons of gasoline. The heat was so intense that he had to be interred with parts of the driver's seat and steering wheel fused to his bones.

Although inert, I'm sure that spot beneath her ear is just as delicate as it was twenty-four years ago.

I open my eyes. She lies quiet and still.

My palms tingle. After this handful of moments, I will never again hold her, never again smell her, and never again taste her calming chemistry.

I unclench my fists. We used to love each other and it wasn't wrong. It was what we needed, then. It was what saved her, what saved me.

It's what I need, now.

It is the terror of my future bereft of her that presses my lips to her cheek, and spurs my hands beneath her shirt.

Kissing her neck, feeling the fullness of her adult form awakens a part of me I thought had died long ago with our Father. All this time and I have craved nothing else. A door that I'd locked shut opens inside me. My hand tremulously touches the curve of her breast.

I shift myself to fit snugly against her. I trace the sumptuousness of her lips with my thumb and press my mouth to hers.

A strangled sob escapes me and I straddle her. I want nothing more than the tangibility of her flesh against mine. I've distracted myself for so long with weak substitutions, guests unwilling or unable to give me the deliverance I seek.

I know what I've wanted all along. She and I and nothing between us.

Unzipping my slacks with one hand, I slip the other beneath the waistband of her pants. Unfettered, I find her still hand and press her fingertips against the dampness growing between my legs. My fingers graze the thatch of hair adorning her mons and I guide Angeline's cooling digits beneath my underclothes to the place that makes me tremble from the inside out.

I moan, bite my lip to keep from crying out. I am lying on top of her, bucking uncontrollably as the density of sensation smothers me in its indifferent embrace. The taste of warm copper floods my tongue and I suck my lip to tease out the pain to pepper the pleasure.

Removing my hand from her, I step from the bed and strip off my clothes. The air is cool, dry, and still and my skin is hypersensitive to every minute current. I glance behind me; the door to her apartment remains unlocked. Quietly, I pad over and turn the lock into place.

Pulling off her sweater and undershirt is the hardest part. Her shoulders are stiff, but with some maneuvering, the clothes fall away. Something slips from her pocket – a crumpled piece of paper – I want to look but can't stop. A lightness in my limbs speeds my movements. I peel off the rest of her clothes. Her skin is as dry as notebook paper. With a flush of embarrassment and exhilaration, I realize I'm panting.

In the grey light I kneel beside the bed, study every angle, contour, and crevice of her. The cheap carpet feels like whiskers against my knees. The constellations of freckles against the creamy sky of her skin remain the same. Angeline inherited mother's face while I inherited father's hands. A wave of revulsion, sharp shame, my arms wrap around my torso. My eyes shut and my teeth grind together.

Is this what it felt like for him? Was it while Mother was dying from a tiny time bomb ticking cancer into her bladder that he first considered the undiscovered joys of incest? Angeline and I lay on either side of her while father whispered to the hospice care nurse in the hall. Shrunken and desiccated, smelling of illness and piss, mother told us to care for each other, to care for father. To be patient and to love.

I cover my face with my hands; press the plump base of my thumbs into my eyes until bursts of color ignite against the black backdrop of my eyelids.

She kissed us, held us, said her love lived in us, then sent us away. Father went in to her and the calm nurse with the IV trailed respectfully behind him. I held my sister's hand as his disembodied sobs slashed us open like razors. Angeline buried her face into my shoulder, and I wrapped my arms around her and cried into her hair.

Was it on the drive home? The black weeks after the funeral of which neither Angeline nor I remember anything? He pulled us out of school for a private tutor. Was it then that he began to recognize the carnal possibilities embodied in two daughters who desolately orbited him like dead stars? In our grief, the sudden absence of our tutor was barely noticed. In our pain, his invitations into him and mother's bed seemed a minute yet tactile substitute for her absence.

Nestled in sheets that still carried her warm smell, he made us play games. Weeks later came the cage.

I pull my hands from my face. Open my eyes.

Angels don't exist, Anessa. No one is coming for us.

No abyss. No angels. No emptiness.

My hair has fallen from its rushed and loose ponytail to swing like silk against my aching skin. Slight ripples of pleasure throb toward the pulse point between my legs.

That's all there is.

The crumpled wad of notebook paper lies a few inches from me. Her suicide note. The answer to the question. I pick it up, unfurl it slowly as if something poisonous will crawl out at me. Four words. The paper torn in tiny strips where the pressure of her hand ripped through the page to leave black graphite bruises.

I HEARD HER SING.

The words seem to echo from the page and seep into my marrow. How did I not hear her? How could Anessa know—and it hits like a sledgehammer to the sternum.

Anessa did want an audience. A confession means nothing if there's no one to hear it.

"You knew." My breath is a shallow whisper. "All this time, that mask of childishness was just an act, a way to placate me, wasn't it?" I place a hand on the swell of her nearest thigh. "A way to keep me off you." Something gelatinous squelches between my fingers. My fingertips are meat hooks digging into her leg.

"You could've stopped me. You could've asked." I turn to her; see the shadows of congealing blood growing along the length of her underside like moss on a felled tree. "But you didn't."

Climbing into bed, I straddle her hips, lean above her with my hands on either side of her shoulders.

"Because you're a monster, just like me."

I probe the still damp cave of her mouth with my tongue. My lips trace the delicate architecture of her neck and shoulders. Her formerly slight contours are abundant and eager to fill my hands. Her thighs are smooth and hairless. I rediscover her. Still, she tastes of seawater and blood. I trap her thigh against me, bury my hands into her hair, and grind myself against her flesh.

There is life in her stiff caress and death in my kisses. With every heartbeat, I can hear her whispers of delight and cries of pleasure, all those sweet sounds she always made just for me and never for father. An exquisite twist of pain flares at the base of my abdomen and slithers its way up my spine. My stomach tightens. My rhythm against her is uncontrollable, unstoppable. The cheap mattress springs creak in time to our movements. I can't stop. I don't care if they can hear us.

I wrap myself around her like a constrictor. Her bones bend beneath the press of my embrace. I give her everything I am. Ever was. Could be.

We are grains of sand in an ocean of feeling.

Time is nothing here. Time is a cage that we have escaped. You and I, dear sister, momentarily separated on either side of youth and age, of innocence and excess, of life and death, have become the angels of a liminal world. Ours is a non-place of twilit grace, the space between our legs, our mouths, our still and shouting hearts.

Yours. Always. I have been and never will be anything else.

**

I slip back into my clothes and tuck the crumpled bit of paper into my sweater pocket. A precious keepsake. I gingerly pick away the hairs stuck to the bed sheets. Taking some antiseptic wipes from the bathroom, I wipe her down before re-dressing her. With one hand, I toss the cloths into the toilet. I cover my mouth with the other and giggle hysterically.

I walk over to the window and pull the curtains apart. The sky dims as dusk approaches. The sun is little more than rippling garlands of brassy shadow. I feel heavier. Sustained.

Turning from the window, I head toward the door. Tammy and her forms are waiting; the business of death must be conducted. Breathing slowly, I soothe my nerves with the memories of my sister's sex and the silent blessing of her confession. There is calm, yes, but beneath my placid surface is a hunger for the captive's secret song.

She'll sing for me tonight. She'll sing for my sister and me.

Wailing Woman
Ken Goldman

Timothy Frasier

Red on the Head

It was just past noon as the sweltering Georgia sun scorched the large, whitewashed chicken house. July heat radiated off the tin roof while a thousand chickens and one twelve year old boy cooked beneath the roughhewn rafters. Just fifty yards away, a yellow, two-story farmhouse stood guard over a dirt road, which saw no more than three travelers in an average week. The road was lined with massive oaks that predated the century old farmhouse by over two hundred years. Along the road, out of earshot of the noisy chicken house, there was not the slightest hint of highway noise. Even the birds and insects were hushed in the bleak, drought baked forests and windless countryside.

Wilbur Spur peered between the oak slats of the chicken house toward the back porch of his home. Tall for his age at six feet, he wore a pair of dirty bib-overalls soaked with sweat and worn out work boots that he'd outgrown six months earlier. His wet, shoulder length hair was the most unusual shade of red and likely considered beautiful had it not been so filthy. He turned and stared at the chickens. Light streamed through the semi-darkness from the countless holes in the tin roof. One of these beams of light struck his light blue right eye, giving him a demonic appearance.

He hated the chicken house. Anytime his dad was on the road and his mother had company, she would yell for him to go see to the chickens, and then he was locked out of the house. Wilbur hated chickens—though not as much as he hated his mother. He felt the urge to pee and pulled his penis from his bibs. A brown speckled hen cackled loudly and fluttered away when he directed the hot stream toward her head. As his stream fizzled, the acrid smell of piss and chicken shit burned his eyes, nose, and throat. He left his member out as he returned to his vantage point and resumed staring at the house. His stomach rumbled as an involuntary belch gave him a second taste of the bologna sandwich he'd eaten for breakfast.

The backdoor of the old farmhouse opened and his mother's "company" stepped out onto the back porch. He wore a pair of black dress pants but was shirtless and barefoot. The small, bald man looked soft; unlike his father, a big rawboned man.

His dad always wore a smile and had time for Wilbur on the rare occasions he was home. The only other friend he'd ever known was Bear, a black German shepherd who had been his constant companion until hunters shot him two years earlier.

The man stood on the edge of the porch and lit a cigarette. Wilbur turned his head away, seething with anger. He glared at the chickens and heard their snickers. "How's this for funny?" he asked as he kicked the nearest chicken so hard that something popped inside its body as it sailed twenty feet back into the midst of its peers. It lay motionless as the other chickens squawked and scattered. Within moments, they forgot about the commotion and went about their usual cackling and scratching. Some gathered around their fallen comrade and began their inquisitive pecking. He knew that in a short while there would be nothing left but feathers.

Wilbur heard the screen door slam and knew without looking that the man had returned to the house with its big window fans. He also knew the man was probably enjoying the cool air of his parents' bedroom. With its small, window air-conditioner, it was the only room of the house that was truly comfortable. He got to sample that cool air two nights ago when his mother called him into her room to rub lotion on her body. He ran from the room when she slipped off her robe and revealed her nude body. He could still hear her laughing as he reached the bottom of the stairs. Wilbur felt a tingling, looked down, and realized he was getting excited. Ashamed, he stuffed his penis back into his bibs and tried to zip up the long broken zipper. Giving up in a rage, he stormed forward, kicking and stomping chickens till he'd killed nearly a dozen. Exhausted, he fell down to his knees and planted his palms in the grayish-white chicken shit covering the floor. He cried from deep inside, gut wrenching sobs, till at last there was nothing left.

A voice from back in the chicken house called out, "What cha' crying about Red-on-the-Head?"

Wilbur looked up as chill bumps covered his hot, sweaty skin. The only one who ever called him Red-on-the-Head was that clown from the carnival two years ago. But he was dead. The sheriff and his deputies shot him when he charged at them with a knife.

Wilbur slowly stood on trembling legs. He ran his hands over his face and through his hair, oblivious to the smears of white chicken shit left in their wake. "Who's there?"

"You know who I am. Still wear my beauty mark?"

Wilbur felt nauseous. The bite scars on his right shoulder began to itch, though they had healed long ago. "You're dead. You can't be here! Them's the rules!" Wilbur strained his eyes, peering through the dust and distant shadows. He thought he could discern a shape near the wall but wasn't sure.

"I never was one to follow rules. You should know that. I've thought about you a lot since I died. I found I had a taste for redheads when I bit you."

Wilbur leaned forward and threw up. He felt cold even though the temperature was well over a hundred degrees.

"Feel better now?" The voice was much closer.

Wilbur turned in panic and slammed his weight against the door, but it didn't budge. "What do you want?" he managed as he turned and strained his eyes. Movement in the shadows to his right nearly stopped his heart.

"We're just alike, you and I. Just look in that mirror behind you."

The boy looked at the dust-covered mirror that rested above an ancient, disconnected porcelain sink, relics from the days before this building became a chicken house. Cobweb tangled feathers and dust now filled the bowl. He slid the side of his palm down the mirror, disrupting the dust but leaving streaks of chicken shit in its place. In the cleanest part of the mirror, he spied something that left him mesmerized. A clown with tangled red hair and a streaked, grayish-white face snarled back at him in horror.

"See what I mean?" whispered the voice, hot on the back of his neck. "We're the same. And with me in your corner, you can do anything you want. Cause, see . . . I like you. Not just the way you taste . . . but you. Does that make sense, Red-on-the-Head?"

In the reflection, Wilbur could see movement just over his shoulder. He remained silent in his terror.

"Don't worry 'bout me, boy. If I wanted to bite cha, you'd done been bit. Tell me now, what is it that bugs you more than me? Could it be that candy ass bopping your whore of a mother under the air-conditioner? In there screwin' and gettin' nasty while your daddy's out making the living. And you know what she wants to do with you, don't cha?"

"Shut up 'bout that!" his fear now forgotten.

"How many times has she strolled naked through the house in front of you? You usually turn your head . . . but not always."

"Shut the hell up!" He spun and took two angry steps as a dark shadow zipped behind a stack of old tractor tires off to the left side of the room.

"You come over here and I'll bite you good!"

Wilbur's fear resurfaced and he remained still.

"It's just a matter of time before she lands you in the sack, and you know what they'll call you then, don't cha? I'm willin' to get you out of this situation if you listen to me." The voice came from behind Wilbur this time as the faint sounds of carnival teased him. The whispering of laughter, carnies enticing suckers to play their rigged games, hungry clowns calling from the shadows.

"Why would you help me?"

"I always pay my debts. I took a bite out of you, so I owe you for that ounce of tasty flesh. Besides, this is the sort of thing I do . . . or did!" he laughed. "Is that choppin' axe still stuck in the old stump?"

"Yeah," he muttered.

"Well, that's your ticket, Red-on-the-Head!"

Wilbur grimaced as he felt a gloved hand gently rest on his shoulder. The smell of cotton candy overpowered the odor of chicken shit.

"Let's go get that axe, boy!"

Wilbur paused and turned back to the mirror. A large, bloodstained smile framed his teeth, which appeared unnaturally long and pointed. His nose was bulbous and turning a dark red. Hunger suddenly replaced fear. The blood in his mouth tasted better than the cherry cobblers his mom fixed when his dad was home.

Wilbur exited the chicken house, yanked the axe from the old stump, and walked to the screen door on the back porch. His mother's friend had forgotten to hook the latch so he entered and tiptoed to the bottom of the staircase. He stood silent as his anger faded and he was unsure what to do. Then the broom closet door behind him opened, causing Wilbur to spin about, almost losing his balance as the axe handle banged the wall.

"Quiet, boy!" whispered a shadow in the closet. "What cha' waitin' for? Get up there and take care of business!"

"That's my Mom," he whispered as tears began to trickle down his face. "I can't hurt my Mom, even if she does bad things."

"I didn't want to tell you this, but I think you should know. Your daddy won't be coming back."

"What do you mean? Daddy said he'd be home soon! He called two weeks ago! I heard him say it myself!" Wilbur's voice began to rise.

"Don't forget where you're at, Red-on-the-Head!" he hissed. "Your Mommy needs special attention you see. She's still young and quite a looker, if I say so myself."

"Shut up!" Wilbur growled.

"That soft belly in there on top of your ma is a banker. He's willin' to take care of y'all and even see to the mortgage. All she has to do is be his whore two or three times a week."

"My dad will kick his ass when he comes home!"

"Well, you see, it's like this, Wilbur. Your daddy's got him a woman in Texas and he's not comin' back. He told your ma that the same night he talked to you. It seems he's as much chicken shit as that stuff on your face."

Unable to contain his rage, Wilbur rushed up the stairs and kicked open his parents' bedroom door.

"What the hell!" the naked man yelled as he rolled out of bed and stood facing Wilbur. Fear registered on the man's face as he spied the double-edged axe.

"Wilbur!" his mother yelled. "What's that on your face? Shit? Go down to the basement and get a shower!"

Through his rage, Wilbur could hear the fear despite the authority in her voice. She got out of bed and stood next to the man, making no attempt to hide her nudity. "You heard me. Get your ass downstairs, now!"

"Is Daddy coming back?" His words were slurred from the mouthful of teeth that still seemed to be growing as he trembled with rage. His bloodshot eyes bore into his mother. She turned her head for a moment, regained her courage, and returned his stare.

"Your dad's done found himself a new piece of tail. What? You expect me to rot away the rest of my life in this hellhole? I'm just twenty seven years old!" She shoved her ample breasts out and twisted her hips to the side as to emphasize her youth and sexuality. "And act like you got some damn sense. John here is going to be your daddy as soon as the divorce is final."

The axe fell to the floor as Wilbur stared blankly at his mom.

"You heard your mother, *Wilburn*! Get out of here!" The man sensed the danger had passed, turned, and smacked his mother on the butt. She jumped and giggled, aroused by having an audience.

"Wait a second, John. Wilbur needs to learn a few things. He can get his shower later if he wants to watch." She said in a childlike voice as she towed the man back to bed. She fell back onto the mattress and looked at Wilbur to assure he was watching.

The man turned and climbed onto the king sized mattress. He crawled slowly toward her on his hands and knees, as excited as her to have someone watching. As he reached her, Wilbur scooped up the razor sharp axe, darted forward, and grabbed the man's ankle with one hand and lifted his thrashing body above the bed as easily as one would a small child. Then, with perfect timing, he sliced off the man's penis and scrotum between the kicks of his one, free leg.

With a snicker, he tossed the doomed man to the floor, picked up the severed parts, and tossed them in his mother's lap as she now sat upright screaming. "Looks just like a chicken neck, Ma!" *Where'd that come from?* Wilbur wondered. That sounded like the dead clown, but it had come from his own mouth. His mother fainted and fell back on the bed.

Wilbur turned back to the man. "Got the perfect name for you, feller! From now on your name is Slick! Get it? Cause your slicker betwixt the legs than my cousin's plastic doll!"

The man staggered to his feet and screamed as he saw his reflection in the dresser mirror. His eyes were fixed on his bleeding groin so he didn't see Wilbur swing the axe. It struck him just below the shoulder, nearly severing his right arm. He crashed screaming into the dresser, shattering glass and rocking it nearly to the point of tipping over.

"Oops! Seven years of bad luck!" he chuckled.

"Please!" the man pleaded. "Help me!"

"Why would I do that, dumb ass? I'm the one what hurt cha!" Wilbur reached down, grabbed the man's dangling arm, and ripped it free. The man screamed again as he kicked his legs in the broken glass as if trying to get on his feet. "By the way, the name's Wilbur, not Wilburn." He looked at his mother and laughed. She had awoke and was sitting up in bed but slouched forward with her breasts dangling. Her face was pale and her eyes blank. She appeared much older than she had moments ago.

"Them titties don't look so proud, now!" The voice was not that of a twelve year old. He lifted the severed arm, sniffed, and then tore into it like it was Thanksgiving at Aunt Lucy's. In moments, the bones were picked clean. The banker stirred on the floor. The blood loss was merciful as he showed little reaction when Wilbur tore into his throat, ripping flesh and severing arteries.

"'Bout time to fix supper," his mother said as she got out of bed and staggered to the door. "Make sure you clean up. There's nothin' worse than smelling chicken shit while you're trying to eat."

Wilbur raised his blood soaked face and growled at his mother, the urge to see how her flesh tasted was almost overpowering. Oblivious to the danger, she turned and left the room. He turned back to the man and ripped open his chest. After several minutes, he stood up and belched. Belly full and rage dwindling, he headed to the basement, leaving a trail of gore as he dragged what was left of John by the ankle. When he reached the ground floor, he could hear his mother preparing supper, although it was only a little past two.

When he reached the basement, he took a long shower. Feeling clean and more himself, he walked to the mirror.

"Oh!" he gasped as he saw the reflection of a pale face with red, rubber ball nose. A large, exaggerated smile was wrapped around teeth as pointed as a picket fence. He caressed his nose softly and was amazed as it returned to its original shape and color. As he wiped his hand over the rest of his face, the rest of his features also returned to normal.

"Ain't it a kick?" said a voice from behind several boxes of clothes.

"What am I?"

"You . . . my dear boy, can be *anything* you want to be. I passed this gift to you, just as it was passed to me a long time ago."

"Anything?" Wilbur stared at the scar on his shoulder.

"Did I stutter, boy?" Movement behind the boxes turned one of them over.

Wilbur looked at the old Polaroid taped to the corner of the mirror. In the picture, Bear was laying on his back in the mid-afternoon sun with an eight year old Wilbur lying on his side, facing his dog, with his arm draped over the its barrel chest. He remembered that day as a smile spread across his face. It had been taken just weeks before Christmas during one of those rare, warm days that are sprinkled in during winter.

He got dressed, exited the basement, and retrieved a can of diesel and matches from the shed. Wilbur sloshed the diesel through the house on the ground floor, careful not to get any on his mother as she went on cooking wearing nothing but an apron. He lit the diesel and stood in the front yard as the house became engulfed in flames, and then turned away. He didn't bother to look back to see if his mother escaped the inferno. He didn't care.

The long dormant wind came to life as if it had been waiting for a sacrifice. It whipped the black column of smoke eastward. Thunder rumbled in the darkening West as a drought breaker promised relief to the thirsty land. Wilbur slipped off his clothes and fell to his hands and knees. Lightning struck a tree in the distance causing him to flinch.

Wilbur's soft fur was as dark as the smoke overhead as he stood on four legs with ears erect. The West wind carried to his nose the scent of cotton candy and he bounded forth into the storm.

Julienne Lee

The Gate

My head buzzed like crickets singing to a heat wave as I opened my eyes. Above, a raven cried. Blinking, I saw a canopy of green and dappled gold concealing the sky. The air was cool and moist where I sat, leaning against a tree. In the overhanging branches the raven croaked again, strong and hoarse, head cocked in my direction, its black eyes studying me, so intelligent; shivers crawled up my arms and nape. The raven took flight in a sudden flap of glossy feathers as I struggled to stand; my body cramped with chill.

Searching for a familiar path, a recognizable tree or rock in this forest, I struggled forward. I had no hunting rifle or walking stick. There was nothing but looming trees and dense foliage. Memory was buffered behind the ache in my skull. I had no recollection of coming to this place, only a lingering sense of urgency—I had to be somewhere . . .

My gut fisted when a smoky shadow darted between the trees to my right. I stood frozen, eyes searching. Unclenching my fingers with an exhale, I dismissed it as an animal, perhaps another raven. I returned to puzzling out my situation but there were no pieces to even begin. No memory, just blackness. The longer I searched my memory, the more vexed I became. My hands trembled from nerves and cold, the knuckles scraped raw. My clothing was torn and filthy and I resembled a beggar - or a prisoner. Beneath the layers of dirt smearing my ratty jacket frayed brass buttons dangled; the waistcoat was long beyond hope, the fob absent of the pocket watch I knew should be there. My trousers were stained and torn, and the hosiery below my knee was shredded to flap at the ankles. Searching my pockets for a handkerchief to tidy my hands, a yellowed square tumbled out to the ground. Snatching at it, I held my breath, squinting at the parchment that unfolded into a worn and tattered message. It appeared to have been very hastily written and was nearly illegible, the ink faded and blotched where not properly sanded.

Dearest Eliza,

107

I fear that Master Phillip is in danger . . . The Villagers have discovered his experiments. I cannot persuade him to stop, nor to flee . . . lost to reason . . . terribly outraged . . . I have helped some escape confinement but . . . I can feel the ghosts of this place . . . despair of betrayal . . . Dearest you must . . .

Your Beloved Alfred

Ice rolled down my back. Who was Eliza? Alfred? Whose letter was this? My heart skipped. And this Phillip? Why did I have this letter? More questions tumbled through my head. Who-What-Who-Why-Who . . . Who was I?

A hard cry tore from my throat as black shadows blurred between the trees around me. Cringing away from them, the letter clutched to my chest, I felt small among the ancient trees. The dark shapes moved, flitting randomly. The sounds of the hushing wind through the leaves encircled me, carrying a low vague murmur that crept up the vertebrae to the base of my skull. One shadow shuddered right up into my face. Without thought, my fist swung out, passing through the insubstantial form. I stared in disbelief at my hand. This was irrational! I bolted. Letter clenched in my fist my legs pumped, flimsy shoes striking uneven ground, slipping over boulders, and gnarled roots. I stumbled, scraping flesh on rough trunks. Thin branches whipped, stinging my face, but I kept running. Clambering up the stony embankments, heart thudding in my ears, a tattoo to the rising murmur, I ran harder. The angry noise dogged me like a swarm of black flies.

I stumbled through nettled bushes, toppling to my knees into a clearing. I fell to my hands, panting on all fours, gasping for breath. I listened. The murmur droned behind me, waiting, worrying my mind over what manner of creatures pursued me. Rubbing the sweat from my brow, I scanned the clearing. There was a craggy burnt out building. I stumbled to my feet, chest still laboring, eyes searching.

My mind itched painfully as images stung me like an attacking wasp. I recalled a stately Manor house looming over grand well-manicured lawns, with a scrubby herb garden bordered by a low wall. The lawn that rolled out from under the house and out buildings had been pristine, with white graveled paths slashing through the lush green grass. There had been an orchard tucked away somewhere on vast grounds; the pungent ghost of ripe fruit mingled with the acrid scent of things long burnt drifted to me.

In the midst of the clearing, ruins rose up in craggy shards from the wild flora. Stones, blackened and tumbled, supported flowering vines that crept along empty door and window frames, drooped from charred ceiling beams and adorned what used to be a solid chimney.

Rooted, I dared not turn back into the forest, yet my feet were adhered to ground.

Do not go there.

The thoughts clung to me with a chilled sweat. And somehow, I knew the house would be far more terrible than the shadows that harassed me. The longer I stood there, the harder the coil in my gut writhed. Something deep and unnatural, unseen flickered over me, knowing, tasting, inviting.

I must Know.

The decaying structure called to me with seductive promises of knowledge of secrets best left unknown. Shadows droned at the forest edge, and I let myself be pulled toward the ruins. The draw was intoxicating, the lure to investigate, to dig deep beneath the surface. And yet there was a deep sense of repulsion of things I might not want to know. My eyes flickered across the tree line where the shadows hovered, and I dashed toward the tumbled stones—perhaps here I could seek sanctuary from them.

Amid the scrubby weeds, broken stones, and other debris, I felt I knew this place. I lived here. A sharp snap drew my attention to the ground. My foot concealed what looked like bones. They were scattered all over the ground beneath where I stood. Drilled skulls, jawbones, femurs, teeth—all strewn and stuck in crevices, or partially exposed in earthen nooks.

Was this something to do with Phillip? Had he caused this terrible scene? I began to feel suffocated as a shroud of sorrow descended over me. I was compelled to flee from this horror. I scrambled desperately to be free of the place, making for the tree line opposite of where I had entered the clearing.

The ruins whispered to me all the while, calling me back. I rushed through the trees, alert, should the shadows find me. The murmuring was still there, but it seemed less oppressive than the eerie tendril of the ruined manor. I pushed onward, deeper, hoping I might stumble out to another clearing or maybe the village.

This time I could feel them before I saw them. They moved like whispering raven wings, appearing like muted ash. I hurried forward, ever away from the clearing. The shadows flitted between the trees on either side, keeping pace. If I turned, I would have been forced to confront them, so I ran, weaving between the trees and struggling through dense bush. Awareness came slowly. I was being herded, but I couldn't stop moving. I was too afraid of what would become of me should I stop. Time lost, I went on.

I could feel my shoes loose against my feet, and one of the soles gave way, catching on a stone. I tumbled; bouncing off sharp rocks, ricocheting off trees, gouging pine covered soil and over more exposed roots, ever downward as the ground sloped.

I crashed against the base of a massive, gnarled trunk and only then gave into stillness. What more? My head lolled—I was battered from crown to heel. I looked down at my shaking fist sporting deep gashes, smeared with dirt, and still clutching the letter. I stared at it awhile, then sniffling, my trembling fingers refolded the precious scrap, blood smeared and soiled, I placed it back in my pocket.

Eyes closed, trying to contain the encroaching madness, I struggled to stand, leaning heavily on the tree that had broken my tumble. Its bark was deeply creviced, my fingers splayed over it, absorbing the texture and age of it. I looked up.

Stumbling backwards a few steps, I collapsed. A face. A face that was formed by the curve of the tree's bark. A Man's face, yet not a man. It stared at me, eyeless, but I could feel it observing me. Fear rippled down my arms and made my bladder weaken as I stared back. I knew this face. It was the face of one of the Ancient Gods. I knew not who I was, but I did know Him. And I knew He was there, watching me. I could feel it as even the hair on my fingers rose.

Trembling and scuttling away, I could see the shadows closing around me. So many! So many more than I had imagined. I locked my eyes on the God, knowing not where else to look, swallowing the rising hysteria.

"WHAT DO YOU WANT OF ME?" My voice was shrill and cracked.

The murmuring droned louder and I grew dizzy, looking in all places at once. They whispered closer, droned louder. I trembled and cowered, darting glances to the Mask of the Old God "Help me," I rasped "Please!"

A gateway shimmered into existence within the trunk of the Great Oak. Gnarled roots interwoven with stones formed an uneven ramp descending into the ground. My head shook of its own volition. Was it Hell?

The shadows continued their slow approach. *This* was Hell!

Scampering forward on all fours, I clawed my way toward the escape offered. But the second my outstretched fingers met the arch of the Great tree, they sizzled against a barrier, and I was yanked upward, held suspended just before the Arch, face to face with the Old God while the Shadows closed in. Grunting and flailing, a shock struck my forehead.

Memories crashed through me, rolling, spinning so that bile rose and descended in my gut. Wealth. Arrogance. Bored Curiosity. Experimentation. Obsession. Crossing some inner Threshold. Disconnection. Burning, driving need to know more. Words of caution, discarded. Faces of people I had known. Neighbors. Faces attached to bodies that I desecrated in the name of Science. Lives snuffed out. Angry faces, uproar, tearing at me. Smoke, stinging my eyes and nose, as I was dragged out of my laboratory.

I was Phillip.

I had been a man of science, obsessed with the pursuit of natural philosophy, flared by the arrogance of my rank and wealth. Alfred. Oh Dear Alfred, my friend, my manservant. I sobbed. He had tried to speak reason to me. I squeezed my eyes shut against that memory. "No, please!" But the memory was forced on me. I could not move, suspended as I was. Alfred. I had caught him writing the letter to his Eliza, entreating help. In a fit of rage, I'd had him thrown in the cellar—my next experiment. And he had died with his disbelieving eyes trained on my face. Frozen in betrayal, as I'd cut him open, looking for—for I wasn't sure what I had been looking for. Grasping for something—that connection that people had to one another. Surely, surely it was something in the blood or bile, something tangible that I could study. Something I could create in myself. That connection Alfred had to his Eliza, to the villagers. That kindness in his heart.

And then I had seen it too late. Far too late. It was in his eyes, those kind old blue eyes, *not* something tangible at all. He had that connection to me. It was what I had been looking for, and could not recognize it. The empty blue eyes.

My chest heaved as I wept, witnessing my own ghastly deeds. It was too much. *Too much.* "Alfred, forgive me."

The force holding me aloft dissipated and I dropped to my knees. The shadows quieted, watchful. I looked at them, and through the wavering of my eyes, I could almost, *almost*, see familiar faces. I looked back to the Path that the Oak offered. I moved closer. The coolness of the air was like silk over my face. It caressed me, drying my tears, whispering to my soul.

I understood. I was being offered Sanctuary, relief. I looked back to the ashy forms. They waited. Would they find Sanctuary? Had I ripped that ability out—broken their connection, trying to steal it from them?

I looked at the gate, rising to my feet. I struggled to remember the lore of the Forest Lord. Would there be judgment beyond? I didn't know. I wasn't sure I could face that.

I stepped back, hands trembling. "I cannot."

The Gate snapped closed with a violent implosion, sucking the light into itself, as the shadows descended on me. I screamed, spinning away from them falling backward against the Tree, suffocated by blackness.

***

My head buzzed like crickets singing to a heat wave as I opened my eyes. Above, a raven cried.

In His Head
Ken Goldman

Steve Bates

Straw Man

Bonnie Clark tended a garden, and she tended it well. "Compost to make the plants sweet," she was fond of saying when asked her secrets. "Bone meal to make them strong."

For Bonnie, gardening was a solemn ceremony. When she entrusted a seed to the soil, it was as if she were investing a measure of her soul into the glad earth. She sang the garden's secret litany of root growth and bud formation, bore its stigmata when insects and drought assailed it. After she harvested a luscious summer melon or a gaudy yellow dahlia flower, she found it profane to part with her creation for mere coins.

One fine autumn day, which proved cool enough to keep the fall crops tender yet mild enough to turn fruit into gold upon the trees, a hawk came to visit. Its familiar shadow caressed the pale green surfaces of plump cabbages, eased across the wide rows where Bonnie pushed her wooden wheelbarrow, and toyed with gnarled limbs in the orchard. In near silence, the proud bird settled upon the shoulder of a scarecrow, not ten paces from Bonnie.

Bonnie's mother had advised her that hawks rarely appear close to humans, other than to take advantage of cultivated land that makes field mice such easy prey. Hawks often hunt in clusters of three or four, riding the thermals in a timeless dance above the earth. *This solitary bird, with its snowy breast, has been here before. It is much too smart to be scared by my scarecrow, for sure.*

"Have you ever seen a prettier spot?" Bonnie said, as if addressing a neighbor at a holiday picnic. The hawk deigned not to notice. It tilted its sharp head in short, jerky motions, assessing threats, and opportunities instant by instant. Bonnie joined it in surveying their surroundings, relishing the patterns of cicada conversations, inhaling the rich odor of recently tilled earth, and contemplating the serenity of the rolling hills beyond.

The view was unchanged from the day so many years past when Bonnie's mother dispatched the young maiden to town on an errand. It was there that she chanced to meet Frederick

Thompson, an apprentice carpenter with a promising future. Bonnie's father put an end to their brief courtship. Bonnie confronted her father in anger once; he struck her and forbade her to broach the matter henceforth. The Thompson boy wed Bonnie's nearest neighbor, Sylvia--though he, like Bonnie's father, died much too young.

The scars from losing Frederick remained fresh and raw within Bonnie, even in her fifty-fourth year. Night after night, she stared into her fireplace, recalling that drizzly afternoon they met, longing for one more glance at his easy smile, and wondering how fate could be so cruel as to propel him into her neighbor's arms. But Bonnie forever loved the land more than any man.

Many were the sun-drenched days when young Bonnie toiled at her mother's side in the garden. They spoke little as they planted, thinned, and watered, her mother imparting but two essential lessons season after season: One, "Waste nothing; whatever you cannot eat or use in your home, return to the soil." And two, "Suffer not a weed to live, but do not cut it above the soil. Remove it head, body, and feet."

As a dark cloud occluded the sun, Bonnie noticed the hawk shift its position on the shoulder of the scarecrow, sinking its talons deep. "Take care now," Bonnie said. "My straw man is not a sturdy one." Bonnie knew these birds well, having watched them operate with ruthless efficiency many a season. They betrayed not the faintest hint of guilt at killing. Then again, they likely experienced not the slightest taste of joy in it, either.

"We are not all that different, you and I," Bonnie said at length. "We cannot always say where our next meal will come from. But we make do, don't we?"

Without warning, the hawk leapt into the sky, executed two graceful turns and became one with the woods. Fragments of straw cascaded from the scarecrow's sleeve. Bonnie knelt to gather the pieces. "That won't do now, will it?" she said to the figure as she hastened to repair the damage.

Bonnie Clark was fair-haired, stout, and sturdy as a fence post, with a round face, a weather-lined forehead, and large gray eyes. Most townsfolk would describe her as ordinary, and Bonnie would not argue with that representation. But she would abide no ordinary scarecrow. Not like the ones, her neighbors displayed, designed to frighten only small children and each other with their carved pumpkin heads or ghoulish faces painted crudely on burlap. More often than not, the neighbors' scarecrows could be found stretched out in mock crucifixion. Bonnie's straw man displayed its arms at odd angles, like a live man. Its clothes were a live man's, though degraded by age and weather. One could surmise that its topcoat was once black; its buttons had long ago abandoned their posts. A ragged plaid vest covered a faded red shirt. Beneath a rope belt, it wore frayed trousers and animal skin boots. Gloves provided lifelike hands. Its straw hat covered a pink gourd that Bonnie had decorated fastidiously with steely eyes, narrow eyebrows, a tiny nose and a tight grin.

"Now, my fine sentinel," Bonnie said, wiping her hands on her gardening apron, "wish me luck on the morrow when I go to market, will you? I must sell our crops for silver coins lest let the taxman take all this away."

***

Bonnie returned the borrowed mule and cart to Sylvia and completed her journey home on foot with a sack on her back and dread in her heart. Instead of the coins she needed to pay the taxman, she navigated the muddy ruts in the lane bearing only used clothing and winter supplies. The market attracted many sellers but few buyers this day, so she had been forced to barter to avoid returning home empty-handed. As she approached her cottage, crafted from the very stones that her grandfather had cleared from the field that became her garden, the home seemed like a mirage that could vanish under the influence of a single malevolent cloud.

What shall I do when the taxman comes, she wondered. She had always believed that the land would provide for her, that it would feed her body and soul and would produce enough income to pay her taxes and obtain necessary goods. Her mother had promised her as much. *Maybe the taxman can wait for spring*, Bonnie hoped.

She sought solace in her garden, thinning her lettuce plants. The variety she favored emerged as pale green seedlings in late summer, and with each day the tender tissues expanded ravenously. They borrowed color from the autumn sunsets until they displayed a fiery red hue. Bonnie would harvest single leaves or entire plants as her dinner and the market required.

116

Bonnie spotted a weed hiding amid the plants; she reached into her apron and withdrew a long, sharp knife. Recalling her mother's lesson about weeds—"head, body and feet"--Bonnie plunged the blade into the soil, not once but several times, describing a circle around the offender. She upended the weed, roots and all, and tossed it into the undergrowth at the edge of the woods.

In the fading daylight, Bonnie walked the perimeter of her garden. The orchard occupied the north end, the tallest trees taking the brunt of the coldest winds. At the south edge, soaring, heat-loving sunflowers and tomatoes sheltered more sensitive plants amid summer's wrath. Raised beds with tightly packed leaf crops captured the morning light to the east, while rows of wide-ranging plants such as potato vines were a fixture of the western side. At the center, where the land crested slightly, the scarecrow reigned. At its side, Bonnie observed the last slice of sun dissolving upon the nearly cloudless horizon.

This is a bad sign, she thought. *The frost will come soon.*

Sure enough, morning's first light revealed a blanket of sparkling crystals, each one melting the moment it was kissed by the sun's rays. Many of her plants survived; by their nature, they were resilient in the onslaught of the season: spinach greens, lettuce, and root crops enveloped by comforting soil. Other plants perished, as was their fate at this hour: warm-weather melon vines and thin-skinned peppers among them.

Having washed her pans and spoons after a breakfast of gruel and tea, Bonnie examined the clothes that her prized cabbages, pears, and cut flowers had earned at the market: a homespun brown shirt, a broad-brimmed hat, rugged trousers, and tall boots. Suitable for a plain woman like herself. But Bonnie had clothes enough. She carried these items into the garden and displayed them to her scarecrow.

"Look what I bring to you, as a reward for safekeeping my garden," she said to the straw man. With no breeze yet upon the land, the scarecrow remained motionless. "But it would be a shame to dress you in such fine apparel, only for winter to come calling so soon with cruel intent."

Bonnie lifted the scarecrow off the pole by which it was anchored in place. She carried it into her cottage and sat it upon a simply made wooden chair in front of a solid oak table. For as long as she could remember, Bonnie had set the table with two handmade placemats and two chairs, despite the fact that it was rare for a guest to share a meal. Two other chairs were fixed at the far end of the room, facing the broad stone fireplace and hearth. Her small bed was pushed up against the south wall, opposite a modest kitchen and privy. Two homespun rugs covered portions of the rough wood floor—one by her bed, the other above the trap door to her root cellar. Six windows allowed pale light to grace the home from various angles, lending an illusion of generous size. The smell of homemade bread and fresh apple cider lent a joyous atmosphere.

Bonnie stripped off the scarecrow's tattered clothes and proceeded to fit it with its new ones. She employed additional straw and other items at hand to fill out its figure to that of a strapping young man. Finally, she affixed black buttons to replace the hand-drawn eyes that the straw man had displayed through the gardening season. Stepping back, she admired her handiwork.

"You need a name, don't you now?" she said. It took but a moment.

"Mister. I shall call you Mister."

No sooner had the name had left her lips than the line that indicated scarecrow's mouth began to thicken, stretch, and open. "I thank you," he said, plain as day.

Bonnie squinted at the straw man. She lifted a hand to her forehead but detected no fever. She felt chill air creeping around the windowpanes, smelled the sweet aroma of the morning fire, sensed warm blood coursing through her body. Yet still she wondered: *Is this a dream?*

"Did you say 'thank you,' Mister? Did I hear you speak, pray tell?"

"Yes, I did speak," said the straw man. "Did I speak ... properly?"

Not a woman accustomed to denying what she found to be true, Bonnie replied warmly: "You spoke fine indeed, Mister. Fine indeed."

"Good," the straw man continued. "It be good that I spoke to you properly, lady."

The scarecrow turned his head ever so slowly, one way, then the other, as if testing his mobility or examining his surroundings. He began to stretch his arms, and next his legs, though it appeared for a time as if his limbs were asleep or all but disconnected from his torso.

"Please indulge an old woman, if you would, Mister," Bonnie said. "How is it that you appear as a live man, after I fashioned you from straw and needle and thread?"

"I know not," said the scarecrow in a gentle and unassuming voice.

"Well now. I do not know either," Bonnie said as the straw man raised himself to a standing position. "But I welcome you to my humble home. And I bid you make yourself comfortable."

***

Soon the snows came. The scarecrow named Mister ate little, and at times Bonnie wondered if he were only pretending to take meals. Still, she undertook to teach him chores, such as cooking and cleaning. He was slow to grasp the lessons and even slower to accomplish them. But he conducted his duties without complaint, carrying wood in small bundles so that he would not place too much stress upon his straw body, and taking care not to allow his face to come close to the fire lest a stray spark ruin him. Many evenings Bonnie would order him to sit after hours of unabated labor. "The dust will still be waiting for you tomorrow," she would say.

As the days advanced, Mister's face gained a smoother, softer appearance, as if spending time in Bonnie's presence had accustomed his features to those of his hostess. His limbs, so stiff at first, gained flexibility as he moved about the cottage. His typical facial expression, which to the casual witness might appear to indicate an absolute absence of thought, could be interpreted by a more astute bystander as that of a being full of wonder.

Often in the hours after dinner, while the evening's fire still blazed brightly, Bonnie read to Mister. He seemed to listen dispassionately, but on occasion, he would ask a question that demonstrated commendable attention.

"Lady, why did the girl and boy in the story push the witch into the oven so that she would burn to death?"

"The children in the story had no choice," said Bonnie, amused by the scarecrow's inquisitiveness. "Either the witch would die, or they would die. Sometimes, that is the way of the world."

Bonnie believed that the straw man would never gain sophistication, but she was glad for a companion, particularly in the dead of winter, when snow and ice made traveling the lane arduous and her neighbor Sylvia might not attempt a visit for weeks at a time.

One particularly cold night, Bonnie ambled to the chair where the scarecrow sat with a contented smile.

"Come and warm my bed," she said. He followed her innocently. When they were under her thick down blankets, she embraced him and placed her lips to his ears. She instructed him in the ways of lovemaking, and he responded.

Bonnie woke late the next morning. Mister had built up the fire and had gruel and tea waiting for her.

"Be of great care. This gruel be hot, lady," he said.

"Thank you. Thank you, Mister." While yet avoiding his eyes, she inquired, "Did you sleep well?"

"I cannot say for certain if I sleep, or rest, or do neither. I do find myself able to conduct all the chores you require. I hope that pleases you."

"Oh, everything you do pleases me," said Bonnie. "Everything, indeed."

***

After a time, there came a mild thaw in the winter. A sharp knock upon her door could only be that of a stranger; Sylvia and her few other neighbors would simply walk in.

"John Palmer. Tax collector," the visitor announced brusquely, removing a shiny, store-bought hat. "You must pay me five silver coins today, Mrs. Clark."

"Good day, Mr. Palmer. Nice of you to venture so far in a grim season," said Bonnie, wondering what to say, what to do. "Are you sure about those five coins, now? That's quite a lot to ask of a poor old woman, with only her garden, and so far away from the town. Is there no delay to be allowed, or no other form of payment I might offer?"

"There is no doubt about it," said Palmer, who wore a fine dark coat and fancy breeches but appeared so pale and gaunt that a vigorous breeze might whisk him into the next county. He withdrew a document from his vest pocket. "It says right here, on this paper signed by the magistrate himself: 'Clark; five silver

120

coins.' Now, will you kindly present them so that I may continue on my rounds?" The taxman appeared not to notice the seated figure of the scarecrow, yet he maintained an undisguised expression of disdain.

"Yes. Yes, of course," said Bonnie. She struggled to contrive a plan. She had no silver coins. And there was something about this man, this tax collector that repulsed her. He seemed odious and heartless, almost as severe as her father when he forbade her to see Frederick Thompson. This visitor was a nuisance to be excised, like a vile weed threatening to overtake her precious garden seedlings. Bonnie thought of her mother and drew confidence and resolve from that memory.

"Mr. Palmer, I keep my coins hidden in my root cellar. Would you please accompany me down the stairs so that your young eyes can help me tell silver from copper?"

"If I must," said the taxman in a weary voice. "Pray, show me the way."

Bonnie lit a candle, opened the door to the root cellar, and started down the stairs. *Head, body and feet*, she recited silently. *Head, body and feet.*

When the two of them stood in the tiny chamber, Bonnie withdrew the gardening knife from her apron. The blade did its work effectively and with little noise, the taxman's blood mixing with the red earth of the floor. After a time, Bonnie emerged. The scarecrow watched as she located a bigger knife and a sturdy sack and returned to the cellar.

"Come, help me, Mister, if you please," Bonnie said from the root cellar as evening approached. "This is a heavy load."

Mister peered into the dim cavern. "Where be Mr. Palmer?" he asked.

"Mr. Palmer has died," said Bonnie matter-of-factly.

"He appeared quite alive when he descended these stairs," said the straw man. "What misfortune befell him?"

Bonnie thought for a moment. "Remember the story I told you about the children and the witch? This is like that story."

The scarecrow was silent for a while. "Lady, did this man not have a purpose? Was it truly his fate to die today?"

"Yes, Mister, it was his fate. I have lived a long time, and I can tell you that it is so."

The scarecrow asked no more questions. He watched as Bonnie salvaged buttons and buckles and then shredded and burned the remainder of Palmer's clothes. Mister turned his attention to the evening meal, but upon its completion, he nearly spilled Bonnie's plate upon the floor. The following morning, he forgot to commence his chores until Bonnie snapped at him. And whenever Bonnie ventured close to him, the straw man stepped back from her with trepidation.

Bonnie seemed not to notice the scarecrow's change in behavior, focused on the disposition of the taxman's remains. Over the next three days, she stripped all flesh from bone and reduced it to such a consistency that her compost pile would consume it over time. The bones could be ground into bone meal in the spring.

Whatever you cannot eat or use in your home, return to the soil.

***

Over the ensuing days, Bonnie started to experience an odd numbness in her hands and unusual stiffness in both feet. It was as if her extremities had minds of their own and had declared a holiday from their duties. *Maybe it's the weather or my advancing age,* she thought, *or the exertion of dealing with that taxman. He was a tough one to cut down to size, he was.*

Just after breakfast one morning, Sylvia arrived with brown eggs and fresh milk. During periods of winter when the lane was passable, the neighbor would journey out with her mule and cart to obtain provisions for both women. Sylvia was a nervous woman, not fully accustomed to the tribulations of living in the country, even after these many years. She was dark featured, with a sharp nose and large ears. But Sylvia had a kind heart, and she remained cognizant of the fact that Bonnie's only beau had become Sylvia's husband, if only for a time.

"Welcome, neighbor," said Mister. In a gesture that Bonnie had taught him, the straw man removed his hat and bowed.

"Isn't he marvelous?" Bonnie said. "He can cook and clean, and much more."

Sylvia recognized the scarecrow that Bonnie had employed in her garden this past season. "What . . . How--?"

"My dear friend, do not think about it much," said Bonnie. "Life is short and hard, and we must accept the few gifts we receive, mustn't we?"

Sylvia approached the straw man. "May I?" she asked.

"You may touch me as you like," Mister responded. Sylvia laid a gentle hand on the side of his face.

"This—this truly is a gift," said Sylvia. Turning, her tone drew grave. "I came to warn you, Bonnie. I heard in town that the tax collector will come to our valley any day, and he will accept no excuses."

"Do not worry, dear friend, we will manage," said Bonnie.

"Manage? How will you manage?" said Sylvia.

"Perhaps we will strike a bargain," said Bonnie.

The scarecrow spoke. "Friend Sylvia," he began. "Mr. Palmer was here. He went into the root cellar. He did not come back up—at least not as a whole man."

Both women turned to the scarecrow, taken aback by his honesty and directness. Mister displayed no change in countenance, as if he had merely commented upon the weather or the quantity of salted meat in the pantry.

"Bonnie, what have you done?" said Sylvia. "Please tell me you did not kill this man."

"Ah, I would rather you not know," said Bonnie, eyes to the floor. "But what's done is done. Can you find it in your heart to forget what you have just heard, to go on as good neighbors and friends?"

"I do not know, Bonnie. Truly, I do not know."

The straw man examined Sylvia's expression, recognizing surprise, horror, and sadness. Only once—as Sylvia departed—did he look at Bonnie's face, but he could interpret no emotion upon her.

***

In the days and nights that followed, the scarecrow grew quiet and withdrawn, if such a mood could be discerned in the expressions and movements of a man constructed of straw. Bonnie read to him less frequently, slept with him not at all, and took to pacing the floor of her cottage, occasionally speaking harshly to him.

"There is no need to tell my business to the world," she would say. Or, "Be grateful that you have a warm house, rather than freezing in the garden."

What bothered Bonnie was not a troubled conscience, she told herself. She did what she had to do. What bothered her was the numbness and stiffness, which had spread throughout her arms and legs, and an absent-mindedness that she had not encountered before.

When Sylvia next visited, Bonnie begged her to fetch the doctor from town.

"It likely is just the cold in my bones. It is so very cold this winter; I have never felt anything like it," said Bonnie. "But it also troubles me that I cannot always remember what day it is, and whether I have eaten my lunch and such," she continued.

Sylvia, who had always envied Bonnie's fortitude, pledged to travel to town on the next clear, dry day. But the winter would not oblige. Thick ice, then deep snow, blanketed the county all around.

Days would pass without the scarecrow uttering a word. Soon, Bonnie ceased speaking to him, other than to order him to stoke the fire. If she harbored even the slightest remorse for killing the taxman, she was determined not to divulge it to a mere figure of straw. She would stare at fireplace embers for hours on end, but she found it increasingly difficult to recall Frederick Thompson's face.

Eventually, Mister broke the heavy silence: "Our firewood be almost depleted, lady. It be my purpose to keep you warm. What shall I do?"

"Get the ax next to the woodpile," she replied. "Take it to the woods. Cut down a tree and chop the trunk and limbs down to firewood. And be quick about it."

"I will do as you wish," responded Mister, "though plentiful snow and strong winds may damage the lovely clothes you brought to me."

"I have rags enough to replace them, if need be," said Bonnie.

As the scarecrow approached the door, he turned to Bonnie. "Lady, forgive me for asking, but what will happen to me if I am overcome by foul weather or attacked by some fearsome animal? Would it be my fate to die, like the witch in the story?" He hesitated before adding: "Or like the taxman?"

"That is no concern of mine," said Bonnie. "I created you. And no doubt I can create another, or many others, from straw and string I have about the cottage. Now, out with you!" she ordered the scarecrow. "Go to your work."

Mister found the ax and trudged toward the woods to commence his labor. He felled a substantial tree, chopped it as

124

Bonnie had demanded, and stacked the wood. The task consumed nearly two days and two nights.

Mister reentered the cottage carrying a small bundle of wood.

"Careful you don't catch a spark," said Bonnie in a faint voice, as if spoken from great distance and requiring significant effort. "That would be the end ... of both of us."

Mister retreated from the fire and resumed his chores. Bonnie did not venture from her chair the rest of the evening.

***

The days passed, the snows receded, and the spring made a grand entrance. As the sun's rays crested the treetops and poured through a window onto Bonnie's face, she woke from her slumber. But she remained still, as if in a trance. She attempted to rise to start a fire, but she found it too much trouble, as if her muscles had been frozen into immobility by deep winter. *I recall asking for a doctor*, she thought. *No matter. I will make do, as always.*

In time, she struggled to her feet and hobbled about her cottage in short, stiff strides, calling out Mister's name, but he did not respond. She peeked into the root cellar and spied out of every window, but she could not detect his whereabouts.

By the chair where the scarecrow would sit when he had completed his chores, Bonnie discovered scattered straw and a few strands of clothing.

Ah, Mister, where have you gone? This is a sad day, for sure, she thought.

Bonnie longed for the familiar comforts of her garden. She padded slowly toward the front door, removing her favorite hat from a peg. She pushed open the door and encountered a scene that seemed to burst from the pages of a storybook, with a cavalcade of glorious scents, birds chirping enthusiastically, and sunlight reflecting brilliantly on dissipating dewdrops. Yet her body remained maddeningly sluggish, and her mind tended to drift from the task at hand. Focusing all the energy she could muster, she inched toward her garden, passing the bright green tips of daffodils breaking the soil's surface while breezes as soft as lovers' whispers swept the newborn season across the land.

It was late afternoon when Bonnie attained the center of her garden and placed a weary hand upon the tall metal pole that had supported her scarecrow in seasons past. With supreme effort, she turned, straightened her body, and leaned upon the pole just so. The hook gripped the back of her shirt.

She turned her head slightly to her left, then just to her right. Finally, she gazed straight ahead at her handsome garden and the unspoiled lands to the west. Presently, the familiar silhouette of the snowy-crested hawk appeared before her. The bird circled the garden before descending and sinking its talons into Bonnie's shoulder. It rested there for a substantial interval before returning to its vigil in the skies. Bonnie remained motionless, a thin smile fixed upon her face. The minutes passed. Then hours. And days.

In truth, it was the prettiest spot in the county.

Richard Farren

Barber Brunswick

Brunswick closed the door and waited a heartbeat for the lock to click into place. Only once he knew the room was secure did he look across to the man sitting at the table.

The prisoner was silent. He looked up from the table, his eyes red—a deep red accentuated by the fluorescent strips of light overhead.

"May I?" Dr Brunswick asked. He stood for a moment, his hand resting on the back of the chair. When there was no response, he pulled back the chair and sat down. This close he could smell the man – a thick musk of piss and stale sweat that drew yellow stains on the paper suit he wore – and wondered if forensics had found anything useful on the man's confiscated clothing.

"Tell me about the boy."

The man smiled. His teeth were small, white as porcelain, perfectly even. "What would you like to know?"

Contact lenses, Brunswick thought, *he must be wearing contact lenses* – that would explain the red eyes. He looked across to the large mirror and then cursed the mistake. Not that the man didn't already know about the observation window – an hour ago he had smeared the glass with his own blood and then licked it clean.

Brunswick put a folder down on the table between them. The man showed no interest in the contents.

"They think I am play-acting," the man said. "They think I am trying to pretend that I am mad, but you do not think that, do you?"

"I'm only here to make an assessment about your mental capacity to answer questions."

"But you have been watching me, Dr Brunswick?" The man slipped the name across his teeth. Brunswick suppressed a shiver.

"You have been observed," Brunswick agreed. "We want to understand you."

The man laughed, hard and sharp and the noise slapped against the walls of the small room.

"You want to *understand* me? That is very noble of you. What about the others, do they want to understand me?"

They just want to tear you apart, Brunswick thought. *They've seen the remains of the boy and they just want a few minutes alone with you.*

The man raised his hands, his wrists held close together as if bound by handcuffs. He pulled them apart. "I assume I have you to thank for this?"

"I find people respond better when they're not in shackles."

"And how you would you like me to respond? Should I tell you about my terrible childhood? How my father abused me before finally casting me out?"

"Would you like to talk about that?"

"What do your years of training tell you, Dr Brunswick? Are you trying to decide what label to give me? Sociopath? Psychopath? Bi-Polar? Dissociative? Are you trying to decide what box to tick for me?"

Brunswick relaxed. "That isn't how it works."

"Enlighten me, doctor. How does it work?"

"I'm here to help you."

The man smiled. "What if I do not want to get better?"

"So you do think you are ill?"

"Is that not how this goes?"

"Have you been in this situation before?" Brunswick asked. He tried to watch the man's reaction, but it was hard to stare into his eyes: *His red eyes.*

"Are you frightened of me, Dr Brunswick?"

Brunswick held his silence, and in response the man simply smiled and nodded, as if he understood what Brunswick had left unspoken.

Brunswick opened the folder and shuffled the pages inside to buy himself a few seconds of thinking time. He wondered what everyone crammed into the small room behind the one-way glass thought of the situation.

He looked up from the papers and stared into the man's eyes. He felt his lungs close up. His ribs ached at the action.

The man's eyes were blue. They had been red before, he would swear to it. He remembered that clearly and yet now they were a deep cornflower blue and for some reason Brunswick found this new colour even more disturbing than the last.

The man smiled, and as Brunswick watched, the colour of the man's eyes returned to red.

A trick of the light, Brunswick thought. Just a trick of the light or maybe the man had been given some medication that had affected the colour of his retina and now it was wearing off—because eyes didn't just change colour.

"Let's--" he stammered and then tried to take a hold of his emotions. He took a deep breath. "Let's go over what you say happened."

"I killed him, is that not all you need to know?"

Brunswick turned around in his chair to look at the mirrored glass.

"Tell me how you killed him."

"Slowly," the man said, and smiled.

"Why?"

Brunswick had spoken to murderers before. He had spoken to rapists and child molesters and gangsters who would put a bullet in the back of someone's head for no other reason than they felt they'd been slighted. He'd sat in a cell with the serial killer, James Hanley, and listened to him recount each of his kills. But this man was different from all of them.

"The boy," Brunswick said. "Why did you choose him?"

"He was there. That is all. If it had not been him it would have been someone else."

"That's not good enough." Brunswick heard his voice rise. Not quite a shout, not yet, but there was frustration and anger in there and silently he cursed the man's ability to get him to react.

"That's not good enough," he repeated; Soft, in control.

"You want to know if I am insane."

"Do you think you are?"

For a moment, the man's eyes switched to blue and then back to red again. The change happened in a heartbeat so that Brunswick could easily tell himself it had not happened.

"Tell me your name." Brunswick shivered; a patch of cold air inside the room touched his nerves.

"Which name would you like?"

"Tell me what other people call you," Brunswick said, rushing his answer.

The man in front of him smiled – the man with no name and no identity despite the fingerprints they had taken and the photographs that had been circulated.

"Someone will know you. Someone will recognise a photograph of you and tell us what we need to know. Why bother trying to hide?"

"Am I hiding?"

"You tell us you killed the boy and yet you say nothing about who you are or who he is. You can't say why you attacked him. You're hiding because you don't know, or you don't want to face up to knowing, what you've done."

The man pushed his chair back and stood up. Brunswick felt his heart slam against his ribs. He looked across – the panic bar ran around the inside of the room at waist height. He could reach it, but his mind clogged with the terror of this man's presence, clouding his thoughts.

The man took a step back, away from the table. Brunswick noticed that he was barefoot. He should be wearing white paper socks but had either cast them away or someone had forgotten to provide them. The man's toes were gnarled and ugly.

"I frighten you."

It was not a question, but Brunswick nodded anyway.

"Why, Dr Brunswick? Why are you so afraid of me?"

Don't answer that. Don't speak. But Brunswick heard his own voice in the small room, as if it had come from somewhere else, from *someone* else. "Because I think you know what you have done and you enjoy it."

"Is that your professional opinion?"

Brunswick shook his head – the assessment didn't come from books or experience, it wasn't logically thought out. It was instinct. Gut reaction.

"If I am not insane, Dr Brunswick, then what am I? Why did I kill that boy?"

Evil. The word rose to the top of Brunswick's mind and he batted it away. Evil was not a clinical diagnosis. Evil was a *News of the World* headline.

"What if you are right?" the man whispered. He smiled – like a teacher watching a pupil finally understand the lesson, finally seeing all the pieces click together.

Brunswick felt despair slip into the room. There was no treatment for evil. No books to explain how to contain it. No court system to regulate it. Evil just... was.

He looked back to the mirrored glass, willing movement behind the screen. The man understood what he had done. He was lucid, cogent. Even if he could not ultimately be held responsible for the murder, he could legitimately be questioned about it. Any formal assessment of medical competence would not happen today – it would take weeks and months whilst the man was in a secure unit awaiting trial. *I've done enough*, Brunswick wanted to say, *let me out of here*. Part of him understood that he could simply stand up and leave, that he could bring the interview to a close, but another part of him realised that he had to wait until he was released.

"You *want* me to be insane. That would make it easier for you."

Brunswick started to shake his head – he never wanted that diagnosis for anyone – but he stopped. If the man wasn't insane, then what did that leave? That he truly was evil?

A single spot of bright red blood appeared on the white of the man's paper suit, just below his throat. The drop of blood blossomed on the material. Spreading, but never losing the virulence of its colour.

"You're bleeding. I'll get someone to attend to you."

"You are a doctor. Can you not fix me?"

Brunswick shook his head. "Not a medical doctor."

The man's eyes shifted – red to blue. "Help me," he whispered. And the voice was not the strong confident tone of the man who had been in the room with him for the last twenty minutes. It was weak and plaintive; a sound bubbled up from someone deep within the man.

And then he smiled and Brunswick knew that the man had deliberately allowed the voice to escape. Brunswick watched the man's eyes shift back to red, as he knew they would do, and he waited until he was sure he knew who he was speaking to before he asked his next question.

"Who was that?"

"Nobody."

"Everyone is someone."

"He was nobody," the man said; "Nobody when I found him and he is nobody now."

The man paced, measuring out the limits of the room in long strides. He passed behind Brunswick and although it took every nerve in the doctor's soul, he managed to avoid turning in his chair to track his progress. That would have given the patient the power he craved.

The footsteps halted directly behind him.

Brunswick felt each hair on the back of his neck slowly unfurl and rise to a sharp point. A sensation ran down his skin – as if a fingernail trailed gently over the surface. He repressed the shudder his body ached to release.

"*You* are nobody," the man whispered, his lips so close that Brunswick felt the chill of the man's breath on his skin.

Brunswick closed his eyes and searched his mind for a prayer. He was not a religious man, but over the years, he had attended enough weddings and funerals to be able to knit together a few words. The sentiment was simple: *Dear Lord, protect me.*

"*You* are nobody," the man whispered again, "and *He* will not protect you."

"Our father, who art in heaven..."

"He will not protect you," the man insisted, but Brunswick thought he heard something new in the man's voice – fear? Could it possibly be fear?

"Thy will be done on earth as it is in heaven."

"Be quiet. They can hear you. What will they think of you – the mad Dr Brunswick who lost his mind and started trying to exorcise his patients? They will put you away. Maybe you can have the cell next to mine." The man laughed, but now Brunswick was certain he could detect a tremor in the man's voice – a fracture in the arrogance that had been there before.

"Give us our daily bread..." Brunswick said.

"Help me," a voice whispered.

Brunswick smiled, and although the man still loomed behind him he knew that if he had been staring into the man's eyes he would have seen them shift from red to cornflower blue, and he had an idea that this time it was not the will of the demon, which had allowed the other voice through.

"Who do you think you are?" the man shouted. "Who do you think you are to pray at me?"

And still Brunswick stared at the plain white wall. His mind filled with images that he knew the demon placed there: the battered body of the dead boy; snapshots of other victims; the

132

spots of blood on the man's white suit; and the back of Brunswick himself, hunched up in the chair using all his willpower not to turn around and raise his hands to protect himself.

"Look at me," the man commanded.

"For thine is the Kingdom."

"Look at me!"

Brunswick felt his body shifting in the chair. The tendons in his neck creaked as his head turned slowly round. He tried to remain still, but his body was no longer his to control. He shut his eyes—clamped them tightly down.

"Look at me!"

He felt pressure upon his eyelids, as if someone had placed their thumbs on the delicate skin and was slowly pressing down upon the soft jelly of his eyes. Explosions of red, yellow, and blue fired across his vision.

"Who do you think you are?"

Brunswick smiled. "Me? I'm nobody."

Somewhere in the station, an alarm went off. Footsteps clattered outside the corridor and Brunswick had enough time to wonder what the emergency was before he heard the rattling of the interview room door. *They're here for me*, he thought, and immediately clamped down on the sense of relief that flooded through him.

The rattling stopped and fists hammered against the door, shaking it in its frame.

"Who are you?" the man asked again.

Brunswick kept his eyes tightly closed. It was becoming easier.

He could hear voices outside the door. People shouted orders – he thought he heard someone bellow, "Get him the fuck out of there. Now!" and then the whole room rolled as something heavy crashed into the door.

"Not long now," Brunswick said with a smile.

"You cannot do this," the man said. "I will not allow it."

"You and whose army?" Brunswick said, and the playground retort felt like a perfectly aimed blow.

The room shuddered again. It felt like he was caught in the heart of a warzone. That the trembles, which rolled across the room, were the result of munitions dropped just outside the building.

Then he was listening to horses scream – trapped in battle. He heard children cry. He heard women and men ripped in torture.

The years peeled back. He heard voices shout in French and Italian and Arabic and Mandarin. A voice cut through the babble. "He's going to fucking kill him if you don't get him out of there now!"

Too late, Brunswick thought. *The man was dead a long time ago.*

Finally, he opened his eyes. The man lay on the floor. The collar of his paper suit was thick with clots of blood. Black pits sank into his face where his eyes had been.

Brunswick looked down at his own hands. They were covered in blood.

Stephen McQuiggan

The Wretched Blessed

THURSDAY

I was glad when she died even though I had promised to take her place. I doubt if Harriet will ever truly forgive me for devouring her corpse but I thought it fitting that a woman who devoted her life to eating should go that way.

Obviously, I've kept some over for the weekend picnic and Harriet would have welcomed that; she was always so thrifty. Who knows, maybe old Marcus will have a crispy bit to suck on. That reminds me, I must really send the old goat his teeth back, after all it's been so long since the incident with the matches, and I feel he's been punished enough.

Tonight I shall offer up a small prayer for Marcus to behave himself at the picnic. Perhaps he will sing for us again, like he used to when we'd drown the newborn.

I think of Harriet constantly now, but she is just a photo in a frame. She watches me adoringly from behind smeared glass. I will return her gaze until sleep takes me.

FRIDAY

Harriet danced on the forecourt as we ate our sandwiches, the moths caught up in her frenzy, swooping excitedly above her splendid nest of white hair. She was a bonfire spewing forth winged ashes, and her eyes, dear God her very eyes bulged with terrible secrets. The rain fell, burning, but it only added to our pleasure.

The beauty of that place never ceases to move me. The lights, the smell, the flags that fly like torn flesh from bone, and the voice of the wind in the deserted shop, pleading, demanding.

It was Andrew's birthday so it was he who gave himself to the blade. I can still see his smile as I gorged on his juices. There are special moments in life, precious moments. God gave us the past to ease the burden of the present. I will always remember that smile.

And the taste of his heart.

SATURDAY

My father was a sin eater and he grew fat on my indiscretions. My mother worked in a factory; she told me she made sacrifices. I miss them so much, their kisses and their beatings, but I can stare at my wall and make them appear whenever I wish. I can manipulate them; make them do exactly as I wish.

Tonight they will suffocate on my fondness, drown in nostalgia so sickly sweet.

They are my only family. I am barren of all things save contempt. Harriet was my wife, my only. She used to whisper to me, "You're nowhere Uri, nowhere." It was love at first insight. But now her grave is silent and all the days have merged. The traps are filled with strangers and I must empty them soon or the meat will turn as putrid as my thoughts.

I watch the walls settle, grow still.

The show is over.

SUNDAY

I caught a glimpse of my reflection this morning. I never realized I looked so old, so unkempt. My eyes are beautiful though, and such a handsome nose. My teeth are yellow and brittle, like the candy that blighted them. Pale blue veins for lips that have only kissed the dead, and a sprinkling of ashes to crown my skull; hair or cobwebs, I neither know nor care.

I was never vain. How could I be?

There are webs in my room that run their thin sticky fingers along my skin.. No matter how much I rub and scratch they will not go away. I feel their tiny tongues but I cannot see them. Once, thinking they were candy floss, I tried to eat them and got a chewy surprise. Now I only watch them sway under the weight of a spider suckling on a blood bag insect.

My mother always called me her little scarecrow.

Uri the scarecrow, always watching, always frightening people away.

How they would all laugh.

And oh, how they fucking screamed.

MONDAY

All the trees are dead so the oak is naturally worshipped. The others are burnt demonic creatures, buried alive, thrusting their black fingers through the earth in agony, begging the indifferent sky for mercy.

I sit under the oak and regard my blistered hands and my ragged nails. If you let your nails grow long enough you can grow a suit of armor, a coffin to bury yourself in. My fingers are scorched too, especially the one that bears my wedding band. That finger is my petrol trigger. The rain has stopped and a nonflammable rainbow spills out above me.

I can hear the old men who perch in my tree, and I can sometimes hit them if an egg shaped stone is handy and luck is on my side. The tree grows all the way to Heaven for I have seen the angels descend to feed the ancient ones. They were given sour breads and cheese and I fought with the rats for the pleasure of those holy crumbs that fell from the branches like manna.

One day I shall climb the oak and wring their scrawny necks. One day I shall feast on that divine platter and God shall be my waiter.

I must be sneaky. I must offer them gifts in order to get close enough. I will hoard my precious berries, oh yes, hoard my precious berries and then we'll see.

TUESDAY

I have a hump on my back that contains all my confidence, locked safely away from the many faced Others. They gave me my hump as punishment for daring to dream and I accepted it meekly because I believed I had sinned.

I still cry, but there are no fat maternal strangers to comfort me. I cry because I let down my father's God. The God of dry men, the bland merciless God they nailed me to when I was young. The God who gave me my hump. Now they tell me He is electric, like a computer their Jehovah; they worship their own platitudes. I am the three stages of Man; the man they liked, then pitied, then feared.

God still hates me. Outside the sky is blank as if God has spilled his milk in his wrath; the milk of all kindness. The world

137

has disappeared, been erased, while I sit and wait. I see His childish hand tap the window, his cold breath prepare to blow away the surplus of my soul. It is a tramp's breath, fetid and sickly.

I have two berries now, one hard and white, the other soft and purple, and there will be more to come. I have hidden them well. Soon I will have enough to confront Him. Soon I will scream in His face.

WEDNESDAY

Silence is hiding, trying not to breathe, becoming dark, merging with nothing, fearful of, and in, the silence. It was never quiet in the service station was it Harriet?

Ah, the times when our companions died the slow death of drink and we would laugh. Do you remember the stern man with his neck covered? What could he possibly have been hiding? We chased him away and our laughter fell like casual vomit; you said I was a man that day.

I'm so cold now, that day seems so hot, and so far away, a distance measured in Celsius rather than miles. I am so cold and so quiet. Father taught me to bite my tongue, but I worried that if I did I would cry out in pain and shatter the holy silence into a million tiny pauses. Silence like an eternal Sunday.

In the dark of the grave, and I know for I dug my own, it is silent save for the scuttle and gnaw of the insects. Here it is quieter than the grave. In my solitude, I have gathered many secrets. I will tell you one now.

It is not silence they crave, merely yours.

Be still. Hush. Count to ten. Remember.

THURSDAY

My granddad's hair was a dandelion, one puff of wind and it would fly away; one o'clock, two o'clock; my grandfather clock. Now when I think of him he is old and sparse, his hair combed over the pink, vulgar expanse of his head. His skull was almost pornographic; the strands of hair lay taut across it like fine lingerie.

I'm glad I killed him even though he was innocent, even though that skull housed secrets.

138

Granddad taught me how to burn things when I was just a little boy. A crooked, friendless boy, all alone on the big farm without as much as a kitten to play with. Everything in nature is farmed. We all pray to God. The burning was my childhood solace, keeping me warm at night.

Granddad always called it wildfire, as if there were any other kind, as if it could be tamed, domesticated. I loved the flames, loved the little grabbing hands punching the air to a song that only I could hear.

The trees were ablaze and she danced among them, her white dress fanning out behind her as the leaves caught and fell smoking on her hair. Dance sweet Harriet dance! Over the roar I heard her song too.

FRIDAY

My berries multiply in their hideaway and I grow confused. Faces slide in and out giving me no time to say hello The angels say I should try to hang onto something solid and I will do what they ask, for how else will they ever trust me. They know nothing of my designs.

Solid. Firm. Focus.

Coke! I remember Coca Cola! It fizzes up my nose, sparkles in my beautiful eyes, before escaping on a pillow of hot air too big to hold in my mouth. Is this what they mean by magic?

I will transform myself. Already I feel my flesh liquefy. I will escape, ascend, and sail on that pillow through the invisible bars they surround me with when I sleep.

They whisper, wake up one-ninety-one.

But if I did, they would never.

SATURDAY

I hear them talking. I think they may suspect; my head hurts, I find it hard to play innocent. Just a little longer, a day or two, and then throw the old man down. Father would be pleased; he always held the devil's claw.

The things I ran from all my life, the women, my parents, myself, all wore the specious garb of self-loathing, all of them wore the devil's face.

Now he lurks in crawling things, things with too many legs that hide beneath my pillow. Satan is alive, the morning star still burns in the consecrated heavens, and his real name is conscience.

SUNDAY

It's all leaving me!
All I'm left with is the horror.
It's a cold feeling, but only sometimes. Sometimes it scalds. It has the bald, brittle feel of a carapace, the whisper of spider hair. If I could smell my heart right now it would smell of black iron blood. A flabby heartbeat, arrhythmic, bloated. If it burst there would be a deluge of filth.

Shh! I can hear the thin membrane crackle. It tastes like the acid knife that stabs my throat when I run from father. It tastes of primal desire. It is all it thinks about. I feel so angry, if you hated me so much then why did you let me live daddy?

I don't know my name. My name is now a number and there are so many numbers, constantly multiplying like the rage within me. I feel it stirring, stretching, scratching, ready to rise and roar. When my rage returns to its slumber, my life will be in ruins, and because the beast wears my face no one will believe I'm not to blame.

MONDAY

I can see the moon outside my window. It holds no mystery for me. The moon is just a big stone. The mystery lies in my past.

Shadows lunge out of the murk, become more distinct, but I try not to look. They are all Harriet shaped. The gnawing scrape in my gut warns me not to remember. These ghosts that flit in and out of my mind tease me with half mouthed portents. I fear I have created these shades.

I am not one-ninety-one.
I am a man with tablets hidden beneath his pillow.

TUESDAY

I found more tablets today, squirreled away beneath the mattress. I must have stopped taking them; though for what reason I have no idea. I feel I have been away for such a long

140

time. Perhaps I hid the tablets because I heard myself calling from so far away.

I'm back in this tiny room with its too bright pastels and its stench of antiseptic. A Spartan niche with a desk and a stool, a single bunk, and a heavy, heavy door that not even a breath could pass through. Sometimes I can hear the orderlies laugh though; such wicked humour always finds an outlet.

The single window is too high to afford a view but I can see a tree branch at its edge. There are straps on the bed and marks on my wrists and ankles. I fear that when I am away they tie me down at night.

They have given me this book to write in. The doctors have told me it will be therapeutic, that it will help me. It is such a beautiful thing. Like a prayer book. Sacred. Its pages have the cold sheen of fine marble with an almost imperceptible skein of blue veining them.

It is a holy book, a relic, but already it has been marred, tainted by some crude hand. It has scrawled ugly spider sentences across its cream expanse.

That is the work of my treacherous hand when I am not here. I know that without even reading it. I am too frightened to read it. I might find out why I am here, and if I did, I might go away and never come back.

Take the doctor's advice. Small steps. Start at the beginning. What's my name? My name is lost. Unless this is it on the front of my smock.

My name is one-ninety-one

.

WEDNESDAY

The tears blur the ink and smudge the gorgeous paper. Would that I could so easily blot out the memories that awoke me today. The orderlies came with their sticks to beat me but on finding me in such a state, they fetched Doctor Anderson who spoke quietly to me and gave me an injection. I must write this down to repay his kindness to me. It will be my last will and testament. I am going away for a long, long time.

If you are reading this doctor, do you know if I can hide in madness? Is there peace in insanity or will she discover me even there?

We had all gathered in the little flat above the shop to celebrate

141

the opening of the garage, of *my* garage, deep in the countryside; my little goldmine. Even my father was there, still in his work clothes. I find it almost impossible to visualize him without his dog collar or a bible in his hand.

Harriet was so beautiful that day, much too beautiful for a little crookback like me. And yes, I tired of hearing that, and of seeing the shock in stranger's eyes when she introduced her husband.

I felt blessed, for a time.

That morning had been our grand opening and my brother Marcus, and his rigid wife Janice, had been our first customers. He rolled up in a brand new bottle green Jaguar and filled the tank.

"Wasn't that awful good of him," said Harriet.

"Yes, wonderful. He really looks out for me," I agreed. I knew I had been upstaged. I was used to it by then. Harriet beamed at him across the table.

"More wine Mark?" I asked, trying to hide a grin. He hated me calling him that; thought it common.

We talked so much that day. Talked of dreams and ambitions, real pie in the sky stuff, and I feel foolish thinking of it now, but I had my business and a beautiful wife heavy with my child and my family all around me. It made a man's heart swell, and a swollen heart is liable to burst.

"Of course, when the business fails you'll return to your caretaking duties at the church." My father said this as if it were written in stone.

"I don't think so father. The business won't fail. I'm deter-"

"Look at yourself son. Be honest with yourself. There'll always be a job for you at the church, remember that."

I saw his lips clasp like an old lady's purse, locking my future within. Why could he never be happy for me? He was the real hump on my back. I've felt his crushing weight there all my life.

I rose from the table standing as straight as I could, and though he remained seated, my father still looked down on me. "Get out of my house!" I said.

Everyone fell quiet, their voices still echoing in the wine glasses. I lifted a dessertspoon, the closest thing to hand, and pointed it at him. "Get out you arrogant old fool!"

I was waiting for Marcus to intervene, to take my father's side and, God help me, if he had I would have run him through, spoon or no spoon, but he didn't say a word.

Neither did my father.

He dabbed at his mouth with a napkin in that over precise manner of his, retaining a dignified silence that infuriated me. I wanted him to mock me, to reveal his true self in front of the others, but he was too clever for that. In his own time, he got up and walked out, and claimed the victory.

I went to go after him but Harriet blocked my way, the bulge of her stomach acting as a barrier. "You're going nowhere," she said, "nowhere."

I sat back down and stared at the cooling pork. I felt her foot rub against mine and when I looked up she whispered to me, "I'm so proud of you", and that was the best moment of my entire life.

I should have known it would be fleeting.

The following Sunday was Andrew's fifth birthday. He had grown so big and strong; I often thanked the Lord that he hadn't turned out like his runtish dad, that he resembled more his athletic uncle.

It was a scorcher that day. I shouldn't use that word. I'm sorry. If you are reading this Doctor Anderson I apologize; I take no pride in it, as you once thought. It was a glorious day and we decided to have a picnic under the oak in the backfield. My grandfather came, wheeling himself out of bed for the first time in months.

"I wouldn't miss Andy's big day," he explained, although I expect he was really showing his support for me; he never got on with my father either.

Later that morning Marcus arrived bearing a hamper large enough to satiate a crusading horde. When no one was looking, I threw the dog-eared sandwiches I had made into the bin.

"We'll never eat all that," I said.

"All the more for me then," said Harriet rubbing her enormous belly; she was only half joking.

"She's eating for two now," said Janice, and something in her voice made me uneasy. It was not the voice of a concerned sister, nor even that of a jealous, childless one". It ignited doubts in my mind that had had grown damp with neglect.

You would never have taken my Harriet and Janice for sisters, much as you would never have taken Marcus and I for brothers. One thin and awkward, with a shyness so severe it could be misconstrued as arrogance had I not been so ugly, the other a joyous spirit, straight, tall, and attractively confident. In the natural scheme of things, it would make more sense if I had been with Janice and Marcus with . . .

I remember Andrew flying his kite on a murmur of wind. I watched him as he laughed and sang to himself and the song stirred up bitter memories and my doubts were doubts no longer.

I watched my wife as she hunkered, red faced, over the hamper trawling for sandwiches and wine, saw her wince as she struggled to right herself underneath the weight of the food and the child within her, saw the wince replaced by a lightning grin as Marcus rushed to help her, saw that grin transform into a hungry smile as my brother furtively touched her belly the way a man touches a secret treasure to make sure it is really there.

The air turned cold, chilled by my blood, as he returned her sparkle and then busied himself with the paper plates. Janice was staring at them, then at me, and, for a moment, before she looked away, I saw the same suspicion on her tight little face.

Rising from the plaid blanket, I went to my wife as through the tangles of a drunken dream. As I reached to touch her shoulder, the shadow of the leaves dappled her pale skin so that it looked diseased, corrupt. She turned, her smile dying too quickly when she saw me. The one she replaced it with could not mask her disappointment that I was not my brother.

I knew. I knew in that instant.

"It's his child isn't it?" The accusation didn't seem to shock her as much as my knowledge.

"What?" Her laugh was too thin, too hurried, too forced. She pulled cling film off the chicken legs and her hands were trembling. "What *are* you talking about Uri?"

"You heard me."

"Don't be so silly dear and give me a hand, or we will all starve to death. Does anyone fancy some quiche?"

"Tell me the truth you bitch!" Even the birds fell silent.

"Not in front of Andrew. You'll ruin his big day."

I could hear my...I could hear Andrew, still singing as his kite tried to escape in the static air. I floated up there with it, buoyant with that song, and gazed down on a childhood long since blown away.

When I was a boy, the big cat that prowled the orchard behind our house gave birth to a knot of shaky kittens and then abandoned them. I couldn't sleep for worrying. In the middle of

144

the night, I went out to the old dustbin where they huddled and, wrapping them in my coat, brought them to my room and hid them beneath my bed.

They would not stay still, darting out from every angle, and Marcus came in and saw them and told father about them that morning at breakfast, and father was very angry.

"It's a sin to put such a burden on your mother," he said. "Another six mouths to feed."

"But Sir, they only eat an awful little-"

"That's what they assured me when you came along."

He made me put them in a bag, one by scrawny one, and take them to the river. I begged my brother to do it but father said it had to be by my own hand, said that was the only way to make it mean something.

I carried that squirming sack all the way down to the stream behind the orchard, and all the way I could hear their thin pleas and the scratch of claws on canvas, and I felt like I carried a heart before me, a beating heart, and I guess I did; my own has never really beaten since.

As I dropped them beneath the calm water, Marcus sang a happy song that mocked my tears. It was then that I realized I hated him more than my father. That song now burst from Andrew's mouth and chased the streamers on his kite.

I took Harriet by the shoulders. "Andrew. He's not mine either, is he?"

"Listen little brother, I think perhaps the smell of all this wine has went to your head." Even now, Marcus tried to belittle me. Janice was quiet but alert, as if a burden had been lifted and she was wondering who was next to buckle under its weight.

"They're yours Marcus, aren't they? Both of them. Yours." For the first time I can remember my brother looked more afraid than disgusted of me. "Just giving your little brother a helping hand as usual, eh?"

Harriet began to cry. "Uri-"

I punched her, hard, in the face, and the harsh crack that echoed across the field was the crack that split the dam.

Despite the horrible things I did that day that is the one that haunts me most. It seems trivial compared with what followed but it's where I leapt the line, and after that I could never go back.

I'm sorry doctor, I can write no more today. This hand is too

145

heavy with blood.

THURSDAY

She picked herself up and walked quickly away, breaking into a run as she neared the garage. Janice left too, silent and stern, but with a gleam in her eye as if she'd landed the punch herself. Andrew ran past calling his mother's name; he didn't even look at me.

I sat back down, trembling, the rage within me curdling to sickness. The world was moving in fast forward and I felt if I didn't hang onto something I would spin off, but there was nothing left to hang onto. Marcus stood above me, his shadow molding the remaining sandwiches. I wanted him to hit me, to light the touch paper.

"You couldn't let it be," he said. "You had to play the victim. You don't care how many lives you ruin, you twisted little fool. Why couldn't you just leave it alone?"

I rocked slowly until his specter left me, and when I was alone I cried. I cried so hard I turned myself inside out, cried until my face was dry. Then I got up and walked to the garage, knowing in my heart what I was going to do but with no tears left to mourn it.

I saw Harriet through the window, her face swollen and bloodied, the strap of her white dress torn where I had grabbed her. She looked like a fallen angel. I saw Marcus hold her, comfort her, whisper snakes in her ear, and something lurched inside me. My grandfather was polishing the Jaguar and his sidelong glance told me he already knew, had always known.

Lifting a hammer from the toolbox by the door, I burst in and struck Marcus in the mouth as he turned to protect her, his teeth spilling like loose change over the counter. I turned on the pump then dragged my wife out to it, kicking her each time she tried to get up as I doused her in petrol.

I kept hearing my father's voice saying it only meant something if you do it by your own hand.

I fumbled with the matches, flicking them on her until she ignited. Her hair flashed and vanished. She flailed across the forecourt like a deadly star. Her touch was flame and she spread the word of her passing until everything was engulfed and grandfather was beating her, trying to put out her melting body.

146

Her smoldering embrace seared his eyebrows.

I picked up the hammer and caved in his skull. Andrew was yelling something. I turned to him next.

I can't do this. This is torture not therapy. It would be better to forget. But how can I forget that I pulled my brother's child, already half cooked, from my wife's belly. How can I forget I ate it.

When I saw she was dead, I wanted to swap places with her. I thought if I consumed her, I would consume her soul and she would live on within me. The only sound I could hear above the inferno was the crack of her bones on my teeth.

I was damned, even then, I knew that; but I would not go meekly into Hell.

I locked Marcus in the cage where the gas bottles were kept, leaving him a piece of Andrew to feed on. I knew the family from the neighboring farm would come when they saw the smoke so I sawed through the boards on the plank bridge across the ditch in the backfield and filled it with glass and wire. Later I thought I could hear Magee and his wife calling out in pain and I harbored ideas of eating them too, whenever the sweets ran out in the garage.

I was chewing on them maniacally, the sugar rush fueling my frenzy, for they tasted as cloying as my thoughts. I felt them rot my soul as well as my teeth.

One of the last things I remember is the old oak. It was the only tree not charred or wasted. I sat there and listened to the birds, or the sirens that sounded like birds. All kinds of detritus had snagged in its branches. I saw plastic bags wriggle and writhe in its grasp, forming faces like old men, like judges, and I wanted to climb up and beg for mercy, or to stop their condemnation once and for all.

I heard Harriet's voice, "you're going nowhere Uri", and I stayed my ground. But she was wrong, I was going to Hell. Or maybe it was coming to me.

I sat under the tree until I awoke here. Doctor Anderson, this journal has become my suicide note. I cannot live with this. I can taste her still. I will take my horde of tablets and leave for good, to death or madness I neither know nor care.

I too am burning.

I *am* one-ninety-one

FRIDAY

We are the rats that rustle in the hedgerow unseen. We are the flies that consume the dung. We are blessed.

Sometimes the angels speak to us, reassure us, tell us to forget the war, but it haunts us. We think they understand. They give us special sweets that float us away to a secret place where pain is just a rumor. They give us manflesh and strong tea. Food fit for a funeral.

They fade through bolted doors where we cannot follow, not yet, but they promise that one day we will. They gave us a book to write in, a holy book for its pages are as white as they. A black pencil. We will write a book of prayer and dedicate it to you.

We will pray for your sorry soul.

Ro McNulty

Extinguishing the Flame

Up on the moorland, the wind tasted of salt. Eli Moran was playing football. The sky was slate-coloured, and the cold raised goose bumps all across Eli's and his two teenage brothers' skin. The older boys stamped their feet and ran on the spot for warmth; Eli put his hands in his pockets, shivered, and watched the clouds of his breath being torn up by the wind.

Their house was high in the hills, a steep scramble above Whitby Bay and the nearest civilization. Up here, Eli and the older Moran boys felt like the lords of all they could see. Eli was ten years old. He played in goal, in between two piles of coats and backpacks. When his brothers scrapped and forgot about the game, he would gaze out over the hills, down to the little redbrick fishing town and Whitby Bay itself.

He'd never admit it, but he made an awful goalkeeper. He was cack-handed, his fumbling movements lacking the sureness to get to grips with the spinning ball, which in any case seemed to him to be far too capable of bruising him even if he did manage to get in front of it. Anyway, football was boring. He liked the rugged moors, which still seemed dangerous and wild compared to the Wiltshire fields, from which his family had moved the previous summer.

"We should move *up north*!" His mother had said to his father one night, in the dining room at their old house. "Imagine how big a property we could afford up there!" Then Eli's father had both laughed, and said "*up north!*" again and again in unfamiliar accents, so that it sounded like '*op narth*'.

Eli liked stories about monsters and knights, and the northern hills and rivers set his imagination on fire. Besides, his brothers were good company, and they would take turns to carry him if he grew tired of walking.

"Eli! Dive!" The ball sailed a broad arc over Eli's head. He didn't even mind going to fetch it. It was as far from his brother's watch as he would allow himself to wander. He liked feeling useful, and loved the chance to tussle around in the wet bracken and gorse. He would march back, football tucked firmly under one arm, caked in mud and grass stains, feeling rugged, and a little bit older. There was always the chance, too, that he would find something, some treasure, lying waiting for him on the moor; a long, firm stave of a wood that might be oak, or a fist-sized rock, or green bottle-glass that had been worn as smooth and round as a precious stone by the rain. Once he had found a fox's skull. He'd kept it in his pocket all day, telling no one, until he got home, when he and his father had made it into a waxy candleholder and lit up his bedroom like a dungeon in a gothic film.

This time, he hadn't seen where the ball had landed. It had disappeared over the ridge of the hillside, down into the deep valley below. It was beginning to rain, blurring Eli's vision, like mist on the edges of the landscape.

Wiping his eyes, Eli began to pick his way down the slope, winding crabwise in between the rocks and coarse thorns. A badger set gaped from behind the roots of a tree, like an open mouth. A stream chuckled over its rocky furrow, throwing itself over waterfall after waterfall towards the valley floor. Eli felt the icy water on his hands and knees.

At the bottom of the valley, he could see no one. There were a few twisted trees, and the stream had joined a fast, shallow river that danced over the smooth, flat stones of the valley bed. Eli suddenly felt very much alone. Hs brothers and their game on the hilltop felt like a world away. He was often gone for an hour at a time, so they wouldn't come looking for him. The slopes loomed above him, seeming far too steep now for him to climb his way back up, isolating him, and allowing only the narrowest streak of grey sky to be seen.

And something was in the valley with him, watching him from the far hillside. It was black, with four tall, spindly legs and a long, thick, snake-like tail. At first, Eli thought it was some sort of huge deer, but its body was horrifically, skeletally thin; its spine was arched around a deep ribcage, the curve of every bone visible. It had a long neck and a tiny, flat head, which seemed to Eli to be blank and featureless. The rain was setting in harder now, the freezing spray making his spine shiver like a cold finger. There was no one here. He felt utterly alone, a desolate fear forming cold, icy words in his mind:

They don't love you. They can't hear you. They won't come for you when you cry out.

"Eli?" He started at the sound of his brother's voice. When he looked back to the creature, he could see nothing but the shadows of trees through the rain.

***

It was always too hot in the Jobcentre office. Gareth could feel himself sticking to his T-shirt. His skin prickled as if something was trying to touch him. His heart rate began to climb in his tight, claustrophobic chest. He couldn't breathe. His back hurt. He felt sick. A fan buzzed somewhere. A fly's wings rasped against the window. The blinds were twisted out of shape at the edges.

"I'm sorry, Mr Austin, but part of your Jobseeker's agreement was that you would apply for apprenticeships as, and when, they came up. We can't continue your Jobseeker's Allowance if we deem you not to be actively seeking work." The girl that Gareth and his cock had named *little bitch* peered over her thick-rimmed glasses as she addressed him with a clipped, prissy southern accent. *Fucking stuck up slut.* Gareth noticed that her breasts in their tight white blouse were resting on the desk. He couldn't remember when he had last been with a woman. Her sexuality seemed to mock him, like an itch that he couldn't scratch. *They shouldn't let them dress like that in here.*

"Well of course I lied on fucking form didn't I? Fucking everyone lies on the fucking forms. You just put some shit in the three boxes. How the fuck am I supposed to claim otherwise? I'm too old to be pissing around with fucking apprenticeships." Gareth spoke more loudly than he had wanted to, and now people were starting to stare at him across the office. His head felt fuzzy in the heat. He couldn't think properly.

"Mr Austin, you need to calm down right now, please. You can make a new claim by ringing the Jobcentre Plus phone line but it will take a few weeks to process. Because of your abusive behaviour towards staff we must ask you not to come into this office in the meantime." They were looking at him, all the poor, shabby claimants waiting edgily on the benches to be called, and the benefits advisors, in shirts and glasses, turning their heads, craning their necks, and staring at him. *Straight at Gaz Austin, judging me. They all want to see me lose my rag and scream at that fucking bitch so they can all be better than me. They can't*

151

just fucking give me my money and leave me alone. They have
to see me fuck it all up

Gareth felt a twist in his gut, like fear. A wild animal in a trap, lashing out.

"What am I going to do with no fucking money? How the fuck do you people expect me to manage? I've got my son..." Gareth stopped dead.

The girl was silent. Very slowly, she began to type into her computer. When she turned back to Gareth, her expression was grim.

"Mr Austin, we have no records here whatsoever, that mention you having a dependent child."

***

When Eli woke up the next morning it was raining harder. From his bedroom window, he could see the black creature stood at the bottom of the garden path, just beyond the low hedgerow and behind the little gate that separated the lawn and flowerbeds from the moorland. At first Eli closed the curtains. The way the creature's eyeless face stared up at his bedroom window made him feel like he was being watched from behind as well as in front. He got back into bed, pulled the covers around himself, and screwed his eyes tightly shut.

He hadn't managed to fall asleep before his father bounded through the creaking door.

"C'mon tigger. Bounce yourself out of bed now and come on downstairs." From under the bedclothes, Eli asked his father if anyone was in the front garden.

"Nope. Your mothers flustering around the kitchen and I'd imagine Jake and Dan are still snoring away, waiting for their wonderful dad to come and throw a bit of sunlight on the situation. Do you want to come and help? It's great fun."

Eli got up and checked the window himself. The black creature still stood by the garden gate, it's flat, blank, unmoving face pointed upwards towards his bedroom window.

He wished his father would leave the room. His cheeriness suddenly seemed disingenuous to Eli; somehow empty and false.

They don't love you. They can't hear you

Eli went downstairs to the dining room. The creature was still waiting at the bottom of the garden path. He could see it watching him through the French doors as his family ate their breakfast. His parents and brothers laughed and bantered around him, seldom speaking to him, their voices seeming hollow and soulless, like liar's voices. Eli hardly even heard him. His eyes were fixed on the black thing's faceless head; it's eyeless stare.

After breakfast, the living room as his brothers took turns to play on their videogames. Eli twitched aside the curtains and felt it watching him through the window. He turned his back, knowing it was there. His brothers shared the games console between the two of them but never included Eli. He ran errands for them, silently, when they asked for snacks from the kitchen, or he sat on the arm of the sofa, saying nothing, not looking out of the window. The two brothers had always had a special bond. It was well-known.

They can't hear you.

He caught a glimpse of the black thing through the kitchen window before his father caught him looking in and shut the door. He and Eli's mother were talking in angry whispers over the sink, and Eli's father seemed to start when he saw their son staring at them, or past them, from the hallway. The black creature stared past them both, back at Eli. He couldn't hear what they were talking about.

They won't come for you when you cry out.

At midday, Eli made up his mind. He quietly left the house and walked slowly down the garden path. The creature waited for him just across the gate, an arm's reach away. Eli could make out every rib and vertebrae on its body. It looked starved, like no living thing should ever look. Up close, it was more like a huge dog or a cat than a deer, with soft paws and a slender, sloping build. Its legs seemed too spindly and thin to support it.

Its face was bony, not flat as it had seemed from a distance, although it had nothing that Eli could recognize as features. Its stare came from beneath a jagged ridge over two depressions that almost looked like they could have held eyes in them. A row of fine teeth seemed to hang down from where Eli would expect to see a chin, or at least where the face stopped; the creature had no bottom jaw.

There was no malice about it, although its blank, featureless stare made Eli's skin tingle. It watched him almost curiously, expectantly, with an intensity that made Eli feel a little anxious

153

that he might startle it. It was trembling gently, the cold rain stinging at its taut skin. Eli reached his hand out to touch it but it sprang away with the speed of a coiled spring.

At that fleeting moment the loneliness that Eli had felt as his family had laughed so falsely around him became a feeling of sorrow that was almost too much to bear. None of them would follow him when he left. Eli imagined he was the only person in the whole world who could see the creature. It had watched him, waiting for him, whilst the others had scarcely even known he was there. *It chose me*, thought Eli.

Eli opened the gate, and turned back to the house one more time. His mother stood in the kitchen window, looking past him. Just for a moment, Eli wished she would call him back into the house, out of the rain and away from the lonely, hungry creature past the garden gate, but when he met her eyes she just smiled and waved from the other side of the glass.

They don't love you. They can't hear you. They won't come for you when you cry out.

So be it. Eli followed the creature.

***

It was a meanly small house. Its red bricks were blackened around the plastic front door. One window was boarded up, like a black eye.

Some kids had mistaken the building for abandoned, and nearly burnt the whole house to the ground one night before Gareth had woken up. He remembered the smell of smoke, the sounds of laughter and windows smashing. The council's maintenance work had been half-hearted, and the house's facade was still boarded, blackened and crumbling. Perhaps they thought it was abandoned too. Gareth had never believed any of them.

Gareth swore as he tripped on a paving slab in the lifeless front garden. At the door, he carefully hid two cans of super-lager, in a translucent white plastic bag, behind the front step in the garden before he opened the door.

Inside, the house had been left to the flies. Gareth felt the greasy air settle on his skin. He hated the house, and never came back here if he could find any other place to go. The floor and walls were the same bare plastic, blistered and bubbled from the

154

fire, streaked like a melting candle. *They'd never given a shit*, thought Gareth.

Something soft gave way with a sucking sound under his booted foot.

"Scotty!" he shouted, coughing, his chest hurting. "There's fucking dog shit everywhere! Can't you fucking look after it?"

Through an empty doorway, an enormous, hideously malnourished black greyhound sat coiled on a bare mattress on the floor, partly covered by a bundle of filthy clothing. It didn't rise to greet its master but instead eyed him lazily through the doorway as he coughed and spat on the carpet. The dog's big brown eyes always seemed to Gareth to be filled with contempt, judging him silently.

"Scotty?" Gareth spoke more softly now, hoarse and spluttering.

"I'm hungry," came the reply. The bundle of clothing moved slightly. A tiny, black-haired boy of about seven or eight lay with his scabbed arms wrapped limply around the dog's ribs. His cheeks looked hollow and emaciated, and his clothes were smeared and frayed. His half-open eyes regarded Gareth with the same reproach as the dog, accusing him, wanting him to be where he hadn't been.

"Yeah we ain't got any food though Scotty. They cut my benefits and all." Gareth had a pit in his stomach. He dreaded seeing his son. He turned away and walked into the narrow kitchen but Scotty followed him through the doorway, blocking his exit.

"I'm hungry."

"Look, don't start this again alright? There's not ought to eat."

"I'm hungry." Scotty stared demandingly at Gareth. When his father turned away without replying he grabbed him by the waistband of his jeans and began tugging, repeating; "I'm hungry. I'm hungry."

"Look Scotty..." Gareth was beginning to feel his skin shudder, the knot of pressure on his gut.

"I'm hungry. I'm hungry. I'm hungry. I'm hungry. I'm..."

"Scotty..."

"Hungry! I'm hungry! Hungry! Hungry! Hungry!" Scotty began to stamp his feet as thrash at the walls with his dirty hands. His eyes were closed, and from the slithering bulge at the back of his

155

sweat trousers Gareth could see that he'd soiled himself. "Hungry! Hungry! Hungry!"

"I know! I know you're fucking hungry! What the fuck do you want me to do? We've got no fucking money!"

"Hungry! Hungry!"

"Shut up! Just shut the fuck up!" Gareth hit the child, feeling smooth, warm skin and the ridges of cheekbones under his hand. Scotty fell to the floor. He sat where he had fallen, breathing heavily, staring up at Gareth with furious eyes. "All you fucking do is sit around all day shitting your fucking pants and dribbling! What the fuck do you want me to do? I'm sorry you were fucking born, alright? Is that what you want?"

"I'm hungry." Scotty's voice was quieter now; shaking with anger.

"I'm sorry you were fucking born!" Gareth went to kick his son but turned at the last minute, lashing out at the kitchen cupboard instead. The door splintered and empty beer cans and plastic bags spewed onto the floor. "Here! Here's your fucking food, you worthless little shit. Why don't you fucking eat this?" He stooped down and threw a handful of litter into the boy's face.

"I'm hungry! I'm hungry!" Scotty was crying now, his nose running thickly over his hollow face. Gareth grabbed a heavy vodka bottle from the kitchen worktop, stepped over the howling child and slammed the front door so hard on his way out dry flakes of blistered paint fell from the ceiling, dusting Scotty's mop of dark hair white.

***

Eli let the black creature lead him across the sodden moors until his house seemed the size of a little toy. The thing always stayed ahead of him, springing between rocks and up slopes, then waiting, its stare unwavering from Eli until he drew nearer, and then prancing ahead again. At first, Eli thought it was taking him back to the valley where it had first waited for him, but when they reached the flat, scrubby plateau where he and his brothers had played their game, it turned instead towards the bay.

Eli watched the rain falling out to sea, in a thick bank that looked like it was made of metal. Whitby Abbey was black on the far cliff. Its empty archways looked like jagged bones. Still, the creature's gaze never left Eli until he began to move again, caked

156

in mud, half-sliding down the boggy slope towards the road and the town itself.

Eli's mother had taken him to the seaside before, and to visit Whitby Abbey, but he and his family had never strayed far from Whitby's cobbled shopping streets and a few favourite cafes. Eli had never liked the way the big, tattooed men in the town had eyed him from the pub doorways, and he had always walked quickly, in his parent's shadow, with his eyes cast down. He hated when his brothers or his father would laugh loudly in the busy streets, and the people near would become quiet, or would stare and whisper to each other in their strange, unwelcoming accents.

This time it was different. Eli didn't feel the eyes boring into him as he passed the groups of bitter-looking men. No-one seemed to take any notice of the lone boy, or his alien-looking guide. He wandered if they could see him at all.

The creature trotted ahead of Eli, just fast enough to force his pace and make him pant for breath. The cobbled streets, the fish-and-chip shops, the little white pavilions, all seemed to Eli like the flesh of the town. Where they ran out were its bare bones. This was where the black creature was leading him; under the looming shadows of tower blocks and across concrete and tarmac. Up on the far hillside from Whitby abbey, the squat blocks of flats and tiny, dirty red-brick terraces held something that seemed much, much older than the postcard harbour side. Whitby's waterfront was full of people who didn't see the town as Eli now did; shiny, smiley people like his mother and father. It was a lie

Eli's guide waited at the high-walled mouth of an alleyway behind two rows of little red houses. The creature cocked its faceless head. It had come to him, no-one else. He would follow it. Tufts of sharp weeds up to Eli's waist had clawed through the cracked concrete underfoot, as if the Yorkshire moors themselves wanted the town back.

Half way down the alleyway, the black thing jumped onto its hind legs and began to paw at the back wall of a meanly small house. Eli shoved a dustbin up against the wall and began to hoist himself over.

***

It was dark before Gareth returned. Scotty was still lying on the kitchen floor, but when he heard Gareth he scrabbled on his hands and knees to get away. Gareth caught him by his hair

"C'mon Scotty fucking get up. Stop pissing around. I'm trying to get out the fucking door again." Scotty screamed wordlessly as his father began to drag him towards the black staircase.

The bathroom was at the back of the house. It had one window, boarded with cardboard where the heat of the fire below had smashed the glass. The bath itself was stained to an off-white yellow, with a thick smear of brown rust from where the water had pooled in the bottom and more streaks of rust around the rim where it had overflown and gushed onto floor. The wooden boards under the lino had been too damp to burn. Instead the floor here was crumbly, bubbled and rotten. Thick cobwebs hung from the shower curtain rail down into the belly of the bath itself, and a black spider the size of Gareth's hand floated dead in the pool of water in the bottom of the tub. It was cold in the bathroom. Gareth could see his breath in the air.

The pipes screamed, and the taps spluttered and spat out red-brown flakes before the stinking water was belched from the guts of the house and began to fill the bath tub.

Scotty spat and bit at Gareth as he pushed him to the floor and tore of his clothes. "There, now fucking wash the shit off yourself. I'm not having this anymore. I'm sick of it. Can you wash yourself, Scotty? Can you fucking do that by yourself? Then when you're done go to bed. You'd better not fucking still be up when I get home."

As Gareth descended the stairs he could hear the wet slap of the water smacking the bathroom floor as Scotty writhed around in the filthy bathtub. He was howling wordlessly. He didn't know where he was. He only knew that he was naked and the water, the freezing, screaming, water was rising over him.

Gareth shut the door quietly as he left. He could hear Scotty's screams follow him down the street, as he walked away from the house.

***

Over the wall, the back garden of the little house was a waste ground. Eli didn't see the black creature jump over from the alleyway, but it was sat coiled up and watching Eli blankly on the other side when he fell with a thud from the high wall, as if it had been waiting for him all along. Eli noticed that it's trembling had become a violent shaking.

Broken glass and dog mess had killed the lawn, staining the dead grass a pallid yellow and leaving great patches of bare, black earth visible. The back wall of the house was ensnared with thorns that stretched up to the first floor. One window was boarded up. This was *up north*, Eli thought, what his parents talked about when they thought he couldn't hear. The land of the gruff, tattooed men in the pubs, with the unfriendly accents, that stared at Eli and made him hate the sound of his own voice. This is what the creature had shown him. The dog shit, the dead garden. The thing pawed at a patch of black mud that looked to have been a heap of earth until the rain turned it to a quagmire.

Eli began to dig at the wet earth with his fingertips, and then to pull away great handfuls of black mud. He fell onto his knees next to the black animal and began to scrabble away at the soil, digging faster and faster. The wet dirt caked his knees, his arms and his face as he pulled away at the earth of the dead dump of the lawn until his palm brushed the torn remains of a wet translucent plastic bag pulled tightly over. . .

. . . over something hard, and wrinkled, and waxy. He cried out. The black thing watched him, head cocked, shaking. Sticking out from the churned mud where it had been buried was a little hand, the size of a small child's, wrapped in a carrier bag. The skin was slack around the stunted, broken bones, and had coloured a frostbitten blue-black around the snapped fingertips.

***

"I'm cold."

"Leave me alone."

"I'm cold."

"Go away," Eli murmured, wrapping the bed covers around himself and screwing his eyes shut so tightly that they hurt.

"I'm cold. I'm cold."

"Please..."

"I'm cold." He could feel something icy and hard in the bed with him. Something with wet, slack, sallow skin, and brittle little bones that clicked and snapped as its little, muddy, blue-black

159

fingers began to tug at the bed-clothes. Something that shuddered, wanting his warmth. Something dead.

"I'm cold. I'm cold. I'm cold..."

And its eyes... its green eyes had appeared suddenly in the darkness of the bedroom doorway and frozen Eli still in fear. It had stared at him from the darkness, its glare seeming to howl silently at him, the words shrieking around his mind again and again; *it's your fault. It's your fault. It's your fault.* The plastic bag had been pulled roughly over the thing's head, its hand caught inside so that its spindly arm had become twisted and broken, but the eyes still smouldered beneath the wet, see-through plastic.

"Please!"

"Cold! I'm Cold! Cold! Cold! Cold!" The lifeless thing began to slither damply over the bed. Its limbs creaked as it tugged at the sheets, pulling them away from Eli, making him see it. "Cold! Cold! Cold! I'm cold! I'm cold!" Its throat rasped where it had screamed its voice to shreds and no one had heard.

"No... Just leave me alone!" *It's your fault. It's your fault. It's your fault. You weren't there. You weren't there. You weren't there.*

"Cold! Cold!" Eli screamed out as he felt the terrible, sodden weight of the murdered child slumped on the bed. No one heard him. *You weren't there. It's your fault.*

***

By the time Gareth came home the morning light was beginning to shine weakly under the cardboard in the window frame, shimmering on the pools of water that streaked the bathroom floor, glinting on the dust in the air. Scotty's body was blue, beginning to blacken in places. His eyes were open, gazing through the bathroom doorway, and for a fleeting instant Gareth thought he was still alive. The child's skin sparkled in the water, although no steam rose from his cold body. Scotty's head rested delicately on the edge of the bath, and an inky bruise was beginning to roil across his hollow cheek where it had led against the creamy acrylic.

Gareth stooped next to his son, and gently covered his face. Then he closed his eyes, remembering the flames, as if their little house was burning all over again, though the room was cold, and damp.

It was Scotty's dog that Gareth turned to. He grabbed the thin, beautiful creature's long neck and smashed its fine snout and tiny skull under his boot again and again until its big, soulful, brown eyes filled with blood. He hated the dog. He hated Scotty too, in a way. They had needed him so terribly.

**

"Have you spoken to Dan yet?"

"No. I've been at work all week. You know that." Eli's father spoke slowly to his wife, aggressively patronizing, weary and sick of the sound of her voice.

'Well I just thought it might benefit them to hear it from you. You know, you're their role model and everything. A positive male influence'. Scotty's mother's tone was jolly, and riddled with sarcasm. A lie.

"If you want to discipline them then do it yourself. You're the one that wanted to move up north in the first place. I told you it was a deprived area, and now, lo and behold, our teenagers are going off the rails". Eli's father spoke in a grating whisper.

"You always do this," Said Eli's mother, suddenly letting her temper show. "You absolutely refuse to take any part in anything, to take any suggestion I make seriously, you just nod and say whatever you think I want to hear, and then the first thing that goes wrong you think you can get away without any responsibility for anything. You're like a ch... a *fucking* child." She hissed, savouring the exciting taste of the illicit word. The kitchen door was closed, blocking the big house out.

"Temper, Alice." Eli's father stared into his coffee cup, one side of his mouth beginning to curl into an insidious, triumphant grin. Eli's mother washed up as if she was trying to strip the paint from the china, throwing the plates onto the draining board with a violent clatter.

"Is Eli up yet?"

"Yeah. I think he went out somewhere."

"Great. Good parenting, there." He gave a martyred sigh. "Do you know where, Alice?"

"What? Like you ever take an interest in him? He's probably up on the moors. He's off in one of his dream worlds again I think.

Playing some weird game or other, out in the rain. He took his duvet with him."

***

In the little house's garden, the ghost of Scotty's greyhound still lay coiled over the muddy mound, waiting when Eli returned. The black creature raised its maimed head as the boy came scraping down the high wall. He knew that he would find it here. He still felt the same shudder, the same feeling of being watched from both in front and behind, when its eyeless face gazed at him. He felt like he could read the eyes that should have been there; big, faithful, brown eyes that he didn't want to disappoint.

Slowly, Eli draped his quilt on the ground over the wet earth. He knew, without understanding why, that a blanket was a better thing to put over a child than a gravestone. Carefully, Eli folded in the edges of the quilt, and tucked them in around the mud of Scotty's grave.

The black dog curled up, and tucked its head between its dainty front paws. No longer eager, or abandoned, no longer with the terrible, unspoken sense of hunger, or cold, or loneliness, or an unmet need, it seemed to sleep.

Amy K. Marshall

Lluvia cae . . . The Rain Is Falling

Sorrow Was Like The Wind.
Lluvia cae
Lluvia cae
Her fingers trailed the sheer curtain. Her grey-blue eyes gazed impassively past the window—out into the weather, losing focus among the trees that crowded up against the cabin. Behind her, the woodstove popped and crackled. Outside the rain continued—blown, tossed in sheets against the wind. It would be dusk soon. She sighed and shifted, her gaze wandering skyward. The crisscross of cedar and spruce boughs, the billowing mass of clouds, heavy-hung with precipitation and blued on the bottom, obscured the demarcation between day and evening. Only the incessant ticking of a clock on the mantle above the bright-sounding woodstove marked the minutes, the hours. Beside the mantle on the rough-hewn log wall hung a calendar; only the pages, torn away one by one, marked the days, the months.
"February 14, 1926"
The tiny cupid lithographed in the space beside the phase of the moon looked out of place on the Winchester Rifles and Ammunition calendar. Around the date, today's date, a drawn red heart stood out even across the room. Her lip curved into the ghost of a smile.
He would come.
She knew he would come.
He had promised.
She was promised.
Soon
She turned from the window, her gaze appraising the tiny cabin: Sparsely furnished, but still cozy and warm. The curtains over the windows were clean and she had pressed them. She had washed the dishes and put them away in the sideboard that had arrived with her on the island. The rough floor fairly shone with cleanliness. She had lugged the cabin's only rug, an elaborate Oriental affair, outside the day before during a brief respite from the rain, to beat it of its dust and spruce needles.

163

She reached for the cup of tea that continued to grow cold on the counter beside her. Thoughtlessly, she took a sip; her nose twitched. The tea had grown much too cold. Soundlessly, she set down the cup and crossed the room toward the kettle atop the woodstove. She wrapped a cloth around the kettle's handle and lifted it. The cast iron was heavy in her hand, and she shifted the weight slightly before returning to the cup to warm the tea within it.

"Thank you."

She heard his voice as if it were right beside her.

She turned and saw his dark brown eyes smiling at her behind the steam of the tea he lifted. The lines around his eyes creased with his smile and he winked at her lightly before taking a sip from the mug.

"You make the best tea."

"Flatterer," she spoke the word playfully, not unkindly.

"I couldn't stay away."

She felt her mouth go slightly dry. "I don't want you to stay away."

He closed his eyes, eclipsing her view of his soul as he leaned toward her. She struggled to steady her breathing. His breath was warm against her lips. She held her breath—

Lluvia cae

Lluvia cae

The wind shifted, driving the rain against the glass. She stood alone within the room, her hand still holding the kettle. Her gaze flickered down to the teacup and her breath caught. She pulled her hand back, raising the kettle, stopping the water from overflowing it and spilling across and down the counter.

"Oh, no..."

She hurried to replace the kettle and dashed back with a dishtowel. She tossed it onto the counter, furiously sopping up the water, picking up the teacup and ignoring the bright burn of ceramic against her fingers.

"What have you done?"

"I'm sorry—"

"Stupid girl," he spoke the words harshly, unkindly.

"I'll clean it up." She offered more words by way of apology.

"Have you burned the water as well?"

Her hands trembled against the cup she offered.

He took it silently and drained it.

"Passable," he snarled.

She hazarded a slight smile.

His blue eyes darkened. "But only just."

"Of course." She managed to whisper the words.

He closed his eyes, eclipsing her view of his soul, as he leaned toward her. She struggled to steady her breathing. His breath was hot against her neck. She held her breath—

Lluvia cae

Lluvia cae

The wind shifted again, the roar through the treetops as the cedars struggled and spruces clung, their roots spread wild upon long-fallen timber and shallow dirt. She stood alone within the room. Turning toward the sink, she wrung out the dishtowel; she watched the tea stream from the fibers, watched the brown swirl slightly before falling down the dry sink. Into oblivion.

It was with an unsteady step that she crossed the room. She balanced her cup before she sat in a chair before the woodstove. She placed the cup on the small table beside the chair and picked up a book. Her hands were still unsteady as she opened the book to the page she wanted.

Soon

"Read it again."

She felt her cheeks redden and she ducked her gaze back into the book.

He shifted, his dark eyes never leaving her. "Please. I love to hear you read."

"Stop." She giggled the word and held up the book as if it were a screen against him.

"Please," he said again. She could hear him sit up on the divan, heard his feet brush the carpet.

"You're being silly," she admonished him.

"I'm completely serious," he assured her. He hesitated and she slowly lowered the book enough to look at him. "I miss your voice." His own voice dropped to a whisper around the words.

"I–" Her voice sounded unsure.

He slid from the divan and sat at her feet. "Just read a little."

His arm slid around her leg and he rested his head against her knee. He did not look at her, but kept his gaze trained upon the woodstove.

"Just a little," she agreed.

He turned his face up toward her. She felt her heart hammer in her breast. He shifted closer, his cheek warm against her knee. He sensed the change in her breathing. He closed his eyes, eclipsing her view of his soul as he leaned toward her.

Lluvia cae

Lluvia cae

"More of this nonsense."

"My chores are done." Her protest was timid.

"A waste of time. There are other things to be done," he snarled. "Yet, here you sit."

Her hands trembled as she closed the book. "I'm sorry," she managed, "I–"

"Of course you're sorry," he mocked her, his blue eyes narrowing, "you ARE sorry."

She bowed her head and looked quickly away.

He ran a hand through his thick black hair. The hand closed, momentarily, into a fist and she cringed. He noticed. "As if I would lay a hand on you!" he snapped.

She winced.

"Say it!" His voice was a bark.

She jumped, startled.

He strode angrily across the room, his hand back and threatening.

"No!" she fairly wailed the word. "You wouldn't lay a hand on me!"

The hand flexed into a fist once more. He stood, his gaze glowering down at her. He nodded once. She felt her heart hammer in her breast. He stepped closer, his hand warm around her wrist. He sensed the change in her breathing. He closed his eyes, eclipsing her view of his soul as he leaned toward her.

Lluvia cae

Lluvia cae

She rose from the chair, too distracted to read. Outside, the light waned. Her gaze wandered once more to the clock on the mantle. Afternoon was nearly spent. Evening would soon be upon her. She brushed her hands across her skirt briefly before stepping toward the woodstove. Silently, she opened the door and cast in more fuel for the fire. After closing the door, she reached up and turned at the flue. Her efforts were greeted with a roar that matched the wind outside as the fuel caught fire and burned brightly, warming the cabin.

He would come.

He had promised.

She was promised.

Soon

She turned from the main room and walked into the bedroom. It was a tiny space, taken up mostly by a brass bed and a large dresser with a round mirror. A neat, white lace bedspread stretched across the bed. The wind shifted and the rain whipped momentarily against the bedroom's only window. She straightened the items on the bedside table before she fussed a bit over the bedspread.

"I could stay here forever." His hand gently brushed back a lock of her hair before he leaned toward her. She drew back slightly.

"I would never want you to leave."

He lightly traced a finger down and touched softly between her breasts. She felt every synapse sear at that touch. "I will always be here."

His hands were tangled in her hair. His lips were tangled against hers. He was warmth and weight and assured gentleness. He drew back and gazed down at her, his dark eyes shining. She felt every part of her respond to his touch. He shifted closer. He closed his eyes, eclipsing her view of his soul as he leaned toward her.

Lluvia cae

Lluvia cae

He snored heavily and shifted in his sleep. Moonlight streamed through the bedroom window and she turned her gaze toward it. Moonbeams danced along the neat, white lace bedspread, and she pretended the beams were enough to warm her with their yellow-white glow. He muttered and shifted again.

Across the room a bit of light caught against her sewing basket. Beside the basket was a pile of what had set off his latest tirade— un-darned, damnable socks. She shuddered. He had railed and threatened, berated her for laziness.

"I could go on forever!" he hissed.

She quickly bowed her head and said nothing.

His finger, sharp and urgent, pointed at her. "I will always be here!"

His hands had tangled in her hair. He closed his eyes, eclipsing her view of his soul as he leaned toward her.

The moonlight shifted silvery white. It sparkled suddenly silver against the sewing basket. She found her feet as she rose from the bed and moved toward the basket. Her hand closed around her mother's scissors—a wedding gift. She stood with the scissors in her hand and stared at her reflection in the dresser's mirror. She closed her eyes, eclipsing her view of her soul before she moved toward him.

Lluvia cae

Lluvia cae

She was startled out of her thoughts by a knock on the cabin door. She smiled and pulled her fingers quickly through her hair, pinched at her cheeks twice, and hurried from the bedroom. With quick feet, she crossed the cabin's main room. She stopped at the door, her hand hesitating on the handle. Out of habit, she took the safer path.

"Who is it?"

There was no answer.

Her hand twitched against the knob. She could hear nothing but wind and rain beyond. She opened the door slightly and peered out. No one greeted her on the porch. She frowned and pulled open the door. The trees crowded up against the cabin. There was no one visible on the trail that led to her porch. She took a step out and her foot struck something. She looked down. A carved, red cedar box sat upon the porch by the door. She bent to pick it up. It was heavy in her hands. A piece of rough cordage circled the box. An envelope, spattered with raindrops and bearing her name in neatly rendered script, lay between the cordage and box.

"Hello?"

Her call went unanswered.

He would come soon.

He had promised.

She was promised.

Soon

She carried the box back into the house and closed the door with the softest of clicks. She set the box on the table before the woodstove and untied the cord. Her fingers removed the envelope, setting it to dry before she would open it—afraid the words would be lost in the rain. She pulled the box into her lap and set her hands along the lid.

"I gave you my heart." His voice, sharp and wounded, pointed at her.

She shuddered. Her mind playing tricks; impossible, his voice. Her breath caught as she pulled the lid from the box. Within, a human heart, twisted in blood and viscera, shone silkily in the waning light.

His lip twisted and his voice was a snarl. "Now, I give you his."

Her hands trembled. Her gaze snapped to the basket of all that remained of him. Little by little, she had fed him to the fire.

"He isn't coming."

Her heart hammered. Waves of terror prickled across her flesh.

"You were already promised."

She felt the ghost of his hands close against her shoulders. His voice was icy breath.

"I will always be here."

She leapt to her feet and turned, the box tumbling, spilling his heart against the carpet. His blood twisted among the fibers.

"And you with me..."

He closed his eyes, eclipsing her view of Oblivion as he leaned toward her.

Editor's Note: *Lluvia cae* is Spanish for "rain falls."

Mike Jansen

The Copper Oasis

At this parallel, close to the equator, the day was long and sundown was short followed by inky darkness. Mick knew stories of Old Earth in which was mentioned the bright band of stars called the Milky Way and the way the moon lit up the night sky. There were few stars in this part of the galaxy and any radiation was largely obscured by dark clouds of dust, far away in space. The three small moons, asteroids really, did not reflect any significant light from the sun and they usually flew by too fast to cast even shadows. At night, the cold was intense and the temperature sunk to far below freezing.

He rode through Dry Vale during the hottest part of the day. The blistering rays of the sun and the extremely bright atmosphere drove the temperature up to well over one hundred and twenty degrees Fahrenheit, detrimental to both man and horse. Over time Mick had learned to protect himself by staying in the shade at these times, for instance in a wind and sand carved cavity in the rocks, just big enough to shelter both Mick and Holly, his trusty, decrepit transportation.

Mick only spent the hours just after dawn and right before dusk on the ranch. It was actually a set of three low, concrete buildings and a tall watchtower. The buildings were pitted and scarred and the pits and crevices in the gray concrete were filled with reddish desert grit. The steps of the steel stairs had been polished to a silvery sheen by all the times that Mick had climbed the tower to observe the desert.

This day started just like the previous four-thousand-seven-hundred-and-forty-two. Mick tied Holly's bridle to a piece of a steel railing that had once been part of the fourth bunker, which now was just a dust filled crater. He climbed the tower as always, his backpack on his right shoulder, left foot first and ending with his right foot after sixty-and-two stairs. The platform had an unimpeded view of the desert to all sides. To the far north, the Blue Mountains, snow covered. To the south there was desert as far as the eye could see. The east was a rough stone plain that also housed the pile of stones Mick used for shelter. The west was a gradual slope up toward a plateau that extended into a dried out highland that in turn stretched out for a thousand miles or more.

The tower reported no special occurrences for the past day, so Mick set himself in the middle of the tower, folded his legs under him and started his lonely vigil. As soon as the sun rose over the Blue Mountains he took his black Stetson and placed it on his head, just far enough to protect his eyes against the rays of the low hanging sun. More time passed and slowly the air above the desert started to swelter. Occasional wind gusts created short lived dust devils. Mick noticed the dust plumes at the peaks of the dunes and knew a sand storm was coming. It almost distracted him enough to miss the moisture trail that appeared in the higher atmosphere, but his focus was sharp and he traced the path of the object as it descended towards the planet. He noticed the flames spring into existence the moment it hit the lower atmospheric layers. The object changed course and Mick sat up straight. This was no meteorite! Something artificial that was capable of changing its trajectory. He tracked the fiery trail coming from the northeast and going to the south west, straight to the Dry Vale and as soon as the object disappeared beyond the horizon, he estimated its coordinates and started counting.

Mick got up, said goodbye to the tower and descended the stairs. Almost at the bottom of the stairs, a muffled crash sound that seemed to come from far away reached his ears. Holly was waiting for him patiently. Mick checked to see if his saddle was still properly in place, checked the saddlebags and his trusty rifle. He took the reins and guided the loyal steed toward the desert, past the treacherous dust pools and the ancient ruins from even before he could remember. The wind force increased slightly and fine grit hit his face. He took the cloth bound around his neck and pulled it up until only his eyes were free. He estimated that he needed a few hours to reach the impact site based on his estimation and the time it had taken the sonic boom of the impact to reach his ears. He knew it would be the hottest time of the day and it would be near Devil's Gorge, dangerous terrain on a good day. Deadly for the hardiest of life forms this planet had reared, especially when the glowing desert wind came howling down from the highlands and through the gorge.

Riding through Dry Vale was a challenge. The soft sand hid sharp stony ridges that could cut clothes and flesh and the

171

sweltering air hid the true shape of the surroundings. Mirages showed flat sand over nasty potholes and small heaps of sand could be just that, or the top of a Sand Slith burrow, a native insect-like creature that could reach a length of a dozen feet or more.

The sun beat down mercilessly and Mick was happy he wore the Stetson to protect his head. The covering had been a gift from Wild Bill, the first he had welcomed on the planet all these years ago. Wild Bill was the only survivor of the crash of the *Preston Charles*, a battle cruiser that had zigzagged through the atmosphere, mortally wounded, until it crashed into a row of high dunes. The ship rose several dozen feet above the highest dune and the characters ".les" were just visible above the sand.

Mick remembered vividly the grey face of Wild Bill as he arrived at the smoldering remains. Bill had erected a temporary shelter of loose metal plates from the ship. He had dragged supplies of water and food from the wreck and collected crates and containers. On a flat piece of the dune there was a row of thirty-eight graves, each adorned with a large metal shard and a personal item of the deceased.

Mick had helped him reach a safe place, helped him settle in and waited with him until a rescue party would come and retrieve him. When they finally said goodbye, Bill had given Mick his hat: "I'm thinking you better hang on to this, Mick, it'll help. Thanks for staying all this time."

***

There once was a salt lake in the dried up valley. The last years the lake had shrunk until only a blinding white, bone-dry desert remained. Far away, Mick noticed a thin plume of smoke rising up. Holly automatically adjusted her course to Mick's body and steadily approached the place where the ship had come down.

***

A deep trench in the landscape showed where the ship had touched down first. Mick followed its direction and a few hundred yards further on there was a second trench. The ship had hit the ground at a low angle causing it to bounce along the surface like a flat stone that skips across water. One hour later, they reached the point where the ship had actually burrowed itself into the ground. It was a rather small ship, more like an escape pod than a space worthy vehicle. The rock hard salt had torn off plates from the fuselage, and the passenger cabin had come free from it. Mick carefully steered Holly around the ship, alert to any cracks in the salt. Occasionally the water was deep underneath a thick crust of salt and although Mick was sturdy enough. He knew that the high saline concentration could actually damage him.

***

"Hey!" The voice was hoarse.

Mick localized the owner behind a low salt pillar. "Greetings, stranger," he tried in Standard One. He appraised the stranger carefully: tall, slim, narrow pale face, thin brownish hair, and large, dark brown eyes. In his mind, Mick tallied up a number of observations: used to low gravity, mostly active with protective suits, hair almost completely gone, low light environment.

"Who are you?" the voice of the stranger sounded suspicious. His helmet had been ripped off during the crash leaving only a few twisted hinges. It had functioned as designed, as there was hardly any damage to the stranger's face, just a few bloody scratches.

Mick recognized the sounds as an archaic form of Old Earth English and he replied in kind: "I welcome the visitors to this planet. Mick's the name. Mick Jacobson. Mad Mick to friends."

"I . . . My name is Miles Goodfellow. I don't remember how I got here. Or where I am for that matter."

"You've made quite an impact. A good blow to the head probably, but it looks like you're not seriously injured. Aren't you terribly hot in that suit?"

Miles shook his head in confusion. "No, no, it's cool. I mean, it cools me."

"Good, you'll need that around here." Mick pointed to the ship. "Not much left, I think. Any stuff you want to take along?"

"Wouldn't it be better to remain with the ship? In case a rescue party comes looking?"

Mick lifted his Stetson an inch. "At your service, Mr. Goodfellow."

Miles Goodfellow stared into the distance for a moment, despondent. He walked over to the ship, took some personal possessions and a supply of rations and water.

**

During the trip Mick showed Miles the many wonderful sights available on this section of the planet. Miles trudged along behind Holy. His suit was heavy but it isolated him very well and kept his body temperature at comfortable levels. The crates with his possessions Mick had tied to Holly's back.

"That there holds a Sand Slith," Mick pointed at a smooth stretch of sand. "Nasty bugger reaches a few dozen feet in length and is content to wait for that one single foot step for years."

Miles took two steps back. "Is it safe?"

"Nothing is safe here. We need to leave Devil's Gorge. There's a sand storm brewing." A small dust devil played at their feet to emphasize his words.

"Where are you taking me?" Miles sounded suspicious again.

"Wherever you want to go," Mick answered.

"I saw a green patch of highland as I flew over. And a small village."

"That's Dry Stone. It's a bit of a distance, but we should reach it in a day or two." Mick smiled at Miles who seemed to relax a little.

As they travelled, Mick told about Wild Bill who had spent many years here. And about Jesse James, named after a legendary Old Earth bandit who had performed many daring raids. He did not remain as long as Wild Bill, but Mick had appreciated his company. After that came Stout Stan who in turn was succeeded by Poker Pete.

Miles listened in silence to Mick's stories as they trudged over the hot, treacherous sand. He interrupted Mick only once: "How many people got stranded here?"

"Seventeen," Mick answered without hesitation. "Mellow Miles, that is what I shall call you," Mick smiled at Miles Goodfellow benevolently. "Everyone who has been my guest, I have given a nick name."

"Did they all survive?" Miles asked.

"All of them. We talk regularly."

"Good, that's a relief." Miles remained silent the rest of the trip, focusing on putting one foot in front of the other.

**

At dusk they left Devil's Gorge while behind them a curtain of glowing hot sand was swept up by the wind that coursed down from the highlands.

The night they had spent in Mick's cave. It had turned cold fast and Mick had observed Miles' restless sleep. His suit protected his body, but left his face exposed to the elements and blood-seeking pests. Mick regularly shot Sand Stings from Miles' face. The tiny insects would circle around their prey twice before diving into their intended victim full force with sucking stinger extended. Mick's laser evaporated them soundlessly just before they would touch Miles' face.

**

Early the next morning Mick prodded his guest with the tip of his boot. "Time to go. We should make it to the plateau before dusk." They trudged out of the cave, just in time to see the first rays of the rising sun.

Miles' face had turned red by the time they reached the highland plateau. The yellow, brown colors of sand, stone, and rock were interrupted by green and green blue stripes and patches. The low sun illuminated the steep sides leading up to the plateau, showing the layered structures that were witness to the history of the planet. Mick guided Miles and Holly to the slope leading up. The climb lasted almost an hour and brought them past the peak of the cliff and onto the plateau.

Through the haze of shimmering air, a few buildings were visible far away in the distance. The plateau was deep green with occasional bluish patches. The slight scent of sulfur drifted through the air. With renewed vigor Miles stepped onto the plateau, followed by Mick and Holly who he led by her bridle.

Mick pointed out a few pyramid shaped hills with holes at their tops. "Careful with the small geysers. This plateau is seismically active and scalding hot steam comes out of them, regularly."

"I'll keep it in mind." Miles searched around. "I thought there would be vegetation here, but I don't see anything."

"Copper oxides and copper salts is what you see." Mick snorted softly. "There's a huge copper deposit below these highlands. Water, copper, magma and other assorted minerals, sulfur and phosphorus. Mixed up and stirred it finds it way onto the plateau."

"That explains all the green and blue colors," Miles whispered.

"Wild Bill always liked it a lot. He often sat beneath Hanged Man's Tree at sunrise."

"Hanged Man's Tree?" Miles asked.

Mick grinned. "Bill's own little joke. It's a rock structure that rather reminds of a skeletal tree, a few miles beyond Dry Stone. Bill knew all the stories about Old Earth's Wild West. He also gave names to most of the interesting spots in the vicinity."

"Let us continue. I am curious to see this village."

***

"Welcome to Dry Stone." Mick recognized the expression on Miles' face as disappointment mixed with, probably, desperation."

"I . . . I thought there was a village here..."

"That depends on your point of view. I constructed the buildings as carefully as possible, carving them out of the local rocks, based on Bill's descriptions."

"But . . . these are not real houses," Miles stammered.

"There is shelter from the sun. There's a hot bath. There's a saloon. Unfortunately no Whiskey." Mick winked at Miles.

"How long did Wild Bill and Jesse James and all the others last here? How long before they were saved?"

Mick pondered the question for a moment: "Most had sizeable amounts of supplies and water."

"That wasn't my question," Miles said. "What happened to them?"

"Nothing to worry about," shushed Mick. "Like I told you before: I speak to them regularly."

"So where are they?"

"Sitting beneath Hanged Man's Tree. Wild Bill is not the only one who enjoys the view," said Miles.

"I want to see them. Now!"

"You're the boss, tenderfoot," Mick whistled Holly close, untied Miles' crates and carried them in one hand into the shelter that was carved out of solid rock and that was supposed to resemble a saloon.

In a square space of less than forty square feet and less than seven feet to the ceiling were the remains of Miles' predecessors. A few books, some dead electronics, plastic casings and, rather unexpected, there was a small recessed niche in which more than thirty small, carefully carved green stone statuettes of various creatures were exhibited. Miles recognized a few animals, but most he had never seen before.

Miles picked one up and held it up in the evening light. "What is this?"

"Centaurian Swivelhead. Male, judging by the horns on its back."

"Who made these?" Miles asked.

"Jesse James was a remarkable person. Before he left he gave me his collection and I put it on display here," Mick answered.

"Wait a moment. You just said they were all sitting beneath Hanged Man's Tree, yet you talk of departing and leaving. I don't get it." Miles blinked his eyes.

"It's . . . hard . . . to explain to a human," Mick said slowly. "Perhaps I'd better show you."

***

Mick mounted Holly and pulled up Miles effortlessly behind him. Without any hurry the animal started walking and after a half hour and in the last rays of the setting sun a bizarre mesh of thick copper colored branches, veined with blue and green and yellow layers.

Coming closer Miles saw a row of sitting figures, covered in thick layers of salt like a half transparent cloak. Each of the figures sat with their head resting on their right should as if they were listening intently to something happening above their heads. The faces, vague contours, were visible in the last of the sun's rays. They looked serene, calm, frozen in a state of indeterminate disposition.

"What have you done?" Miles asked. He dropped to the ground and took a few yards distance.

"When Wild Bill had spent three-thousand-two-hundred and seventeen days with me, his heart gave out. His dying wish was to sit beneath the tree, facing the direction in which the sun would set." Mick took off his hat and held it in front of his chest.

Miles noticed the gesture. "He gave you his hat then, didn't he?"

Mick nodded.

"But how can you still talk to him, like you said?" asked Miles. He distanced himself a little more as a precaution. "After all, he's dead."

"At nights like these, when there is tension in the air, that is when he speaks. All the others too." Mick grinned. "Feel the tree, you will understand."

Carefully Miles stretched out his hand towards one of the branches and as he approached it the hairs on the back of his hand stood up. "Static electricity."

"Yep," agreed Mick. "Months after Bill left, I came by again. By then he had been covered by a thick layer of copper salts. There was a thunder storm. And after the storm Bill started talking to me. I suspect that copper saturated water entered his head through his ear." Mick pointed to a slender needle that reached into Bill's ear. "Branch probably broke off and hit him in the ear. Copper deposits followed the neuronal and dendrite pathways in his head. After that all it took was a little electricity to wake up the old man and bring him back to life."

"I don't get it. Bill is dead. They're all dead." Miles was beginning to get very anxious.

"Relax, tenderfoot, I will not hurt you," Mick said. "Your turn will come."

Miles swallowed, and then asked, "Has anyone ever been saved from this planet?"

Mick grinned. "There have been many battles in this corner of the galaxy. All sorts of things float by. But never a rescue ship."

"What does that mean for me?" asked Miles. His face had turned a little paler.

"When your supplies are gone, you will slowly starve or die of thirst. But I will be with you in your final hours. I promise you that," Mick assured him.

Miles was dumbstruck. Dejected he walked back to Dry Stone, muttering all the way.

***

Sixty-one days it took Mellow Miles Goodfellow to accept his fate. No rescue team showed up. He learned to appreciate the setting sun and the many wonderful and vibrant shades of green and blue that its rays produced in the landscape. The ever-changing environment was beautiful to behold and after a while, Miles started talking to Mick again. After all, he was the only person in the area that Miles could have a conversation with.

When the water was gone and his purification system malfunctioned, he resorted to the mineral rich water from the rock. As the toxins built up in his body, his skin turned yellow and he knew his time had come. Together with Mick, he slowly, as fast as his body allowed him, made his way across the barren, green plateau until they reached Hanged Man's Tree. He saw that Mick prepared a nice seat for him and, with a deep sigh, he sat down.

"It's been good, Mick," Miles whispered.

"This is only the beginning, Mellow Miles Goodfellow," Mick said solemnly. "You will have what many people desire. Immortality of a sort."

"I just never understood your part in all this, on this planet, Mick. Will you explain it to me, please?" Tired Miles leaned back against a copper branch.

"Of course, Miles. I am the guardian. I make sure no one leaves this place," Mick explained.

"But why?" Miles asked.

"I do not know the reason, Miles. I'm just following my programming," Mick answered.

"So you are a mechanoid. I suspected as much." Miles coughed deeply and a fine red mist settled on his by now decrepit space suit. "So why help us? Why?"

***

Mick remained silent until Miles closed his eyes and breathed his last breath. He guided a thin copper branch to Miles' left ear, positioned his head properly, and softly pushed the branch through the tympanic membrane so that rich, mineralized water could drip inside.

***

As he rode Holly into the sunset, Mick whispered softly, "Mellow Miles Goodfellow. When you return in our midst I will explain everything . . ."

He softly whistled 'I'm a poor lonesome cowboy' as the sun sank beneath the horizon.

Rocky Alexander

Steel-Toed Boots

When I was a child—I was in third grade so I would have been about eight years old—my pappy came and woke me up out of bed late one night...said, "Put your shoes on, boy! We're goin' for a little ride!"

He didn't let me change out of my pajamas because, "We ain't goin' to Wal Mart or nothin'." A couple of his buddies were there with him, and we all piled into my pappy's truck and another one that his buddy owned. We drove a couple miles to the edge of town and pulled up into the driveway of a big house that I'd never been to before. Pappy told me to be quiet as we all got out of the two vehicles and went through a wooden gate that opened up into the backyard. There was a small basement window just above ground level on a side wall of the house. Pappy told me to crawl through it and go upstairs and unlock the back door. I asked him why, and he just said, "Because I said so!"

That's what Pappy always said when I asked him why.

Kids are small when they're eight years old, and I was even smaller than most at that age, but still the window was barely big enough for me to fit through. I wriggled my little body about halfway through and couldn't see anything inside, as it was so pitch black. I don't think there was even a moon that night. I pulled back and told my pappy I didn't want to go in because it was dark and I was scared, but he smacked me hard on the back of the head and yelled at me, "Get back in there, boy, like I told you to, or I'm gonna put my steel-toed boot up your ass!"

I knew that putting his boot up my ass was the least he would do if I didn't mind him, so I crawled through the tiny window with tears welling up in my eyes. The opening was about six feet or so off the floor, but there was no way for me to know how far it was because I couldn't see a thing in the dark. I backed out once again so that I could reposition myself to go through feet first instead of falling to the floor on my head. I held onto the window ledge for what seemed like a long time before I finally got up the guts to let go, and dropped onto the floor as quiet as a cat. Once I was inside, Pappy told me to go up and unlock the door for him.

It didn't take me long to find the stairwell, and I went sprinting up those steps like greased lightning—*loud* greased lightning that is: *BOOM BOOM BOOM BOOM BOOM!* until I was throwing open the door at the top of the stairs. If anyone else was in the house, no doubt they knew I was there now. I didn't care too much though. I felt scared and wanted out of the basement—out of the *house,* period. I opened the door into a narrow hallway that led to a living room where there was a big glass sliding door with some curtains over it. I scrambled toward the door as fast as I could move, smashing my leg against a table and knocking over a lamp as I went. I didn't even break stride.

It took me some time to figure out how to unlock the door, and once I did I still couldn't get it open. Finally, I realized that someone had jammed a broom handle or something onto the door track to make it harder to get the door open if someone wanted to break in. I remember thinking what a stupid idea that was. If someone wanted to break in, all they had to do was shatter the glass.

Pappy and his two friends were waiting for me as I slid the door open. He smacked me on the head again. "You tryin' to wake the whole damned neighborhood?"

He told me to wait by the door out of the way while the three of them made their way through the house with flashlights and duffle bags. Every few minutes Pappy would hand me something and tell me to go stick it in the back of the truck and get my ass right back in a hurry. One time he gave me a box of cassette tapes to run out to the truck. Once he gave me a typewriter. One time he gave me a big gun. It didn't occur to me outright that they were stealing this stuff. I almost asked at one point but I thought better of it. When I realized that was what was going on, I just figured they were mad at somebody for some reason or another and were taking their shit.

As it turned out, that wouldn't be the only time Pappy would take me for a late night ride. The next time had me crawling through the bathroom window of a grocery store, then a skylight on the roof of another. A record store. A couple of restaurants. Quite a few houses. I got to where I liked it because Pappy and his buddies would tell me how good I was at it...and sometimes I got to keep cool shit that I found.

But one night Pappy took me to a house where there was somebody home. Pappy broke a window in the garage that was attached to the house. I crawled through, and right when I got inside, the light came on and some lady was screaming in the doorway holding a baseball bat. Once she saw that I was just a kid I guess she got her courage up because she ran at me swinging that bat like a wild woman. She got me pretty good a couple times too, before I could get back out through the window. I also cut my hand pretty bad on the broken glass when I was going back out—I still have the scar from that. After that, I didn't want to go on any more late night rides with Pappy and his buddies.

I was nine years old when I told my Pappy no to his face for the first—and last—time. It was just after dinnertime on a school night when Pappy grabbed his flashlight out of the kitchen drawer and told me he needed my help on another "job." I told him I didn't want to go. He cracked me upside the head with the flashlight and told me to go get my ass in the truck. I told him no, then fell on the floor and just sat there bawling and rubbing the lump on my head. He wasn't playing that shit at all. He threw the flashlight at me, hitting me in the head again, grabbed a butcher knife in one hand and my hair in the other, then put the knife up against my forehead and started screaming that he was going to scalp me for telling him no. I was blubbering and begging, screaming, "No, Pappy! Please! I'm sorry!" He pressed the cold blade of the knife harder against my scalp, then dragged me over to the oven by my hair. Then he opened the oven door and stuffed me inside, slamming the door closed on my flailing hands. Then he turned on the gas. He's screaming and cussing me the whole time but I can't make out a word he's saying because I'm so terrified that he's going to cook me alive. Let me tell you this: When a person reaches a certain level of fear, nothing else in the world matters, and I mean *nothing*. You'll do anything to make what's happening to you go away. You'd butcher your own mama if that's what it took. I could barely breathe because the gas had filled the oven almost instantly. I started puking and it didn't seem like I was going to be able to stop. Then my pappy was holding the oven door shut with his big steel-toed boot while he lit a rolled up magazine with his cigarette lighter. At that point, I pretty much just gave up. Instead of hoping to live, my thoughts turned to wondering what it was going to feel like when my pappy lit the oven with that flaming magazine. I figured it was going to hurt pretty bad before I finally died.

When Pappy opened the door wide enough to stick his torch in, I used every bit of strength in my little nine-year-old body in one last act of desperation and burst through the door onto the kitchen floor. I screamed over and over again that I was sorry and that I would never tell him no again. He yanked me up off the cold linoleum by my hair and yelled at me to go to bed. I ran as fast as I could for my bedroom and jumped onto the mattress without even taking my shoes off and pulled the covers over my head.

Pappy didn't make me go with him on his ride that night. He left me alone in my room and gave me plenty of time to think about how tired I was of being scared of him. It was real late when he got home, and I pretended to be asleep when he came in to check on me. I could smell that he'd been drinking a lot. After he closed the door I waited in my bed for a long time before I got up and snuck into the hallway. I could see him passed out in the old raggedy recliner in the living room, could hear him snoring a little bit. The TV was on but it wasn't showing anything but one of those test patterns they put up after a station goes off the air in the early morning hours.

I crept into the kitchen and took a can of charcoal lighter fluid out of the cabinet and found a big box of matches in a drawer. I then went into the living room and stood in front of my pappy and popped the little red cap off the lighter fluid nozzle and squirted the liquid all up and down his body. When I sprayed some in his face, he stirred a bit and opened his eyes and just looked at me without saying a word. Right then I sort of froze and didn't think I could go through with it, but I started thinking about that oven with the choking gas, and in my mind I saw Pappy getting up from that chair and stuffing me back in there and cooking me alive, and then sitting down at the kitchen table and eating me like a Thanksgiving turkey—bones and all.

I struck a match and tossed it on his lap.

At first, he only shivered, as if he'd caught a chill, but after a couple of seconds he leaped up out of the chair and started slapping himself and let loose a high-pitched scream. He didn't sound like a man anymore, but like an excited woman, or maybe some kind of animal caught in a trap. He tripped over the coffee table and fell and started rolling on the floor, and then he

184

stopped and reached a hand out to me and screamed, "Help me, son," but I didn't think there was a whole lot I could do for him, even if I had wanted to, so I only stood there and watched him burn up on the dirty carpet. When the fire started to go out, I squirted more lighter fluid on it, and before long Pappy stopped screaming. Then he stopped moving, and I was pretty sure he was dead.

I was sitting on the hood of my pappy's car when the fire department showed up. The house was blazing pretty good by then. The firemen asked me what happened. I said, "My pappy burnt up in the living room." They asked me how he burnt up. I said I didn't know, but I don't think they believed me because I still had the matches and lighter fluid in my hands.

All these years later, Pappy still visits me here in the hospital every so often, but he doesn't look the same every time he comes. Sometimes he looks like how I most remember him, with his thinning hair and scruffy face and unwavering eyes that always made him appear so focused and determined. Sometimes he is charred black from head to toe, and his skin falls away in ashy flakes that fragment on the glossy floor tiles. Other times he is only a shadow on the wall. Occasionally, I can hear the footfalls of his big old steel-toed boots, and once in a while he wakes me in my bed late at night and says, "Put your shoes on, boy! We're goin' for a little ride!"

William Cook

'Til Death Do Us Part

Hugo sat watching the late night re-runs. His eyes were glazed and the stark light from the television made his flesh look anemic as he slumped in the lounge-chair. He looked at the clock on the wall and rubbed his tired eyes; 2.30 am. Hugo stifled a yawn and looked at his wife propped up with cushions in the centre of the couch. Her eyes rolled in the back of her head and an audible snore came from her inflamed nostrils perched above the duct-tape that covered her mouth.

Hugo looked back at the 20/20 program with renewed interest as a story came on about a local surgeon who successfully separated conjoined twins. The gory footage of the operation showed the surgeon meticulously separating the cranial flesh, bone and then the blood vessels and other viscera surrounding the two exposed brains. Mary-Beth murmured as Hugo turned the volume up. He glanced back over at her and noticed the blood had coagulated at the end of her bloody limbs where he had crudely cauterised the wounds.

The story continued as the journalist interviewed the surgeon in his opulent downtown office after the operation. Hugo was sure he had seen the surgeon before somewhere. He realized that the medical insurance company he had worked with for the last two decades probably had the good doctor on their books. Hell, he'd probably even sold the surgeon some expensive public liability insurance. That must be it, Hugo concluded, and looked back at Mary-Beth again. He had tried to dress her in her own clothes but had settled for an old bathrobe that kept her warm enough. He had cut the sleeves off to stop the blood soaking into the material where her arms had once joined her shoulders. He envied the skill of the surgeon but was happy he had effectively removed Mary-Beth's limbs without losing her during the operation.

***

Hugo had been spending a lot of time recently in the large basement of their ample house. He had taken annual leave and used the three-month vacation to set a few things straight in his otherwise mediocre existence. He had been awake four nights straight and was finally ready for sleep now that the operation had succeeded and he knew he would never lose Mary-Beth again.

He stood and stretched his tired body, making his way to the bathroom to piss and brush his teeth. He looked in the mirror and saw a stranger looking back at him: short but messy black hair, a white pasty complexion, and black rings circling his staring eyes beneath expensive glasses. He looked gaunt and far from the tanned, healthy young executive, he'd been a month ago. He took the spectacles and placed them on the edge of the sink as he brushed his teeth.

Hugo, now dressed for bed, went back to the lounge to kiss Mary-Beth good night. He didn't notice the petrified look of fear in her eyes or the shivering of her body as it passed through the final stages of shock. He kissed her gently on her clammy brow and whispered, "Love you Mary-Beth, beautiful wife. I love you forever." With that he turned and made his way down the hall to the bedroom, failing to notice that his once beautiful wife had toppled sideways, before landing on the plush rug in front of the couch, head first.

**

Hugo stayed awake for a while, waiting for sleep to take him away to a dark place. He thought about Mary-Beth and couldn't help feeling a deep anger and resentment at the way she deceived him. He had found out that she was planning to leave him through a mutual friend that worked at the office. A night out with the guys from work led to drunken conversations and then one of them told him directly that Mary-Beth was "fucking one of the other reps from the competing Medical Insurance Group across town." He dismissed it as rumor at first. After all, they had only been married six months and that kind of thing only happened to other people after years of marriage. However, he had been wrong. As soon as he could, he checked her phone while she was out and found the revelatory text messages from STEVE.

He confronted Mary-Beth and she bluntly told him that she wanted to move out of their new house and that she was going to seek an annulment, failing that, a divorce. He hadn't handled the news well, maniacally reciting their wedding vows as she hurriedly packed her bags. She ignored him as he continued to plead with her, asking her "why?" The final straw had been when she had dragged her suitcase down the steps to the front door, turned and told him that she had never loved him. That she had been banging STEVE since their engagement party and that STEVE was twice the man Hugo would ever be.

Mary-Beth was his wife, no one else's and he would be damned if he was going to let her get away from him so easily. Hugo decided that she would not leave him, ever.

***

Sleep hit Hugo hard. The blackness came but with it marched the nightmares. He dreamed of Mary-Beth. Flashes of her beautiful smile, slow motion visions of her curvaceous body twisting seductively, and then torrents of blood flooded his thoughts. He saw Mary-Beth bound to the workbench in the basement, the fluorescent light above illuminating her naked body, bound with ratchet tie-downs. He could see the rise and fall of her breast slow, with the effect of the strong sedative he had given her. Hugo started to sweat profusely in his sleep as the dream replayed what he did next to Mary-Beth. He remembered the intoxicated numbness he felt as he fired the Black 'n' Decker electric handsaw to life. He held the vibrating saw with one hand and took a giant swig of the expensive cognac he held in the other. He remembered putting the bottle down slowly as if trying to delay what would come next and then, it was as if he fell into a dream, a very bad dream, as he began to remove Mary-Beth's thin limbs one by one. Dark blood gushed from the fresh wounds, covering Hugo and the workshop, in a visceral spray of warm fluid and flesh.

He briefly worried about electrocution but recalled plugging the saw into a transformer before he began. He also recalled the tension in Mary-Beth's body as the angry saw bit into her soft flesh. He watched her smooth skin turn from mocha to chalk as her body slipped into shock. As he put the saw down, Hugo felt the first wave of nausea hit him and he threw up violently on the floor as he picked up the glowing iron resting on the shelf above the workbench. He forced himself to push it hard on the bloodied stump of her shoulder, where once her arm had been. He threw-up again as her flesh sizzled and popped as the crude but effective method cauterised Mary-Beth's horrible wounds. One by one, he completed the process and with a final application of antiseptic cream and bandages, Hugo finished the task and woke from his nightmare.

He sat up in bed trembling as he tried to convince himself the whole thing had been an elaborate nightmare. No matter how hard he tried to convince himself, he knew it wasn't a bad dream. He got out of bed and made his way into the lounge, finding Mary-Beth face down in the shag-pile rug. He quickly, but gently, picked her up and took her back to the bedroom, laying her carefully on her side of the bed, before climbing in behind her and falling into a deep sleep. This time, he dreamed a different dream than before.

***

Days passed and Hugo knew he had to do something. Mary-Beth was no longer drinking the pureed food that he had been giving her through a tube. She felt cold and he began to panic. "I won't lose you again my love," he repeated to her as he lay by her side on the bed and stroked her delicate features. "I won't ever lose you again."

The seed of an idea began to germinate in his mind as he paced the basement that night. The basement was as clean as the day they moved in. He had spent the better part of a week cleaning it from top to bottom. A ten-litre pail of disinfectant and another of bleach were used to mop down every surface. He had carefully wrapped Mary-Beth's limbs in newspaper before binding them with masking tape. The next day he spent the morning sweeping fall leaves into a pile in the middle of the backyard.

As soon as night fell, he poured an accelerant on the leaves and stoked the pile with various pieces of timber and flammable rubbish he had found around the house. He placed the wrapped limbs carefully in the centre of the pyre and struck a match. The flames rose high into the air and he was sure he could hear Mary-Beth's screams as the fire crackled and burned ferociously.

Hugo headed back inside and took Mary-Beth down from her perch in front of the window overlooking the back lawn. A faint smell emanated from her and he realized she had relieved herself. He cleaned her up in the bathtub, careful not to let her slip under the murky water. He towelled her dry and slipped the wedding ring on a gold chain over her bowed head, he had made sure he salvaged it from her hand before he got rid of her useless limbs in the fire. He sprayed her with some deodorant, failing to suppress his disgust as he noticed she was still leaking from various wounds and her skin had the color and sheen of an avocado. He wrapped her in a clean towel, knowing what he had to do now.

Hugo put her back to bed and went downstairs to the garage. He backed the shiny-black BMW out of the garage and headed downtown. It had been easy enough to find out the surgeon's work address, all Hugo had to do was have a quick look online and he had all the contact details he needed to track him down. He spent the following week driving back and forth, spending hours monitoring the surgeon's movements outside the plush downtown office where he worked while not in surgery.

***

Philip Binder Snr, MD was on the homestretch of a successful career in Paediatric neurosurgery and was looking forward to a very comfortable retirement. The last successful operation he'd performed on the Chinese conjoined twins had been the crowning glory of a forty-year run as the principal Neuro-Surgeon at the Portvale Municipal Hospital. He had won various accolades and awards for his pioneering work in the field and was considered by many to be the best.

Hugo had done his research, spending days in the library reading the various publications written by and concerning the surgeon. Hundreds of different medical news archives provided the background of the man via Google and the Internet. The most important part of Hugo's research was the 20/20 story that he'd recorded, when it replayed a few days after the initial broadcast. He'd sit there at night trying to battle his insomnia by watching the feature story repeatedly. Hugo knew exactly what he needed to do so nobody would ever take Mary-Beth away from him again and the good doctor would be the one to help him achieve his goal.

Hugo tried not to notice the slightly rancid perfume as he wrapped Mary-Beth in a blanket and placed her in the boot of the BMW. He swallowed and took a breath of the afternoon air as he opened the garage doors and let sunlight flood in. He tried not to think too much about the damp dark stain on his shirtsleeve, where he had cradled Mary-Beth before wrapping her, as he gingerly brushed some residual flesh from his arm. He went to the rear of the garage and took down the Mossberg shotgun from the gun rack mounted above the workbench. It had been a wedding gift from Mary-Beth's father along with big plans to go hunting in the fall. Hugo had never used it before and lamented the fact that he would never be going hunting with his father-in-law now. He packed the two boxes of shells that came with the gift into an overnight bag and wrapped another blanket around the Shotgun, before placing them both in the boot next to Mary-Beth. "I love you my darling," Hugo said, as he gently closed the boot.

***

Hugo waited in the car with the window down as the end of the day approached. The heat from the afternoon sun made the interior of the car rank with the smell of purification but Hugo remained focussed on the mission ahead. He watched the surgeon's staff leave the small but exclusive office on the town-belt, only a short walk away from the Municipal Hospital. As the last staff member left, Hugo backed the car up to the side exit of the office block and turned the engine off.

He cradled Mary-Beth in one arm and with the other, levelled the shotgun at the doorway as Binder opened the door to leave work. The look of shock on the surgeon's face propelled Hugo forward, bundling the older man back into his office and locking the door behind him. Hugo placed Mary-Beth upright in a chair in the Surgeon's waiting room and the blanket fell away, taking with it most of the decomposed flesh from her face. "I want you to meet Mary-Beth, doc," said Hugo with a too-large smile.

***

Hugo lay naked on the floor of the office and motioned with the shotgun for the surgeon to approach with his surgical tool kit.

191

Mary-Beth lay beside Hugo naked also. Binder Snr's hands trembled as he removed various instruments: scalpel, sutures, forceps, and needles, laying them on a cloth next to Mary-Beth's decomposing corpse. Hugo smiled up from the floor where he lay. "You know what to do Doctor – local anaesthetic first, right?" The surgeon shook his head, still reeling in shock at what was happening in his office. He considered running but looked in Hugo's crazed eyes and knew the man was completely insane. He knew if he did not do exactly what the thin man said, he would be very dead.

His fingers shook with fear as the muzzle of the shotgun jabbed his mid-section, encouraging him to administer the anaesthetic with a syringe into various junctures along Hugo's right side, from the ribs down to the hip.

"Where you goin' doc?" slurred Hugo, as Binder Snr. rose to his feet slowly.

"I need to get some antiseptic wipes," said the surgeon as he made his way to his desk and removed the sterile wipes from a glass wall cabinet behind his leather chair. He looked over his shoulder briefly and saw Hugo grinning at him from the office floor, holding the shotgun at arm's length, pointing directly at the surgeon's head. As he turned back to the bizarre prospect in front of him, the surgeon pressed the small record button on the remote sitting on the edge of his desk. He knew the office security camera would be whirring into life and would at least capture what was happening, even though he felt that he might not get to see the footage or enjoy his coming retirement.

***

The Senior Investigating Officer leaned over and puked into the waste-paper bin next to his desk. The other officers looked away in disgust as the security camera footage replayed the grim surgery. "I just kept doing what he told me to do," explained the surgeon, choking back tears. The monitor buzzed with the low-res footage as the bizarre scene showed the surgeon, hunched over the bodies of Hugo and Mary-Beth.

The sound was barely audible apart from an occasional scream from Hugo, as the Surgeon cut and clamped, sutured and stitched. The officers watched as the surgeon rose quickly from the floor, scrabbling out of camera range to reveal the torso of

192

Mary-Beth joined just above Hugo's hip with a blackened wound laced with tight stitches. Hugo's head rolled back and forth and a blood curdling scream emanated from the computer monitor, flashes of white exploded from the barrel of the shotgun as he fired wildly around the small office, writhing on the floor. The officers continued to watch the footage in silence, as Hugo appeared to lose consciousness. Nothing stirred onscreen and then the sweat-soaked back of the surgeon appeared and bent down over Hugo and Mary-Beth's prone forms.

"I'm administering adrenaline and more painkillers at this point," explained Binder Snr MD, wiping sweat from his forehead with a bloodied handkerchief.

The footage kept playing, the surgeon clearly recoiling from the now-conscious Hugo who had the shotgun levelled at the surgeon's bald head.

"I should've taken that damn rifle off him when I had the chance," sobbed the surgeon. One of the officers patted him on the shoulder and reassured him that he 'did all he could've done.' Binder Snr MD looked far from reassured, as the camera footage continued.

Hugo tried to get to his feet and fell sideways with the dead weight of Mary-Beth's attached torso. His face opened with obvious pain a high-pitched scream exploded from the monitor speakers. He dropped the shotgun on the floor, a flash erupting from the muzzle as it discharged involuntarily. The surgeon quickly darted out of camera range once again.

"This time I ran. I ran out of there as fast as I could and called you guys straight away."

"You did the right thing sir," said the grim-faced Senior Investigating Officer.

The younger officers watched open-mouthed as the monitor now showed Hugo holding himself up on the edge of the surgeon's desk, his arm wrapped around Mary-Beth's naked torso, blood leaking profusely down his thigh from the now-gaping wound that had split open. Hugo seemed to be talking to his grim appendage, kissing the decomposed face, wiping the rancid flesh from its lips. He was also visibly paler, as he started to slip in the dark pool of blood at his feet.

He let go of Mary-Beth to steady himself and the wound visibly split, her limp body tearing away in a spray of blood as the stitches burst where they joined the bodies. As Hugo tried to regain his footing, Mary-Beth's body seemed to twitch and then the limb-less corpse reared up. Hugo's face twisted with terror as he tried to recoil from the swinging corpse attached to his thin frame. Mary-Beth appeared to launch herself at Hugo, the skeletal face animated visibly in rage, black rotting hole of a mouth stretched wide, teeth snapping at his neck.

Hugo collapsed on the floor in the middle of the black pool of blood, the thrashing corpse on top of him, their separate bodies barely discernible now, both covered in slick gore.

***

Two of the younger officers tried to choke back vomit as they continued to stare numbly at the screen. An arm flailed underneath the heaving mass of flesh and blood, then a thin shiny sliver of steel appeared from under the desk, clasped in Hugo's clenched fist. The surgeon's scalpel slashed into the back of his wife's corpse, hacking and cutting at the mutilated wound that half-joined the two together. As the bodies separated with each slicing cut and Hugo pushed the dismembered corpse away from his own eviscerated body, the camera faltered and started to judder as the recording ended.

"What the fuck just happened?" asked the Senior Officer, a shocked look on his face that offered no hope of any understanding. The surgeon sat in his chair, his sweaty bald head clasped between his bloodied hands. Some of the other officers excused themselves and left the office, while the remaining few shuffled uncomfortably and looked at each other for an answer. The coroner, who had been watching proceedings impassively from the doorway, took two steps forwards and dropped the autopsy report on the Senior Officer's cluttered desk.

"Two deaths, one by homicide, one by misadventure. The female's time of death, at least one to two weeks before the male's. Male neck wounds unexplained, although clearly bite marks correspond with the female dental records and the footage you have just witnessed."

"How the hell am I gonna write this one up?" asked the Senior Officer to no-one in particular, shaking his head, hypnotised by the folder on the desk in front of him. He picked up the coroner's report and looked at the folder blankly. He hated cases like this that fell somewhere in between a good old fashioned 'jealous-husband murders wife' and a 'sociopathic stalker-ex who can't let go.' He set the folder back on his desk amidst the surrounding clutter of forms, case files and reference books, then placed his hand on top of it as if he was about to swear on the good book. The coroner leaned across the desk, picking up one of the rubber stamps heaped in a basket next to the 'in-and-out' trays overflowing with paper. He rolled the stamp in the red inkpad next to the phone and bought the stamp down hard on the cover of the report.

'CASE CLOSED,' declared the imprint, now emblazoned diagonally across the cardboard folder. The Officer picked up the folder, waving his remaining colleagues from the room before heading to the filing cabinet. He opened the bottom drawer and filed the report at the back of the other copious files marked "Case Closed." Slowly shaking his head, he repeated, "Case closed," as he took the half empty bottle of scotch from another drawer, unscrewed the cap and drank half of its contents in a single mouthful, not giving a damn if anyone saw him do so.

Chantal Noordeloos

Soulman

Underneath the bridge, on a crisp and cold night at Junction river, sat three figures clad in the shadows of darkness. One, a fat man wearing multiple layers of clothing, tried to start a fire in a self-made fire pit. He was grunting slightly, his breath creating little clouds that looked like wisps of smoke.

These were the three men I was looking for. This was the location where I needed to be for this particular night. The place where men told themselves they were monsters. Blood would flow here tonight, and it was my duty to bear witness.

With silent grace, slow but deliberate, I made my way down to the gloomy area they called home. I peered at them with my good eye, the other hidden under a patch, and only when I neared their seating area, did they take notice of my presence.

"Well, hello stranger." The man who spoke to me was Caucasian, in his late thirties. He wasn't handsome, with his coarse skin and pug nose, but his friendly face and genuine smile almost fooled you into thinking he was, indeed, a friendly man. "Have you come to warm yourself by our fire on this chilly October night?"

"Shit, what fire?" said a second man, dragging out the 'i' in 'shit'. He glanced at the big man who was trying to light the wood in the fire pit. "That big motherfucker couldn't light a fire if he was standing in hell itself." The second man had a narrow face. His skin was black, but it was patchy and even looked white at some parts, as if someone had randomly taken off his pigment with paint scraper. His grin consisted of a few remaining teeth that were brown from rot. Heroin addict. It was easy to spot them. The drugs ate away at their soul as well as their bodies.

"Now, now, master Weasel, let's not doubt the capabilities of our giant friend here," the first speaker scolded with the flourish of a poet. There was something dark in his eyes, something malicious, but he hid it well. "There is a special challenge in lighting the wood on a night like this." From the way the man dressed and the eloquence of his words, it was obvious he was an educated man, one not born to the streets.

196

"Wood's too wet," the third man interjected. From up close I could see he was a giant of a man. What I had mistaken for fat was muscle, though he did have a very fat face. His large chin wobbled on his neck like a canvas bag of lard.

All three men dressed in multiple layers of clothing to keep the cold wind at bay. In the stinging breeze, I could smell it, that sour scent of stale body odor mixed with garbage and smoke from previous fires, the scent of the street folk, the beggars, and the forgotten men.

The large man bent down and held his lighter to the wood. I let out a soft breath, so gentle that no one saw, and the fire flared. A victorious yelp escaped the large man's lips and echoed off the stones of the bridge's foundation.

"I did it," he said, his voice low and deep but with a childish tone. I could see the surprise on his face.

"Well done," said the first speaker, making a grand gesture with his arms as if he were a thespian. "Come and join our fire, stranger," he said to me. "And come and sit, Big Dave, we shall share our spoils by the fire." His hand, clad in a fingerless glove, reached underneath the layers of his clothing and he produced a flask, a memento from his old life. "To keep out the cold," he explained as he lifted the flask to his lips. "Salute."

"Save me some," the man that had been called Weasel said hungrily, his dark eyes eyeing the little flask. "I've been thirsty all day."

"Guests first," said the man with the flask and he handed it to me. "What is your name friend?" I blinked and took the flask from his fingers.

"They call me the Soulman," I answered and took a little swig. The bottle contained whiskey. It burned in my mouth and I hated the taste, but I did not wish to be rude.

"Shit," the little black man spoke again. "Soulman? Ain't nobody ever tell you, you is white, motherfucker?" He laughed, revealing the stumps of remaining teeth. My face was blank and I handed the flask to the big man, who sat next to me.

"Ignore my rude companion," the first man said. "Like you, we have adopted names for our street personas." He pointed at the skinny black man. "That delightful fellow over there is called Weasel. I think the name derives from a combination of his memorable looks and his interesting personality." The man winked at me and the black man spat on the floor. He reached his hand out as the large man handed him the flask.

"Shit," he said again, in the same tone he had said it before.

"That gentleman next to you is Big Dave," the man continued. "I am called Mister Candy." He stuck out his hand and I shook it. The man had a firm grip.

"They calls him that because he likes the children," Weasel explained. He put the flask to his chapped lips and took a swig. Mister Candy smiled a humble smile.

"I don't actually lure them with sweets," he said. "Children are far too clever for such tricks these days. Men like me need to be more creative." The corners of his mouth were twisted in a friendly smile, but the eyes were watching me like a hawk, trying to determine my reaction to his words. I did not give him the satisfaction of reading me and kept my face blank. This seemed to intrigue him.

"Down here we are monsters," he said with a joyful sparkle in his eye, his voice raised an octave higher. "The monsters that gather in the night. Only the darkness tolerates our behavior."

"Hey, motherfucker, who are you calling a monster?" Weasel protested. "I ain't no monster." He spat on the ground and lifted his woolen hat to scratch his mop of tangled black hair.

"Aren't you?" Mister Candy asked bemused. "You are *not* a monster?" Weasel shook his head, but there was doubt in his eyes. Mister Candy placed the tips of his bare fingers on his lips. "Interesting."

"I'm not saying I'm some sort of a fucking white hat or anything," Weasel muttered, "but I ain't no goddamned monster either, not like you and Big Dave." He shifted uncomfortably on the bucket he used as a seat. The fire was burning brightly, casting shadows on all our faces. The wind was cold, and cut through my clothing; it made my skin tingle.

There was a silence, as Mister Candy seemed to contemplate Weasels words. "Weasel is right about one thing," he said after a while. "Big Dave and I are indeed monsters. We are barely human by the standards of the average man. As most homeless do, we live in a different world with different rules." He waved his hand at the small area under the bridge where we sat. There were some old sleeping bags, blankets and cardboard boxes scattered at the base of the bridge, away from the cold wind. It was a sorry place to live.

198

A loud caw stirred the three men and they looked at me in awe as a large raven swooped down and perched on my shoulder.

"Is that your bird?" Big Dave asked, his large chin wobbling as he spoke. I nodded and offered the raven a small morsel that I kept in my pocket. The bird took it carefully. "Did it take your eye?" he asked innocently, pointing at the eye patch I wore over my left eye. I shook my head and that seemed to comfort him.

"That is a mighty fine bird," Mister Candy said. "Big Dave?" The big man sat up straighter when he heard his name being called. "Why don't you sing your song for the Raven?" The large man nodded, running his big meaty hands over his face and he sighed before he began his tale.

"I killed my wife," Big Dave said without any emotion showing on his round face. His bottom chin rested comfortably against his neck. On his head he wore a hunter's cap. The side flaps hung loosely over his ears. "She was fucking other men. A *lot* of other men, so I killed her." He ran his big hand under his nose and sniffed, though not from sadness. "I killed the men too." The eyes, that were set deeply in the thick flesh of his face, were staring off in the distance, reminiscing. A hint of a smile ran over his face as he thought back to the murders and he nodded ever so slightly. Then he turned to me, his face grave once again. "I liked killing them," he repeated. "Didn't want to get caught though, so now I'm here." His eyes met my single one and I nodded. I understood the pleasure of taking a human life.

"We lived in this trailer, right?" Big Dave said, his eyes watery with the memory. "Then one day someone tells me: 'Hey Dave, you know that your wife is fucking Charlie Altman, don'tcha?' And I says 'No'. He laughs at me and he tells me 'everybody knows that'." Something hard appeared in his face, something that showed the lack of self-restraint this man had, the anger like hot lava ready to spill out and burn the world around him.

"Wasn't just Charlie Altman either, was a whole bunch of fellas." He relived the moment back in that trailer; I could see it in his face. He was there and he felt it again, the faded carpet under his boots, smelling that smell of home. There was a frown on his forehead but a hint of a smile played on his lips.

"So I get home early and I see the dishes ain't been done. Again. Bitch never did the dishes. But I always figured it was because she was watching Oprah, not because she was fucking the county." He laughed a little, but without mirth.

199

"I go into the bedroom, and there she is, sitting on her hands and knees and Charlie Altman is sticking his filthy cock in her. His pants around his ankles and the fucker still had his shoes on." There was that hatred again, he was perfectly in the moment. "So I grab him, by the ankles and pull him off the bed." Big Dave made a pulling motion as if he were really dragging Altman from his bed, his eyes round and wild, filled with murder. "There is this real nice cracking sound when his face hits the bed board. I hear Charlene screaming but it don't register. There is blood and I can smell it. It drives me insane and I go all bloodthirsty, like a shark you know?" His eyes meet mine. He wants me to understand, to share that feeling with him. I give him a simple nod in response.

"I want to hurt this guy, I want him to bleed. I want him to die. I am the master of his life and I can take it away." The eyes roll back into the big man's head. He is submerged in the memory and I egg him on, draw him out. He wants to tell his story, he has to.

"So his face is on the carpet. We had this ugly ass orange carpet that Charlene picked out, because she said it would brighten the place up. Charlie is bleeding on the carpet and I have these huge steel tipped boots on. I lift my leg and I start kicking his face until there is nothing but blood and pulp left. His skin bursts open, revealing the insides, all wet and glistening. Bits of his skull are everywhere. It was fucking beautiful." Big Dave licked his lips, his hand was shaking a little as he touched the hat on his head gently, almost in reverence.

"Charlene won't stop screaming, so I go over to her and I wrap my hands around her throat. I have big hands." He held up his hands so I could see the size of them. They are indeed impressive. "Her neck is really small and it's so easy to just... squeeze. She's making these weird noises and her face is some weird ass purple. Then I saw the light dimming in her eyes, I swear to god I saw her life leaving her body. Best thing I ever seen." His hands move to his cheeks and I can see he is crying.

"Charlie and Charlene, they were my first. Isn't it a hoot? Charlie and Charlie. I did the other fellas too, four of 'em. I don't know if there were more. I wish there were. I would kill them too."

He stares into the fire, tears in his eyes, the smile still on his mouth. Weasel hands him the flask and he takes a small sip.

"Beautiful," Big Dave whispers.

"And that is the story of our gigantic friend," says Mister Candy.

"What is your story?" I ask.

"Do you want to hear my song for your raven?" He stared at the bird on my shoulder. "I would not have given you the name Soulman," he said, "Not with the one eye and the raven on your shoulder. I would have named you 'Odin', after the Norse God. Odin one eye."

"I have been called that," I admit. "In the past. But I am not He, I am the Soulman. Sing your song to my raven."

He nodded, eager to tell his tale. "I always liked the little ones," he said, his smile all honey and sugar. "From a young age I used my baby sister for my pleasure." There was a small gust of wind and he wrapped the coat he wore tighter around his body. "I loved them so much I could not bear them to live." He smiled; it was almost a bashful smile.

"I got away with it for a long time. Mainly because I found children other cities. I never *shat* where I ate." His gaze turned up at the sky, seeing something in the dark skies that could only stem from his memories. He was different from Big Dave, more deliberate, more controlled.

"People started to suspect me," he said. There was something mournful about the way he spoke. "My wife was the first to feel something wrong. We wanted to have kids. I needed to have kids." His sharp eyes met mine, wondering if I understood what he was saying.

"Her slowly aging flesh started to disgust me," he continued without shame. "Her skin was so coarse, and her breasts were too big, her cunt too hairy. She would shave for me, because she knew I liked it, but it wasn't the same." He shook his head and inhaled deeply, his chest puffing out, and then he let out a long sigh.

"I found her revolting and all I wanted was a little boy or girl to play with, but she couldn't give it to me." There was bitterness in his tone. He blamed his wife. "Then she saw me talking to a young boy at the carnival, about a year and a half ago. She said I was sick, she said she could see it in the way I looked at the boy. I pleaded with her, denied everything she said, but it was no use. She had seen the man behind the mask."

He sighed and ran his hands over his woolly hat.

"What did you do?" Weasel asked with a wide-eyed fascination. "Did you kill her?"

"No," Mister Candy answered. "I did not. I only kill children and only because I want to kill children." He pursed his lips together and rubbed the palms of his hands against his dirty jeans.

"She told me to get out and I got out. I didn't bother with building up a new life. After the talk with my wife I accepted that I was a monster." He looked at me again, his eyes trying to convince me of his words. "Either I stopped what I was doing with the children, or I just removed myself from this world. I didn't want to stop." He lifted his hands up in the air, palms up to the sky. "Here I am."

"A monster?" I asked.

"Yes." There was a hungry smile on his face. "I am what they dream of at night, the little ones. I am the monster that sleeps under their bed and in their wardrobe. I am the big bad wolf, Mister Candy." His hand reached for his pants and he gently rubbed his penis from the outside of the cloth. "I take them from their safe lives and I play with them until they break." There was a look of pleasure on his face. His song was finished. There was certain simplicity to his cunning. The murders he committed were to quench his lust. My gaze moved to the third man.

"What about you?" I asked Weasel.

He snorted. "I ain't no motherfucking monster," he said. "Not like those two, I don't kill for fun and I don't rape little kids, neither." Disgusted he spat on the ground. "I am just a simple junkie."

"You are bereft of a soul by the very drugs that course through your veins," Mister Candy mused.

"Whatever, mother fucker," the little man looked at him wide eyed and spat on the ground. "I ain't no fucking baby killer." Mister Candy shook his head, but looked bemused.

"You are a shell of a human," he said, "A different kind of monster, but still a monster." His words offended Weasel and the skinny man shifted on his bucket in agitation.

"Stop calling me a monster," he said, his voice high pitched and bursting with nerves.

"It is only a matter of time before you become like us, Weasel," Mister Candy said, teasing. "Only a time before you take that very long butcher's knife of yours, the one you use to rob innocent people for cold hard cash to buy warm soothing heroine, and you run into the wrong victim. Then you will have to choose, the drugs, or a human life." His eyes glinted in the firelight and he smiled a hungry smile at the dark skinned man. Weasel was clearly uncomfortable.

"And soon you would realize it would be so much easier to kill your victims for their money," Mister Candy continued, relentless. "And it would become part of your little ritual. Your monstrous little ritual."

"Fuck you," Weasel spat, "Says you, motherfucker."

"You would kill for your drugs, would you not?" There was a moment of silence.

"That's different," Weasel muttered, feeling reluctant to admit that Mister Candy was right.

"Why is that different?"

"I would not get any pleasure out it?" Weasel wasn't sure of what he said, doubt reared its head, and I could see it in the way he looked from Mister Candy to me, his eyes pleading. Mister Candy seemed intrigued by his words and leaned forward.

"Then who is the bigger monster?" he said in a soft voice. "He who kills out of love of killing, out of the love for his victim... or he who kills to get his next fix?" His mouth curled into a wicked smile, which turned up his pug nose even more. There was nothing friendly about his face now, and Weasel stared at him, his mouth opening and closing until he finally whispered: "I would still say, *you*, white boy."

Mister Candy ignored him and turned to me.

"And you?" he asked, his face sly as a fox. "What makes you a monster?"

"Why do you think I am a monster?" I asked.

"Because you are here," he said, his hands waving at the area around the bridge. "In the darkness. In our home." He looked around the small area again, his face dramatic. "Because you carry that raven on your shoulder. Because you look like a monster with your one eye, and . . ." his voice lowered now and there was a cunning smile on his face, one that indicated that he believed he had won some sort of challenge. ". . . because you just listened to our stories without blinking that eye." He sat back, satisfied with his own words.

"You are right, I am a monster," I admitted. "But I don't think you are." All three faces turned to me in wonder.

"You don't?" Mister Candy asked.

"No," I said, "I think you are all very human. Just because you left your safe little lives, or never had them, doesn't mean you aren't human. All humans juggle with the darkness, you just gave into it." The smile on Mister Candy's face faded.

"Some of you gave in a little more than others," I added, nodding towards Weasel.

"And what makes you think you are a monster?" he asked.

I pulled another morsel from my pocket and fed it to my raven.

"Why are you called the Soulman?"

"Because that is who I am," I said. "I guide the souls of humanity. When a baby is born, I kiss it on the forehead and give it its soul. When a human dies, I take their souls and when a human embraces darkness, I take part of their soul." There was a silence and I could hear the wind rush through the gaps of the bridge and the soft rustle of the reeds.

"Is that why you are here?" Mister Candy asked. "To take a piece of our soul?"

I shook my head. "I took a piece of your soul a long time ago Alfred Woodman," I answered softly. "Tonight I am here for another purpose." The man blinked, recognizing the name he was born with.

"Why are you here?" he asked. His voice was suddenly small. He was afraid.

"I am here because of him," I nodded towards the large man who sat staring at the fire. The two other men stared at him, as if they wanted to see something that I was seeing. But there was nothing there, except Big Dave, who stared into the fire with a stern face.

"I would have suspected you obtained some of his soul, when he first began killing," Mister Candy said, nonplussed. "Why are you here now?" My eyes were fixed on Dave, but he sat very still, glaring into the fire. He knew why I was here, only he knew, and he had not accepted my presence just quite yet.

"I am here because Dave is not quite done yet," I said. "He has yet to make his choices." The raven on my shoulder cawed, a sinister noise that sounded so much louder in the abandoned place. Somewhere in the distance, I could hear the soft rustling of traffic, but here in the dark there was no one but us monsters, and men pretending to be monsters.

"Why would you aid him in making a choice?" Mister Candy asked, his voice unsteady now. "What does that have to do with his soul?"

Weasel leaned in to our conversation. He looked perturbed. "What are you crazy honkies talking about?" he screeched, his voice high with a rising panic. There was something in the wind that whispered of darkness and despair, Mister Candy heard it too.

"You are not here for his soul are you?" he said, his voice barely audible over the soft howling of the wind. "You are here for ours." Our eyes locked together, my one eye and his two and he understood.

"Big Dave has yet to fulfill his task," he said, understanding and accepting. Weasel was about to ask him what he knew, but a brick that hit him on the side of his temple took the words from his lips. There was a crunching sound, the force causing the little man to fall off his bucket and he lay on the ground twitching and clutching his bleeding skull.

Mister Candy did not run, nor did he defend himself. He just stood, stretched his arms in front of him, palms up and looked at me with that sad accepting face of a man who knows he is about to die.

The brick hit him from behind and his knees buckled. I watched him sag to the ground and I saw the great hulking mass of Big Dave standing above him. The large man was crying again, but they were tears of joy. The brick landed on the back of Mister Candy's head again, and again. The grey wool glove was soaked in the crimson of blood, looking almost black on the material. Each blow caused a spray of blood to splatter on the assailants clothing and face and he struck the man with such ferocity that he was soon dripping with the thick red fluids.

From the corner of his eye, Dave spotted Weasel trying to crawl away on hands and knees, his left temple bleeding profusely. With strides worthy of a giant, he reached his other target and smashed the blood soaked brick onto the little man with great force. It took only two blows to kill him, but Dave kept beating him until there was nothing human left of his face. Then he stomped on the body.

When he observed the two pulverized remains of his victims, he looked up at me.

"This is what you wanted me to do?" he asked.

My face was blank, a mirror for him to look into.

"This is what I wanted to do," he said, nodding his head in understanding. The brick fell from his hand, making a small sound on the blood stained tiles. "I wasn't angry at them," he said. "Not like I was at the other men." The eyebrows on his face scrunched together like two thick furry caterpillars. "But my murdering people was never about anger, was it?" he said.

"In a way it is," I said. "But it isn't always justified anger that drives humanity to make certain choices."

"Mister Candy was a bad man," Big Dave said, looking down at his victims, trying to justify his actions. "He got what he deserved." There was hesitation in his face and he looked at the slight frame of Weasel. "Little Weasel wasn't so bad though. I shouldn't have killed him. He was just a little junkie. Didn't deserve to die."

"It is not about deserving, it is about choices," I answered him, shrugging my shoulder, which aggravated the raven and he cawed in protest.

"I am a bad man," he said softly, resting his chin on his neck. "But not a monster. You said we weren't monsters?" he asked me, almost begging. I looked him in the eye.

"Do you think you are a monster?"

He shook his head.

"I think he was a monster," he said, pointing at Mister Candy. "He did things to kids and then he killed them. I only killed grown men, men who sinned; men that fucked my wife, men that did drugs and killed little children." There was a whine to his voice, like that of a little child who was caught with his hand in the cookie jar.

"He wasn't a monster either," I said. "You can't kill monsters. He was just a man." Dave bit his lip and looked at the sky. He seemed hypnotized.

"He did bad things," he said, stubborn as an ox.

"It doesn't matter what a man does," I said. "Death comes for all men. Whether they live a good and clean life, or they sin, they all die. No matter how old they are."

"That is why you are here, right?" he asked.

"Yes." He looked up at the sky again, as if he were searching for something. Perhaps he was looking for something to forgive him for the blood he had on his hands.

"The blood is starting to cool," he said, "It was warm at first, but now it is starting to cool. It is making me cold."

"Blood will do that," I agreed. "When the blood cools, remorse sets in." Big Dave nodded. There were tears in his eyes again.

"They were my friends," he said. "They kept me safe. And I killed them." He wiped his large flat nose with the back of his hand, spreading the blood around and smearing it across his face. "Will it be like this from now on?" he asked, looking at me, his shoulders hunched.

"That is up to you," I said.

He nodded, but he did not look convinced. "Are you taking their souls to hell?" he asked softly.

"That's up to them."

He looked at me with those little empty eyes that were so childlike. I was not what he thought I was.

"I am not here to punish them," I said. "That is not my job. I merely guide the souls where they need to go."

There was a silence between us and then Dave nodded and turned around. He walked to the little area under the bridge. There he rummaged around and grabbed as many things as he could, sleeping bags, blankets, some food and clothing. He piled the treasures on his right shoulder and walked towards the foot of the bridge.

I watched him climb up and disappear from view. There would be a time I would meet Dave again, but it would be much later.

The raven on my shoulder cawed and swooped towards the bodies, to collect their souls. We would have to move fast because my presence was expected elsewhere.

A little girl was about to be born and she needed a soul.

Vincenzo Bilof

Friends with Benefits

The streets of my city are filled with the refuse of sorrowful men. The dark streets are a black wasteland—you won't find any cops crawling around my theater during the evening. Streetlights haven't worked in years. Here, the few homeless who linger in the shadows are the survivors and refugees of capitalist warfare.

With her arm wrapped in mine, Valerie said, "You weren't kidding when you said this place was desolate. It's so dangerous here . . . and beautiful. You'll protect me, won't you?" she giggled softly.

Valerie was proving to be everything she advertised. Our internet relationship had finally evolved into our first encounter. She loved films as much as I did, and I was looking forward to sharing my experience with her; I'd been waiting to see the movie for months after learning its premiere date.

"I will do as you wish," I answered her with a playful smile. "You won't be harmed as long as you're with me."

"It's so quiet," Valerie whispered. "Kind of sets the mood. You're so . . . *Adventurous.*"

None of my other friends had complimented me as much as Valerie had. While I'd never gone to a movie with a female companion before, I couldn't help but blush.

"I take a rear entrance," I explained. "The owners know me here. I hope you don't mind. Are you sure you want to do this?"

I hoped she would resist. I'd already done everything in my power to dissuade her. Whenever my newly acquired friends began to ask questions about my intentions for the evening, I discovered they were all unwilling to see the theater. I preferred it this way. After all, most of them did research before we would see the film. They ask, "Isn't that theater abandoned?" or, "I've never heard of that movie—who's the director?" They were all ignorant about the works of the visionary filmmaker Nick Craster, but I was always more than willing to educate them. Those brief moments of resistance often turned the evening into a game, which always made the experience more pleasant and exciting for me.

Craster's movies were glorious works of art. His movies were the only ones I ventured out of the house to watch. Valerie was well acquainted with his accomplishments; she was an impressive woman.

"A back entrance?" she drew me closer to her. "Now that really *is* exciting. Are we sneaking in?"

"In a way," I nodded. "We can always leave, if you wish. I know this might feel a little awkward for you. I would understand if you want to do something else. I brought you here because this place is special to me. Nobody knows about it, you see, and I've only shared this with a few people."

"I don't think you get it," she said. "I've been waiting for *Cannibal Octopus Three: The Revenge,* ever since the second one ended. You think this one will be as gory as the last one?"

"Well, it isn't the gore that marks the film as visionary or unique, but I suspect there will be plenty." She'd finally disappointed me. These movies were hardly about the amount of violence and gore; "grindhouse" films obeyed conventions and reveled in their depravity. While Valerie believed herself to be a student of the genre, she hardly understood the beauty behind the filmmaker's art. Still, I wanted to add her as a member of my beloved inner circle.

She seemed to sense her moment of failure. Why was she so interested in making me happy? I'd never met a woman who was so interested in my own passions. Mother always told me that women who feigned interest played a game. Valerie wanted something from me.

"I know the movie will be good," she insisted. "The premise is inspiring. I've often thought about writing my own scripts, usually after watching a damn good movie. Of course, I'm not any good."

"Film is an art," I added. "The greatest films allow us to peer inside our souls and consider the human experience. Both of us will share this feeling, tonight. You've trusted me, and you'll be well-rewarded."

"You're a tease," I could hear the smile sliding across her face in the dark.

My world of perpetual shadow and darkness mirrored those recessed hallways within the mind of a mysterious creator. The

209

men and women who engineer the creative process behind the greatest films are benevolent gods who've shared their worlds with us. Humanity can be warped and redefined. We can learn something about ourselves while considering truths we thought impossible. Our imaginations are modified, our souls tickled. Films are the oasis in the desert of human suffering and depravity.

Sheets of old, yellowed paper were stamped into the concrete at my feet or blowing past like windblown dust devils, although there wasn't any wind. A pile of rags seemed to belong to a bum lying against a graffiti-stained wall. I could smell old piss and sour vomit. The homeless suffered the malaise of loneliness and ineptitude. Cheap alcohol and the lingering nightmares begot by madness had built or destroyed this bastion of human suffering. This is where men go to die quietly when the shelters can no longer provide comfort, and the homeless community has cast a man out like a leper amongst the trash. This was the dumping ground for damnation's fools.

My theater is my own personal haunted house. I've brought many friends there, whether they trusted my judgment or not. It takes great effort to befriend another, and while I prefer to be alone, a man can become a howling savage without any companionship. Mother and I talk frequently, but there are things she can't understand or identify with. She doesn't share my love for film or art. Not like these others do.

I simply wish to share my own intellectual ruminations with those who might comprehend. There aren't many who can. I deign to teach others; people can understand so long as their ignorance is alleviated. There have been many worthy candidates, people who might be able to understand the art of film without my meddling, but I enjoy educating others.

Valerie said, "This is the perfect evening. I've never done anything like this. There are *so* many people who just don't understand movies. I can't tell you how many times I've tried to show others, or tell them. But they just don't *get it*. They look at me like I'm the one who's strange—you and I know better."

Her enthusiasm was starting to aggravate me. Why didn't she protest? There's nothing to be gained if I can't explain the nuances of the art to another person. I palmed the instrument within my pocket, and began to wonder if I might show it to

Valerie. All of my plans were being waylaid by her desire to participate.

I tried to think about the movie while I led her to the rear entrance. We stepped inside the cavernous theater, where some of my old friends awaited our arrival. They'd been expecting Valerie, and were excited to meet her, though I would wait to introduce her until after the movie. I'd already explained this to my new guest.

A large hole in the roof revealed the full moon's bulbous stare, as if it also wanted to watch the much-anticipated film. The weather-beaten seats had been gnawed on by rats that scurried into the webbed corners from whence malicious spiders watched with their multitudinous eyes. Valerie squeezed my hand tightly as we walked within view of my five friends, who were scattered throughout the theater, all of them strangers to one another, though they maintained a kinship with me. They wore upturned collars over their faces and hats to hide their eyes. Valerie smiled at them, but they didn't return her courteous gesture. She allowed me to lead her to a pair of seats near the back.

It was usually at this point that my evening companion would become indignant and attempt to flee. Valerie, however, was more than willing to sit down beside me in the gloom.

"This really adds to the effect," she noted. "There can't be a better way to watch a movie. It's like a drive-in, and I like the fact that it's independently owned. It hasn't been tainted by the carnival atmosphere you get at the other theaters."

I had to agree with her. She was clearly an expert in such matters. I thought about the razor in my pocket, and wondered when she might finally start to resist. Where was my opportunity? My other friends had been very afraid, at first, until I educated them. Now, they're all more than willing to share my love for film.

With the blank screen staring back at us, I began to hear the sound I dreaded more than anything in the world, the noise that often tormented me when I began to struggle against my need for friendship. Mother always insisted I should meet new friends, but she didn't understand how hard it really was to find someone whose interests are similar. I've done everything I can to broaden my scope, but my passion for exceptional films have narrowed my opportunities. I've used the internet to find like-minded individuals, but they still never understand to the fullest, and when they resist, I hear that damnable sound.

The incessant ringtone of a cell phone. The same noise that deprived me of my one, true friend and inspiration, Nick Craster. It was a Wagnerian epic that assaulted my senses. Soon, the headaches would start.

I glanced over my shoulder. Valerie followed my eyes. I could make out the outline of her hawk-like nose and the short, black hair that was cut in the manner of a boy. She wore a simple black shirt and skirt; she was much taller than I, and her shoulders were broader. Though she was hardly feminine, my interest in her lay only in what kind of commitment she could make to me as a friend, not as a lover.

"Tell me what inspires you," she said. "While we wait for the movie, I want to hear you talk. I want to know what goes on in that amazing mind of yours."

The ringtone seemed to bleed out of the dusty corners where the spiders hid.

I couldn't help but think of Craster. What would he say about this?

***

Nick Craster was the one who introduced me to grindhouse films; we'd met at the pet store where I've worked as a cashier for the past 110 months, seven days, eight hours, and thirty-seven minutes (as of the moment I sat down to watch the third *Octopus* movie, which I'd been looking forward to because the mutant octopi had been eradicated at the end of the second film). Craster was a prolific filmmaker, whose credits included such classics as: *She-Devil from Brooklyn, Championship Robot Soccer, Cannibal Octopus, Cannibal Octopus Two: The Resurrection,* and *Pandora's Wet Box.* It was my luck that we'd developed a friendship together, one that often involved long discussions into the evening about dream projects and the failures of the movie industry. I provided an attentive ear, and learned all I could about the movies I loved so dearly. We forged a strong friendship almost instantly. It was as if we were inside of each other's heads.

On the evening Craster disappeared from my life, he'd decided we should see a more popular film, although it still belonged to the genre we loved. It was a wild plan: we would see *Nazi*

Werewolf Lords from Argentina, which had garnered a bit of media attention for a rather gory scene that involves lampshades and pregnant werewolves. We would visit an independent theater in the middle of our city's more derelict area.

That night, the theater was fairly crowded. I counted thirty-two people in attendance, though most of them were teenagers. This infuriated Craster. He called it an, "American tragedy that serves as a metaphor for everything that is tainted and corrupt about the capitalist demigods who prey upon the mass-market monkeys and their lust for blood." Craster, you see, was both a prophet and a genius.

Before the film began, Craster left his seat (which was an outrage, because he felt it was disrespectful to the artistic visions of the men and women who made the films, which were designed to be viewed in the darkness of theaters, for anyone to leave a movie while it's being shown. He often compared it to taking a break in the middle of intercourse). He complained to the theater's "management," as they preferred to be called, though the late-night slave-driver was nothing more than an obese mother of four named Carla Jean. I'd read about her in the newspapers a short time after the subsequent incident at the theater.

When Craster returned to his seat, he gripped his armrests tightly. His bottom lip quivered. His eyebrows were furrowed deeply into his eyes, and a little bead of sweat slid from his receding hairline and over his jaw. A child may have feared that his head might explode.

"They need the business," he couldn't stop the spittle that popped out of his lips. "These kids paid for their tickets. They're all seventeen or older. They won't be removed."

The theater darkened, and right before the credits began to roll, some young idiot's cell phone rang; the ringtone was the Wagnerian opera, "The Ride of the Valkyries." He answered it rather loudly. To the caller, he explained where he was, who he was with, and what he was doing. The conversation went on. Badly played piano music played over the theater speakers. Names appeared on the screen in white letters against a black backdrop.

Another cell phone rang.

Two girls laughed.

I understood that several members of the audience were stoned. Almost all of them, I realized, were teenagers. Somehow, this would all be my fault. The complete ruination of an evening Craster had been looking forward to for a long time would be on my lap. Our friendship would end. The entire event had been my idea.

"What is this?" he wheezed.

Another phone rang. Nobody seemed to care.

Craster used to say that multimedia and technology had cheapened films. Anything that was free didn't have any kind of value, and the "art of film" had suffered. He hated young people. He hated technology. What was the point if anyone with a computer can simply download a movie without ever paying the people who created it?

He pushed his fists against his ears and seethed. With his mouth hanging open, he rocked back and forth in his chair. I hoped he wasn't having a seizure because I had no idea what to do.

With a loud, ear-splitting scream, he shot up from his seat and ran. The scream trailed his fleeing presence, and nobody in the audience seemed to care. There was some scattered laughter, but as the movie continued to roll, more phones chimed, and more conversations began.

Three years passed since Craster ran out of my life.

Craster made only one other film since he left me. *Cannibal Octopus Three* had earned itself a one-star review from more than one horror-film aficionado, but none of those "professional" reviewers truly understand the dedication it takes to make a "B" movie. The legendary Ed Wood would have loved the concept behind *Cannibal Octopus*. He would have been upset for not having thought of the idea himself.

I couldn't wait to see it.

***

The ringtone continued to haunt my sense of perception. I surveyed the vast stretches of space between the scattered strangers. I knew each of them personally. Like Craster, I believe art has been murdered by gladiator television and video games. These strangers are dedicated to the visionary expressions of great filmmakers. They sit and ponder the vast, universal

214

questions raised by the metaphorical, wholesale slaughter of nubile teens on spring break on the big screen. Each stranger is transfixed by the courage of independent artists who poured their own money into these financial failures for the sake of blood and art.

"These films inspire me," I finally answered Valerie's question. "You've seen the rough draft of my own screenplay—the one I sent you. You can see the heavy influence these movies have on me."

She began to talk about herself, although I wasn't interested.

"I worked for eight years as a homicide detective," she leaned forward in her seat and stared into my eyes while she spoke, as if interested in my reaction. "Sometimes, when I would come home, I would sit up late at night and watch horror movies. I wanted to see the blood. My real life wasn't enough. No matter how many dead bodies I saw, there was a part of me that felt a rush. Some of the other detectives would get sick if a victim was mutilated, but not me. Another corpse meant another killer, and another killer meant I would be responsible for their capture. For me, murder created action."

Valerie refused to stop rambling. "There were too many sleepless nights. I knew something was wrong with me, that I was different from the other detectives, and some of them wanted to stay away from me. But everything I experienced spilled over into my life. I was easily agitated, and nothing could make me happy. Several times, I asked my husband to please me in ways he never imagined. I wanted him to hurt me. He refused when my requests became more . . . complicated. We divorced."

The ringtone grew louder. Couldn't she hear it? There were so many questions she should have been asking. I kept thinking about her rapidly-moving mouth and the words that tumbled out. The blank screen loomed before us, silent and colorless. Somewhere, a rat tittered. The sweat that oozed through the back of my shirt glued me to the seat. The headache hammered at the blood between my eyes. The pain seemed to grow like a carefully-stoked flame, reaching over the top of my skull and burning along the back of my head.

Valerie continued, "I'm a huge fan of your work, you know. I know I never told you this, but I've followed you for years. I'm actually a bit surprised there aren't more people in this theater. I thought your inner circle was much bigger. I'm not disappointed or anything, I'm just surprised. Do you have more friends waiting for you somewhere?"

Why did she ask all the wrong questions? The ringtone nagged at me, and the razor in my pocket felt incredibly warm against my thigh.

The other five theater-goers had been good acquaintances of mine for a long time. It was a matter of fortune that I stumbled upon them: each drew my wrath with their own shitty ringtone, and I'd discovered that we had much in common. I'm very fortunate now to have so many friends, but such relationships take time to develop. They require careful planning. Sometimes, I might accompany them home. I would retrieve their mail for them. I visited them at their jobs.

I wanted Valerie to join them, but I couldn't grasp what was happening. I seemed to lack control over my own body. The moonlight highlighted her large, beak-nose.

"I have friends of my own," she continued to ramble. "Of course, I prefer to spend time with them in the comfort of my own home. They fired me from my job because they thought I was, well, their words for it were, 'unsavory conduct,' but they really just didn't understand. Not like you do. Before they fired me, I was already following you around. I mean, I was literally following you. I'm sorry if this is going to make you uncomfortable, but I already knew about this place, and I knew you wanted to bring me here. Forgive me if I admit to being a little obsessed with you, but you were the one who inspired me. That's why I have my own friends, now. In fact, three of them are sitting on my couch at home, waiting for me to get back. But you're sharing this with me. This is special to me, and when we leave here, I'd hoped you would join me at my place."

I pushed my hands against my eyes. "I'm not . . . feeling too well . . ." I confessed. "Don't you hear it? The movie's about to start and they won't shut their phones off."

"I always wondered what happened to this theater after the fire. It was all over the news when it happened. You were there that night weren't you? You don't have to answer, because of course I already know. There were a bunch of dead teenagers. I remember there was a woman named Carla Jean who had four kids at home. They said the fire was an accident. But it's still beautiful. I'm so happy to be here with you!"

She stood up then while the pain in my head caused my eyes to water. My vision blurred, and I shook my head frantically. I would do anything to stop the pain. I knew there was only one way to make it go away, but I couldn't bring myself to include Valerie in my intimate group of followers. I wanted her, but I couldn't think, couldn't act.

"I recognize that man!" she shouted suddenly and ran down the aisle toward one of my comrades. The impulse to stop her was overwhelmed by the intense pressure that tortured my consciousness.

I wanted her to leave. The woman didn't belong among my friends; she would embarrass me in front of them. She was a monster of the worst kind. I loathed ignorant fools who believed they knew everything there was to know about their hobby; she was a snob.

While standing nearby one of my old friends, she suddenly removed the man's dusty old trucker hat and placed it on her own head. "Nick!" she shouted at me. "I'm sorry, I made a mistake. I don't recognize him. I thought maybe it was Greg Jensen, or Steve Bracken. They both went missing some time back . . . are you okay, Nick?"

I recognized those names. Were they old friends of mine? And why did she call me "Nick?" Who did she think she was? I became infuriated. I would make a stand against her folly, once and for all. Moviegoers everywhere would be pleased to know that this abomination of a fan was no longer among them.

"Your script for *Cannibal Octopus Three* was amazing," she declared. "I wish I'd read your screen treatments for the other two. I highly recommend that you send your script to a prominent agent, or even another screenwriter! Someone will recognize the talent you have!"

"We're here to watch a movie!" I roared against the waves of pain.

"This man doesn't have a face!" Valerie revealed. "He can't tell me his name because he's dead. Nick, you should have introduced us. I'm here to meet new people, too. You promised I would get to know your friends."

She sauntered back up the aisle and pushed me back into my seat. She dug around in my pocket and withdrew the razor. I could feel her hot breath against my face.

"I really want to get to know you," she said.

"You'll never understand. You're a snob. You don't appreciate these films like I do." I squeezed my eyes shut against the pain.

"You don't know much this means to me. You don't even know where you are, do you? You burned this theater down to the ground yourself. Don't you remember? You've killed all of these people here. You've been doing this for years! Where're the other bodies?"

She'd gone mad.

"Your name is Nick Craster. Look at me!"

I looked upon her leering face. I didn't know what she intended to do with me, but I know what I needed to do to her.

The name rolled around in my head. Craster was an infamous director, and I was a cashier who collected money for dog treats. He was my favorite artist, a man of vision and integrity. I'd had the good fortune of meeting him, and we became quick friends. He left me in a movie theater after an abrupt cell phone's ringtone drove him mad.

Since Craster left, I needed to make new friends. I would listen for Wagner's music, which would always lead me to another fortunate soul.

"*Cannibal Octopus* is your idea," she held the razor in front of her face. "You're the writer . . . you're the man with vision."

It wasn't possible. She had to be wrong. My name was . . .

Valerie placed the razor in my hand and closed my fingers around it. "Share your vision with me. Let me watch the movie with you. It's all I ever wanted. I haven't felt alive in years! I need you to help me. I know I'm selfish, but I'm so alone, and you're the only one who can help me. Share your passions and your dreams with me. Let me live again!"

With my shaking fist, I slowly drew a line of blood across her cheek with the razor. She gasped and shuddered. Her eyes closed, and her full lips parted. The ringtone's volume decreased and the pain in my head pulsed with diminished strength.

"You're an artist," she said with her eyes closed. "I hope we can be friends."

I nodded. "Yes. I would like that."

"Get on top of me," she whispered.

We switched positions, and I drew a similar line of blood across her other cheek.

My desire to see the movie hadn't left me. It was something I could still share with her. I knew everything about all of Craster's films.

"The movie opens on a cruise ship," I said. "There are families on board, and newlyweds. There's a gang of men who're on the cruise because they're going to try to assassinate a congressman, who's also on the cruise."

"Tell me more," she said. "This feels so perfect, Nick. I'm watching the movie with you."

Her eyelids fluttered while I began to peel back a layer of flesh from her cheekbone with the razor. Flaying her was quite enjoyable. She wrapped her hands around my shoulders, and she tried to grind her crotch against mine. I sawed away at the loose skin and removed it. It plopped to the floor beneath the theater seat.

None of the others in the theater moved. They knew I had work to do.

"There's so much blood," she said while arching her back.

The headache was completely gone.

"At the start of the film, I've already laid the groundwork for subplots. There are several characters involved."

She interrupted me with breathy gasps. "We'll always be friends. Always . . . always . . ."

To this day, I believe that she really enjoyed the movie.

William Cook

Aspects of Infinity

I

I remember how it all began, as clearly as if it were yesterday. It was a fine morning, crisp and cold, but full of sun. I woke up to the sound of angels playing music in my ears. I can't be sure of their instruments, although they made the most beautiful sounds I had ever heard. I couldn't see, my bedroom was filled with a blinding white light, the only sense I had was one of sound. I lay motionless in my bed, the waves of crystal light and symphony pervading my every pore. I was a blank canvas as the sounds began to shape the very fabric of my being. Through the lucid choir of nothingness came a word and with it followed another:

'Rise', it whispered, as if a breeze.

'Rise up and face the day for your life has ceased. Your new life is just beginning . . .'

I awoke again, yet unsure of if I had ever been asleep.

***

It is cold tonight. The streets are quiet for once. That 'feeling' is not there, for the moment. Everything is so still and pristine. My breath fogs in front of me, a backdrop of black night. Cold O cold, yes warmth – that is what I need. Three coats over rough layers of cloth. I feel like a freakish character in a Brueghel painting.

Another memory stabs my eyes – a feeling comes running at me, then disappears with my steaming breath into the night. Ice has covered everything; shards and sheets of crystal light illuminate the dark.

The cracks are more visible tonight; under stark streetlight, gaping splits filled with phosphorescent light that weep and spew forth into the black shadows.

There is nowhere to hide.

If there is nowhere to go where it is warm, then there is always the cemetery. Earth always offers sanctuary, so softer and more welcoming than the hard bed of concrete. A manhole cover beckons from behind a tomb; we scurry like diseased rats in burrowed warrens beneath the poisoned city, deep within its gut, beneath the rivers and the broken factories. The steaming creeks and rivers above lap the earth from their banks. Pulling the blistered blanket of glass up, as its wake rocks and stirs our consciousness from mournful sleep and ritualistic instinct. We realise that if we were to be dead --- we would be, yet, we are all drowned. . .

White begins to stain the night as we sleep.

II

We stopped for a while; the others went to forage for maps and food. I rested on a huge marble step that stretched its cold form out for a mile. The building hovering over me above would've welcomed Alexander's drunken torch. Persia never looked so grand and diseased at the same time as this mortuary – huge space cobbled with grey stone, the other surrounding buildings scrawled like feverish charcoal monoliths, deep shadows frame the cold snow of their architecture.

I sit alone on these steps.

I watch the cold clouds reiterate above the grey skyline. There is no blank canvas. Everything is a colour. Everything is a word. I cannot help but interpret and participate in this infinite moment. This morning froze me; snapped me from a dream of thirteen faces — none of which were mine. What is neutral in this God-forsaken world?

I have a newfound faith in sleep that serves me well for everything. Shuts my eyes as light as a thief's, yet still lets me live when I wake. This I find quite amusing. And here we now stand, on the edge of the hill above the dirty little town where I was born; looking across the black abyss to the thrashing, heaving, mass-molecules of space and time, bursting and splashing the city lights.

O where do we go from here?

What will the skies bring us tonight?

We thirteen seekers of the truth, who were once slaves of sin, now stand with countenance and fortitude amongst the teeming hordes of brutish defilers. We think of nothing but the goal that never lets us know its name and in that coveted mystery, we find assurance and spiritual strength. Like Lazarus, we have risen

221

from pools of blood and death to walk amongst the living dead, to have some purpose totally foreign from that of this world. We sight our ships to sea just to have them crushed by quick waves. Others abort the vessel falling fallen while we fall, we set our sights to land and catapult an anchor plated with the fear of missing the mark. We know however, that where it scalps a patch of earth, we may as well dig a place and in it lay our skeletal frames – watching the moon spin off, far away, to an inconceivable distance as steaming black sod frames then blocks the final vision.

In a damp cavern beneath the border, we seek and find temporary sanctuary. Food is shared and words are said; you step from the shadows into the fold of the family. Warm light dances off the sloping dust caked walls. An orange aura fills the chamber and shadows play out their grotesque pantomimes of murder on the walls, but your silhouette is beautiful yet transparent. The reflection of the flame burns brightly in your eyes tonight and I see a hunger there so deep. I feel your skin so warm your touch like silk lips so you who hypnotise like a home welcome me into your arms once again and again and for a brief instant, I am human again. I pledge my undying love to you and everyone as we twirl like dervish dancers begging for alms of love in worlds of pure white neutrality untainted by freedom as we melt sun with the sky to burn bloom buy our place with what and all we've got, which is not much.

My hands do not feel your memory.

My eyes see you in everything . . .

In various sorrows, blizzards begin above the ground. Grinding sand and shingle down the dark corridor toward our empty shelter. To blow the bells and ring the chimes of you, burning pyre-like in my flaming chest, I must climb the highest mountain.

I must record the journey and events of the hours and days to come.

I must record your beauty and your twisted ugliness as detailed and as infinitely as I can, with the last drop of blood as my ink. My heart houses the flint you struck; to live is to die tonight and every lost night from now.

I must record your dying history – your progress, your decay, your thwarted attempts to claim new worlds . . . everything.

Piano Concerto No. 21 in C major - Andante

III

A new day and we brush the ash and dust from our eyes and hair. Our black overcoats increasingly stiffen from the shed skin follicles of her Malthusian moulting, which stick like mortician's wax with every warm breeze of her dying breath. The sun is purple and fills the tangerine hued sky. Its burning eminence pockets the loose change of oxygen, its twisting smile creases, dazzling. We lower our welding masks and shuffle dust clouds off through the churning ghost dance of the early morning day. From half-awake to suddenly wide awake, almost – a lucid kind-of light licks our flesh. It is hard not to forget the ancient promise of real rain --- crystal clear water that is sweet and liquid wet.

O to taste the diamond drops of moisture!

What a bastard of a shadow of a dream!

This is the time when a mind eraser could be put to good use.

We all wish that we could die.

***

Last night I had a nightmare, my memory recorded my thoughts. It started with a noise and then language became apparent. Words crawl like pulsing worms from my mouth. Naked.

All naked we are nude and nice now in the slow fetid time of a clock no longer tick tock tick tock . . . Rain falling like dead sparrows on the roof, so loud and thudding; the water-drops as big as bombs. If you had a weak thin neck, it would snap with their pummelling weight. Old trees cracking twigs arthritic limbs frozen air freezing flays flesh off bare cheeks. Wind whipping strop's slap acid sand grates. Breathless. Diseases abound to burrow faster, yet still we stand and breathe the foul air.

All around – beautiful vampires.

Red lips platinum hair ghost skin yellow tongues lick black teeth.

Everything surrounds and squeezes back – large machines enlarging . . .

223

Everything is a word, but I can't shake the fact that words are so meaningless in the face of such events. I want to wake up.

***

We have ploughed our fields with streets, planted them with ugly tombs of concrete instead of fruit trees. The separation is evident; the direction misunderstood. We the unwilling are urged to remain seated 'til the show is over. Is there any one with just cause why this marriage should be over, speak up now or forever hold your peace in check? Throw twenty different objects together and try to stack them up; a triangular structure is the only form withstanding. Who is at the top? How soon before the objects beneath collapse or eject from the equation? Who ploughs the field does the sowing, yet who is it that reaps and rapes the rewards of our toil?

The separation is evident.

***

On my way through the smashed suburbs, I saw a clothesline swaying in the cold wind, a single tall stick, a rake that strongly held the weight of the world above its rigid head. The pole pushes piles of christened ragged clothes into the wind. It flaps the wet wrinkles of the clothes dry, impregnates their nature to rub against skin. The pole sways privately. Ticking off the time, a pendulous metronome, and supporting it all a blue line and the breeze. The rigid rake has kept its place actively alive by its still and unwavering disposition. By its silence.

***

It feels like autumn now, but the seasons are all mad and messed up.

Burning bark smells like cinnamon sometimes, right now it smells like burning bark. The tree's on fire – the last of them, on this dying street clogged with floating embers and curling balloons of smoke. All the ghosts stand in the mist smoke in silent chastity and broken innocence, shivering at the sight of the steel scythe blade of the reaper. Some peel in fright like snakes, others shed leaves like scales and skin – matt-finished minnows fall – sardines litter the ochre smoky floor; quite hot, then cold

224

blue haze blankets everything and we drift off toward our destination.

Towards redemption, or just another aspect of infinity?

IV

A three storied building offers sanctuary from the searing elements for a while, affording us a vantage point from which to spy all other travellers and assassins. Cold hard concrete swells and sweats its broken crumbling walls under the midday sun. We take turns on watch. I meditate in a quiet corner in the dark – waiting for a sign, a map, a pineapple, a hole in the clouds . . . sleep. The others try to sleep; stirring occasionally, humming, reciting lost songs and poetry, drawing crude figures and signs on the scarred walls. After seven hours, I rise refreshed and wary of the indigo night that is now upon us. I climb the outside window fire-escape ladder, hanging out over the litter-strewn footpath below. The simmering night fluctuates in temperature. All is silent save for a warm breeze brushing between my ear and the wall of the building. The yellow moon is huge and seems to be gaining ground with every revolution, its eerie light casting a sickly glow of gold over the jagged geometry of lower downtown Knotterdam.

From out behind a dead store scurries one of the first mutants we see on our odyssey. He scuttles along on his gammy leg. He looks like he is trying to leg-over a short fence, dragging his idle leg then kind of flipping it to limp along on.

From out behind shadows and shapes, emerge the blackened faces of children.

Screaming with insane mirth and laughter like small dancing skeletons, the children surround their prey like rodents around a corpse. He occupies their ebbing worlds as a target for stones and short relief from their surroundings. His hunched body burns with words, rocks, and perverted piercing stares. Looking up bent over, his face twisted in shadow, he shudders and flops faster to outrun gregarious gazes and the pelting assault of creatures more mindless than he. It gets too much sometimes, in fact all the time, the throwing about of his cumbersome cage. The frustration of a life not knowing why, but most of all it gets too much, because of them. They hate him, they always have, and they follow him wherever he goes. Crying now and limping as fast as he cannot go, he falls down, curls up, in the black dismissal of the world.

I can hear his pathetic moans from the rooftop.

He is sobbing and calling "Esmeralda? Esmeralda? I hang my head with the weight of shame just as the weight of your natural and cumbersome form hung you. Come back to me my love. Come back, to me. . ."

A piece of brick flies from the dark, knocking a splash of blood from his swollen forehead. He lies back and stares at the moon glistening in his weeping eyes, his arm raised, fingers moving in silent appeal. In the pain of difference and of hurt, and of being very much alone, he succumbs to the world around him. The ground flattens and swallows his twisted form, the black asphalt pulsing like a heartbeat – each swell inhaling, gulping.

A bony arm remains, elbow high above the ground. In the sick light, it looks like a withered fire hydrant. The fingers still writhe and click, their lumpy knuckles turn and crack, the torn shirtsleeve slides down the twitching forearm.

From the dark realms of a narrow alley, the squeak of pedals, chain, spokes and bell resounds. In slow moving motion, a child on a bike floats across the stage of the street. The child's head is a balloon – a balloon with huge wide staring black pupils for eyes, button nose upturned, all framed in an ivory countenance as polished as a marble basin. His small arm swinging in timeless motion, it seems to swell and elongate like sharpened bone. I watch his small arm swinging as he pedals, the other hand steering his mechanical vessel. In his toy hand, his hand, he holds a thin shiny curved blade – a scythe glistening like a diamond in the shadows, a razor sharp scythe tinkling off the road, small red sparks dancing behind the black tyres of his bike.

The hand and muscle of the exposed arm is lined up by the boy's front bike tyre. The arm suddenly stands still and tall like a heron on alert, as if aware of its approaching foe, trapped in a quagmire trying to free its tethered form. The boy peddles pedals pedals faster faster, breath puffing in small red clouds of dust from his sneering wee mouth. The white bony arm wriggling above the asphalt, fingers clenching unclenching as if trying to scream. The boy's strange arm upraised now, blade in hand sharp, arm – a swinging arc down and . . . SCHLOCKKK . . .

The moon silhouettes the spinning arm clutching at arm and then disappearing past the window of the light of the moon. The

226

boy tilts his huge head back, laughs, swallows and then blows perfect dust-red smoke rings at the night's weird sky. I look down at the scene, all actors disappear now, as the swirling paper and dust in the gutters of the street stop their discontented stirring. The breeze dissipates, comets stop their blazing trails across the sky, and everything is so quite. I lean back on the wall of the balcony of the roof and slowly let my knees give out under my weight – goodnight sick moon.

Good night.

Cello Concerto No. 1 in E Flat Major, Op. 107 – Moderato.

V

We walk past a flickering transmitter, still crackling with stored power. Static burns the brain cells, buzzing constantly like electric fur brushed up the wrong way. The strange sensation of a foreign body invading every pore and cell. Its life force scratches neon graffiti on never-ending night while all around satellites spin above . . .

A message – another mountain to conquer.

How many days left?

Looking all the time for something that has always seen us, which we will never see, through this burgeoning haze of red dead solidity. O but now I'm letting my emotion override my sensibilities in my search for truth! But what is truth?

Of the heart?

The mind?

The soul?

And what are these names for these things, if such things even exist anyway . . .?

My heart is low, my mind weary, my spirit has wandered on ahead to scout safe passage for our advance, but it is not searching for mystery or treasure. Yet, I pray that it might find some, just something small. A glimmer of shining illusion that we may believe in, to get us through another day and night . . .

A common theme along our journey, that I find quite disturbing, is the pervading impressions of silence that pepper the day and night. It is a dripping tap – even the most subtle of words repeated enough, eventually drives to the point of

227

distraction and attentions the prey. As a tiny twig, broken from a tree, that falls upon water makes ripples that echo its form. However, when such water is not calm, still a bigger branch with more substance is needed to create visible and audible impression. In these moments of absolute peace and lucidity, the shadow of death breathes its name in an epiphany of silence.

This morning, everything moves in slow motion. I awoke to see women beating slow tracks in beauty with leaves swirling at their heels touching sweet white feet. A moist caress glides in their perfumed surrealism. The summer sings optical promises; maybe everything will be all right?

Another vision of Mary – standing on the edge of the Black Forest on the fringe of the camp. An army of ghostly figures behind her, writhing in the mist and the damp leaves, waving slowly, translucently.

Her last good-byes seem forever cast in cold calculus, a flickering hologram.

Fantasien, Op. 116 – No. 7 Capriccio. Allegro agitato

VI

We found an old run-down cabin, just before dusk gave in to night, deep in the foothills of the mountain ranges. Windows doors grey walls torn. A fox skitters 'round the room, sniffing trash, oblivious to our presence. Eye to eye rats in rafters, on mantle, windowsills, within walls – scratching, scratching, scratching through holes; standing still for slash of time, then off again. Seen sniffed snorted disappeared forgotten, room now empty save for moonlight.

The fireplace flickers, then explodes.

The whole broken brown-grey interior illumined, in all its decayed woody brilliance. The flame licked the cobwebs in the grate, blossoms crushing cellophane, sounds that burn sun-burst bright, engulfing envelopes stuffed with wads of cash and unforgettable memories, crackles to ash.

Then back-to-back black.

The visions are becoming stronger while our quest becomes more inconsequential. Nature is casting its archaic spell over our experience of things. We have all experienced a heightening of

228

the senses; the smells of the deep woods and tumbling streams, the clarity of sight and hearing - a leaf so finely cut, a dry twig cracking under the hoof of one of the green deer sniffing the air ten miles downwind in the heart of the forest.

I remember a story that once captured my imagination – a poet at the end of his tether, frustrated with society and (ultimately) himself, walks into the foothills of a vast mountain range in the Americas with a loaded firearm.

No one ever sees him again, no body is ever found.

All he leaves behind are memories and a huge body of verse for the world to do with what it will. The forest has swallowed him; nature has enveloped his very being, distributed his atoms throughout the flora and fauna like so much mulch, and that's all we are . . .

VII

The new day vivisects the dawn, another telegram from hell. Pressures of belief make for sacrifice of sleep --- relief, so hard to shake the madness of life from one's head, without losing dreams . . . grown nurtured there, like lice they hunger, live upon ghosts, teasing and teeming rife with maddening proposals. Wet dam breaks, floods the soul, quenching fires of the fragile heart; blood ferries vessels of shrouded prayer, laps sides of narrow passage, ridges perched precarious --- shelter in the shadows, breeds clinging moss of time --- the dawn buries the dreams in thought, in matter, under the new day.

O thank god for the new day, today!

These small mercies are no mean feat, yet there is still a huge nagging doubt in my nature as to the effectiveness of petitioning the lord with prayer.

Another painful message came today; the great communicator speaks with no words so familiar. I placed the impulse with words so much softer than your cutting spiel of want. I would not hesitate to use you as such, mere words of my own writing, but you would let all of my blood become dust, leaving me dry with tears of loss like water.

A small stream seems to follow us just to remind me – where there was just flat baked dust and soil, a fissure appears and splits, widening as it fills with crystal water, tripping past my shambling leaded feet. It is quite all right to drink; in fact we are on agreement that it is perhaps the best water that we have ever tasted. The sky parts its grey beard for a minute, yawning in bright disinterest and makes the dull colours glow, as they should, for the same amount of time. Flitting birds play and sing all that's natural, the stream babbles wetly, tumbling quietly past us, leading us on into the unknown while the sun shines warmly --- paints everything still, so still and quiet for a minute.

I turn back in the grey, toward the valley below, to check the burning fires glowing as far as the horizon. Suddenly, a waddling duck jets its slick form out from the front of the burrowing stream; I grab its wet neck and wring the painful life from it.

We all have to remind ourselves every now and then that we are only human.

That we are still alive.

    ***

The river frogs choke the highway, croaking to the night.

And the rain it hammers down across the barren blue hue, in its shimmering sweeping black dress. Smoke-like clouds draped above the great flood of blood. Dawn cloud ingrained in this almighty time with blindness. It rained forever in the sweet south and sweet north and sweet east and bittersweet west. Sweat pearls run down my face. An almighty fine wine of the weeping sky falls down on old slumbering earth, snoring with the promise of the BIG sleep in Messianic night. Till that almighty river's shining dawn and passage down stream turned big muddy, where the desert had been --- and Noah might've rowed on out from the banks of old earth . . .

If it hadn't been another dream.

            ***

Near the camp, ripples on the surface of a nearby dam signalled the coming tide upstream as Salmon swam down-stream, furtively kissing the small insects from the mirrored surface of the sky.

We have to close our minds – we have learnt the laws of the forest – and we have to disintegrate our bodies in order to become part of the force of the storm. Resistance is futile and dangerous. The sun glows pale red through the silhouettes of the

230

trees, as we trace its fall, cold sinks its blade a little deeper in the bone, shadows merge.

We build a small fire on the embers of yesterday's.

The pine-needles pop and smoke, the twigs ignite and consume themselves, as the flame's glow casts masks and dancing shadows across our pensive faces. We sip Rosemary tea from warm receptacles; steam curling from our breath, the forest is deathly quiet again save for a stirring breeze swaying the treetops. The chill air defies the approaching storm, the silver clouds above now iridescent in the blue moonlight; they accelerate across the grey plains of the night sky. As their speed becomes lost in the filling of the sky, the trees creak and drop branches and pine-cones from their thrashing limbs. Our fire is scattered, tumbling sparks flicker through the tumultuous bracken and undergrowth, as the wind's momentous fury systematically attacks our camp.

VIII

I know now the third trouble has earnestly begun its unstoppable stoppage. From the wrong mountain that I had wasted three days and nights upon, answering question after question of my silent companions. To be skin-blackened in the blazing light until refuge in a crag brought my skull bloody pecks from all manner of winged creatures. I decided to descend, as I was told that this was not the very tall terrain that I should be on.

Coming down the mountain, I met a virgin who had children; her entourage were all weeping for their lives. I met a blind man who had vision, but no other sense at all. I met a poor man who had given all his wealth away and had nothing else to give anyone – no words, no hate, no nothing at all. The travel down was so much harder than the voyage up the mountain, despite the heavy load upon my weary shoulders. My twelve companions, light as they were; all grasping, clinging, like a thick ball of twitching twine coiled up across my creaking spine.

Coming down the mountain, I met a muse that could not play, sing, or impart gifts of inspiration. I met a clown that never laughed, but who had always been laughed at. I met a married man who had lost his ring deliberately amongst the stony slopes. Now on another mountain, we had ascended, amongst the ranges of the world. Up high on mountain peak, three days and three nights did curse me with its silence, yet the voices they were loud. A cold cave in crags of granite precipice did afford we with sublime providence and writing space in the dark. All about me ravens black and buzzards grey, haunted me with beady hungry stares, while forcing me into friendship with threats of violence and despair. I do not know, nor will I ever, the nature of those creatures that caricaturise the deformity of men.

Coming down the mountain, I was blinded by the brilliance; everything was crystal clear and held a lucid gold resilience. To my dismay, my vision could not offer me sanctuary of allegiance. Thrown from one apparition to spirit deed entrusted --- the golden glow endowed within, soon poisoned all, and ruptured shaking ground. Serenity of peace and mind madness breached the shrunk horizon.

I made retreat in haste and fear of all that I had witnessed.

A martyr's life, of seer and shaman, harnessed by the reins of Sodom.

To lead like the blind scout in disarray. To plot the paths through minefields olden laid, without map or guide to show the way for who has gone before, has gone without, to bleed for wounded souls their pain. To dance scarred by the acid rain's great rocks. To house the children evil shamed. To see the blind-man's tortured fate, in beggar's rags dressed with itching pestilence. To walk the paths with famine as my food, with death as my guide . . . I wove my bleeding heaving wretchedness, once again up the incline.

Were we ever going to find the answers for the great one – we were beginning to seriously doubt the validity of his requests?

IX

In my sleep, I had another dream.

Beneath the old sash window, someone had placed a mirror; it reached from the floor to the frame. Standing naked, head-less – it did not look like me, but then I'd only ever seen myself in reflection, so I presumed that it was. Outside, dry ochre fields – flat as sea – stretch away through and beyond defiant nets of fences. A black bull – horns, big polished lump of charcoal stares at me, snorting breath paints the window. He thinks that I have fresh blades of grass for his consumption, he is wrong. Its huge head adheres to my form, the cadence clear:

I rise to fall – the morning sun stains bronze, the birds song sounds of pipe and tambourine, minus my hands that now burn with the sun in this labyrinth of dawn. Seven figures shimmering with energy, atoms spinning in a spinning mass of form, one stood apart – more material and menacing than the others who had a certain kind of innocence in their immateriality.

***

Given eyes to see a world, we did and so we died. Hunger in the new night's yawn we ate ferociously, like wolf cubs at mother's milk, gorged pregnant with concrete fear.

It was all we could do to stay awake.

Now we are the infected.

Slippery tongues of crass old lands injected in our virgin veins, we have not even begun to begin to see the mud we stand in, to smell it as it is, to disregard its funerary qualities. Buried we have not begun to contemplate this place we are in, this rock we stand on. We see the ocean as a moat, as an eternity, between the setting sun and us. We do not feel the touch of waves all we see is all we are. The transcendence of time, irrelevant in its ticking hue, buoyant on its mocking grin -- grasped by none, aspired by some. It chatters – a bone wind-chime, cracking and tolling each short but endless passing of day. Impeccable revenge: in evanescence two pits dwell -- infinite charcoal voyeurs, watching, always waiting for you. For me . . .

Rain falls – ashen snow of sorts, trying hard to clean it only dissolves and steams. Evaporation leaves a hollow where there once was life. Time keeps ticking off itself, so do we too bring intonation to ourselves.

As we have done, so shall be done to no one, but unto ourselves . . .

What is this place on which I stand?

What is this place in which I dwell?

Is this thought naught but a smell, of what has always been that is not seen? Consummation has stamped its seal on everything, long dead and buried – who wields the stamp with such intent?

Who creased the seal on our bent backs?

Who gave us these dead eyes?

Adagio – Concerto No. 2 in G minor, Op. 10

X

Inside the enclosure, they gave us a street to play with. Everything was ok until we began to think we could not see them.

They were there though.

We worked hard while some fell down; they were not picked up.

We became one, so they said.

Our liberty monopolised, streamlined, they said.

Then came the virus. No fence could keep it out. They contained it well, the chosen few were made to survive, you see, they needed someone to repair the machines that built the machines that mined the metals that made the machines that control our existence. Herein lay the redemption inside the enclosure. Suicide – the only sin-filled option.

The wicked city sleeps for a second as the sun comes up sleuths with blind obedience and subtle reward the day blinks and is gone – swallowed by itself we float like zombies bittersweet voodoo magnet – implants its claws in our broken backs toward the neon grin great endless inanity of night pulls to begin in earnest the spade breaks the earth's skin our quest for delight knows no bounds for fools streetlight sings and slaps the cruising cars like bleeding sunshine shards through weeping tree-lined avenues the cumbersome concrete breaks another face upon goose-steps – goose-steps, across and over while the black mirrored glass of her evening bodice entices the swirling mutants who stumble and ripple with vanity and the tease of undress winding – winding in and out through cavities like a cancer as the darkness covets the flight of our souls and soon, as ghosts, we echo and return with another tattoo from the city's sin emporium.

Journey we go, into a place where lost buildings of time stack against each other in a delicate city of memories. Walking these barren streets, searching for hidden clues, we get lost in the quest of looking for answers to the future, in the gloomy and poisonous back streets of the past. Black galloping pillows of cloud; hasten like advancing sentries of night against the grey sky, proclaiming: the ferocious almighty thunderheads, glory, blossom, and stab the tender side of the West. The East's long sabre draws out and twists, spilling gushing blankets of deep, deep maroon over mortal Earth.

Casting great floods to the West.

Decaying plagues shall ravage the North; moreover, famine bleeds dry the South's cold haven as the East, connotes slow suicide in its prophetic insane seclusion. Green stems from the grey and all the glass age redeems itself back to the crimson beaches, whence it came.

Always hunting, without knowing, for the three properties of motion: the beginning, the middle, and the end.

Life, death, fire, water, earth and ocean.

Bringing in the space of the old: the new.

The idea, the propulsion, the result is seen in all things.

Cause, effect, and result of the action, is a troublesome discourse, when the end is ultimately commotion, destruction . . .

XI

What is acquired at birth falls back to more pure and honest beginnings.

This burgeoning and ever-present death is not really our creation, but more like God's. . . Or something else. Nature does not concern itself with our presence, or the way we practice genocide, murder, rape, cannibalism, and sacrilege. For a while, we lived inside an enclosure in which they gave us a street to play with.

We saw everything, as did the third eye.

There was an uneasy calm about the place. No one spoke. Outside the walls, disease marched across the west desert scratching its long black fingernails along the high tin fence. The fossils that controlled the place stood around nervously; clad in leather jump-suits, their white faces glowing like light-bulbs in blackened sockets, obese ink-pot bodies swelling and twitching at the sounds of the scratching screams, the bloody baseball bats twirling anxiously in their podgy dough claws. Everything was ok until we began to think we could not see them.

They were always there – our imprisoners.

We worked hard as did the other broken bodies. Some fell down, they were not picked up, we saw it all and still the statues rise to meet the falling sky. We became one at that stage so they said; that point between death and beyond or something like

235

that? Our liberty monopolised, 'streamlined,' so they said. Then came the virus, no fence could keep it out but the ones that stood tall around the cities contained it well.

Soon the chosen few were made to survive.

They needed someone to repair the machines that built the machines that mined the metals that made the machines that control our existence. . . and that was then, this is now. It all collapsed beneath the onslaught of the natural night. We tried to forget that place, but for some inexplicable reason it was photographically tattooed on our internal vision.

We could not shake it.

Herein lay the redemption inside the enclosure – acceptance, honesty, awareness, and encompassment.

Aspects of infinity.

Symphony No. 5 in C sharp minor – Rondo-Finale. Allegro

Author Bios

Rich Orth. . . Poet for many years. . . works can be found in the Zombie compilations, Undead Tales & Undead Tales 2. . . also wrote lyrics to Cemetery Girl on the new Demonboy CD Dawn of Demon and has 4 songs on the bands upcoming CD, including This Halloween & Zombie Dance. Won a contest and now has his poem, My Night as Poe walled up in the Poe Cottage in the Bronx NY! Also has poetry featured in the anthologies, in both 21st Century Photography Vol. 3 & Vol.4. Also 5 featured poems in The Art of Darkness! Find me at https://www.facebook.com/orth.chroniclespoetry

Matthew Wilson, 29, is a UK resident who has been writing since small. Recently these stories have appeared in Beyond Centauri, Starline Poets Association and Carillon

David Frazier resides in Merrillville, Indiana. He has been married for 39 years to his wife Kathie. He retired in 2003 and has been writing ever since. He has had a few flash fiction stories published. He has been writing poetry recently, four of his poems have been published in Indiana Horror 2012 Anthology. Three poems are on Circus of the Damned blog site. Three flash fiction stories are in Sacramento Poetry, Arts and Music site (eskimopie.net). Although Gothic poetry is not his strongest, he will have one published at Grantswood Anthology. Breath and Shadow will publish a poem in their fall edition.Magazine. He is currently editing his first novel.

Ken Goldman is a former teacher of English and Film Studies at George Washington High School in Philadelphia He is an affiliate member of the Horror Writers Association He has homes on the Main Line in Pennsylvania and at the South Jersey shore depending upon her mood and her need for a tan. Her short stories appear in over 655 independent press publications in the U.S., Canada, the UK, and Australia with over thirty due for publication. He has written three books : Two books of short stories, YOU HAD ME AT ARRGH!! (2007, Sam's Dot Publishers), and DONNY DOESN'T LIVE HERE ANYMORE

(2012, A/A Productions), and a novella, DESIREE (2012, Damnation Press). He is currently searching out publishers for her novel . . . OF A FEATHER. Ken has received seven honorable mentions in The Year's Best Fantasy & Horror Anthologies, and he has won numerous awards, too many to mention here. Ken is available for readings at weddings, bar mitzvahs, and a subway station near you.

Marija Elektra Rodriguez grew up in a delicatessen, with a multi-ethnic family, where pickling cabbage and knife throwing were taught at an early age. She would scribble stories on butcher's paper which would then be passed on to unsuspecting customers when they received their groceries. She is thirty years old and currently lives in Sydney with her husband (el carnicero), her daughter, and pirate pets.

William Cook: I live in Wellington – the small wind-blown capital city of New Zealand. I have been writing weird stories ever since I was a kid. My first published works were poems in various literary journals in NZ and a few in the States. Back in 1996 I published a collection of verse titled 'Journey: The Search for Something' and had the occasional poem and short story published online, but nothing really of note until 2010 when Lee Pletzers from Triskaideka Books accepted my story 'The Devil Inside' for the 2010 Masters of Horror AnthologyI have since had quite a few Horror shorts published in various anthologies. My novel 'Blood Related,' was re-released by Black Bed Sheet Books Halloween 2012. If you would like to buy a copy of 'Blood Related', either paperback or E-book please visit my Amazon author's page:

Mike Jansen has published flash fiction, short stories and longer work in various anthologies and magazines in the Netherlands and Belgium, including Cerberus, Manifesto Bravado, Wonderwaan, Ator Mondis and Babel-SF and Verschijnsel anthologies such as Ragnarok and Zwarte Zielen (Black Souls). His debut novel appeared in 2011, the sequel will be published by the end of 2012. Obviously he lives in the Netherlands, in Hilversum which is close to Amsterdam. He has won awards for best new author and best author in the King Kong Awards of 1991 and 1992 respectively.

More recently he publishes his work in various English language magazines and anthologies. Website: meznir.com

David S. Pointer has been writing poems for a long time, and he's old enough to remember when Kenny Rogers and The First Edition just checked in to see what condition their condition was in. David plans to check in later to see the human condition here at "Static Movement."

Timothy Frasier is a poet, novelist, and short story writer. His work appears in various literature magazines, the Collaboration of the Dead anthology *Zombies Gone Wild Volume 2*, John Ward Kirk's anthology *Indiana Science Fiction 2012*, and the Static Movement anthologies *Hell, Serial Killers 2, Grave Robbers, Here Be Clowns, Here Be Clowns Book 2, Long Pig, In The Darkness, Dangerous Dreams, Mirror Mirror, Legends and Lore, Noir, Gothic Poems and Flash Fiction*, and *Undead Space*. Frasier lives in Western Kentucky with his wife, Lisa

Julienne Lee loves stories that explore the history of humanity through the art of writing. She lives with her husband and children near Brockville, Ontario.

Steve Bates is a freelance journalist based in the Washington, D.C., area. He was a reporter and editor for The Washington Post for 14 years and has written for magazines and the web. He self-published a nonfiction book, *The Seeds of Spring: Lessons From the Garden*, which won two awards. His website is www.stevebateswriter.com.

Richard Farren Barber was born in Nottingham in July 1970. After studying in London he returned to the East Midlands. He lives with his wife and son and works as a Development Services Manager for a local university. He has written over 200 short stories and has had short stories published in Alt-Dead, Alt-Zombie, Blood Oranges, Derby Scribes Anthology, Derby Telegraph, ePocalypse – Tales from the End, Gentle Reader, Murky Depths, Midnight Echo, Midnight Street, Morpheus Tales, MT Biopuink Special, MT Urban Horror Special, Night Terrors II, Siblings, The House of Horror, Trembles, and broadcast on BBC Radio Derby and Erewash Sound.

During 2010/11 Richard was sponsored by Writing East Midlands to undertake a mentoring scheme in which he was supported in the development of his novel "Bloodie Bones." His website can be found here www.richardfarrenbarber.co.uk

A.A. Garrison is a twenty-nine-year-old man living in the mountains of North Carolina, USA. His short fiction has appeared in dozens of zines and anthologies, as well as the *Pseudopod* webcast. His horror novel, *The End of Jack Cruz*, is available from Montag Press. He blogs at synchroshock.blogspot.com.

John Stanton's stories, novellas, essays, poems, and articles have appeared in *Mount Zion Speculative Fiction Review, The Indianapolis Star, Compuserve Magazine, MIND, Static Movement, Theatre of Decay, Yellow Mama*, and other print and on-line magazines. His photographic art has been used as covers and internal illustrations for *Not One of Us, Black Petals, Twisted Dreams Magazine, RAZAR I* and *II, True Police, Literally*, and the anthologies *Of Shadow and Substance, Requiem for the Damned, Studies in Scarlet*, House of Horrors' *Tales of a Woman Scorned* and *Indiana Horror 2012*, among others.

Amy K. Marshall: I am the Director of The Craig Public Library on Prince of Wales Island, Alaska. I am an Associate Member of HWA and serve on the Library Committee for that organization, and serve on both the Alaska State Advisory Board for the AlaskaOWL Project (BTOP/Broadband Initiative in Libraries), and as Chair of the State Committee for Library Advocacy. I was featured in two Bill & Melinda Gates Foundation videos (2011) that sought to raise awareness of the benefits of technology in libraries (available on YouTube), and was lately the subject of an AP Wire article about the circumstances surrounding my birth in Lawrence, Kansas in 1964. I hold an M.A. in Maritime History/Nautical Archaeology from East Carolina University and am a former archaeologist, conservator, and curator with over 20 years experience in the public and private sectors. I'm also married to an archaeologist and am the mother of two teenagers (which may explain the descent into writing horror).

Greg McWhorter is a pop-culture historian and teacher who resides in Southern California. Since the 1980s, he has worked for newspapers, radio, television, and film. He has been a guest speaker at several universities and the San Diego Comic-Con. Today, McWhorter owns a highly acclaimed record label that specializes in vintage punk rock. He is also the host of a cable TV show titled Rock 'n' Roll High School 101. Most of his published writings to-date are nonfiction pieces related to pop-culture and music. McWhorter's love of classic horror and detective stories have been his main influences in writing fiction.

Michael Lee Johnson is a poet, freelance writer, photographer, and small business owner of custom imprinted promotional products and apparel: promoman.us, and is from Itasca, Illinois. He is heavily influenced by: Carl Sandburg, Robert Frost, William Carlos Williams, Irving Layton, Herman Hesse, Krishnamurti, Charles Bukowski, Leonard Cohen, and Allen Ginsberg. His new poetry chapbook with pictures, titled From Which Place the Morning Rises, and his new photo version of The Lost American: from Exile to Freedom are available at lulu.com. The original version of The Lost American: from Exile to Freedom, can be found at: iuniverse.com. New Chapbook: Challenge of Night and Day, and Chicago Poems, by Michael Lee Johnson: lulu.com. Michael has been published in over 25 countries. He is also editor/publisher of seven poetry sites, all open for submission, which can be found at his web site: poetryman.mysite.com. All of his books are now available on Amazon.com. and Borders.com

Rocky Alexander is an author of horror and dark fiction who lives with his wife in central North Carolina. He spends his days as a professional boxing coach, but at night, from the acres of woods surrounding his house, he can hear the sounds of the zombies, cannibals, serial killers, and a host of other magnificently loathsome things that hide among the trees, and every so often, he catches a glimpse. . .

Chantal Noordeloos is a writer from the Netherlands and a 1999 graduate from the Norwich School of Art and Design (UK) with a major in creative writing. Apart from work, motherhood and a busy social life that also includes -playing in and organising of- regular LARP events, she has been writing stories and honing her writing skills through workshops, seminars and a lot of writing. During 2012 she decided it was time to start her actual writing career and to have her work published. She now participates in several Dutch writing contests and she writes stories for various English language magazines and anthologies. Chantal lives in The Hague with her family.

From Detroit, Michigan, **Vincenzo Bilof** is the recipient of SNM Horror Magazine's Literary Achievement award in 2011. Vincenzo is the author of the zombie novels "Nightmare of the Dead" and "Necropolis Now," the first book in the Zombie Ascension series. Both are available from Severed Press. When he's not chasing his kids around the house or watching bad horror films, he reads and reviews horror fiction. His current writing project includes the new serial, "Japanese Werewolf Apocalypse;" the first episode is available from Severed Press. You can check out his blog here: http://vincenzobilof.blogspot.com/

Scathe meic Beorh, raised in Suburban Florida and on piratical account since 1971, is an author and contributing editor for both Haunted Magazine and Bradbury Quarterly. *Animadvertistine a Deo* and then discovered by Robert M. Price and John Gregory Betancourt, his writing style and content have been compared to authors as varied as Ray Bradbury, William Blake, W. B. Yeats, Shel Silverstein, James Joyce, and J. R. R. Tolkien. He is the author of the story collection Always After Thieves Watch (Wildside Press), the dictionary Pirate Lingo (Wildside Press), the novel The Pirates of St. Augustine (Wildside Press), and the poetic studies Golgotha (Punkin House Press) and Emhain Macha Dark Rain (Rebel Satori Press). His stories and poetry are often found in anthologies and periodicals worldwide (such as Fungi, Morpheus Tales, Bound For Evil, Romantics Quarterly, Black Lantern Publishing, Black Petals, Deep Cuts, The Willows Magazine, and Songs for the Raven). Formerly a Southern Baptist and then a monk of the Eastern Orthodox Church, he presently resides with his exceedingly creative and brilliant wife Ember in a quaint 'Bradburyesque' neighborhood on the Atlantic Coast of Florida.

Paula D. Ashe is a native Ohioan who came to Indiana in search of a flatter landscape. She is an English instructor at Ivy Tech Community College and a PhD student in the American Studies program at Purdue University because she is crazy. A member of the Horror Writers Association, her award winning dark fiction has been published in Nexus Literary Magazine, the Indiana Science Fiction Anthology 2011, Indiana Crime 2012, and Indiana Horror 2012. She also has stories appearing in Serial Killers: Iterum and Hell. She lives with her wife and far too many pets in Northeast Indiana.